Dirty
ANGELS
Karina Halle

D1634887

headline
ETERNAL

First published by Metal Blonde Books in 2014

First published as an Ebook in Great Britain in 2015
by HEADLINE ETERNAL
An imprint of HEADLINE PUBLISHING GROUP

First published in paperback in Great Britain in 2015
by HEADLINE ETERNAL
An imprint of HEADLINE PUBLISHING GROUP

1

Cataloguing in Publication Data is available from the British Library

ISBN 978 1 4722 2884 0

Typeset in Electra by Palimpsest Book Production Limited,
Falkirk, Stirlingshire

Printed and bound in Great Britain by
CPI Group (UK)Ltd, Croydon, CR0 4YY

Headline's policy is to use papers that are natural, renewable
and recyclable products and made from wood grown in sustainable
forests. The logging and manufacturing processes are expected to
conform to the environmental regulations of the country of origin.

HEADLINE PUBLISHING GROUP
An Hachette UK Company
338 Euston Road
London NW1 3BH

www.headlineeternal.com
www.headline.co.uk
www.hachette.co.uk

A NOTE FROM THE AUTHOR

Thank you for wanting to read *Dirty Angels*. Please note that the following book deals with life within the drug cartels of Mexico and as such, it depicts many brutal acts and events that most people wish to believe don't happen – but they do. As a writer, I tried to stay as true to the real-life dealings of the Mexican drug cartels and consulted such books as *El Sicario*, *The Last Narco*, and *Midnight in Mexico*. As a result, the book contains situations that are not suitable for all readers, whether you are 18+ or not.

While this book is written in English, all characters are assumed to be speaking and thinking in Spanish, except where otherwise noted.

TRIGGER WARNING: If you are sensitive to scenes that include or allude to rape, domestic violence, abuse and torture, please do not read this book. While *Dirty Angels* is fiction, it strives to be as realistic as possible to the world of Mexican drug cartels and the mentioned scenes do occur, and frequently. Otherwise, please note the book contains a lot of explicit and unprotected sex, erotic material, violence, and bad language.

For Scott MacKenzie, from Karina MacKenzie.

PROLOGUE

I was running.

I didn't know where, all I knew was that I had to keep going, one foot in front of the other. The wet grass brushed against my bare legs and I wished I'd planned my escape a little bit more. After a month of dwelling on it, toying with the idea, then finally committing, you think I would have escaped my husband's house with something more than shorts, a blouse, and a wallet. At least I was wearing running shoes.

There hadn't been any time. I was already outside when I saw my husband's boring guests arrive. I didn't mean to be. I was supposed to be in my room putting on my dress and making myself look oh so lovely. I'd been looking forward to them coming over for the last few days – they'd break up the daily monotony of a woman captive to her narco husband, a slave to the golden palace.

I'd only gone outside, out the kitchen door, to get flowers for the centerpiece. The maid had brought these expensive blossoms from in town, but I wanted the gardenias that grew at the front fence and created a hedge along the line. When the guests' Mercedes rolled in through the gates, I froze in place and watched as they parked and strolled up to the door. The night sky was minutes away from engulfing us.

After Salvador answered with that big phony smile of his and ushered them inside, I took in the deepest breath I could.

I couldn't think. I couldn't chance changing my mind. I needed to act, and act now.

I grabbed a few sparse blossoms off the hedge and walked over to Juan Diego at the front gate. I knocked on the glass of his booth, making him jump in surprise as he'd just started to read his tabloid, and told him I was going outside along the hedge to get more flowers. He was reluctant – he had orders to keep me inside, though Salvador always insisted it was to protect me from everyone else. But there was never anyone to protect me against Salvador.

I waved my flowers at him and put my hand on my hip. I had only been the wife of Salvador for two months, but I was going to use that while I could. I needed to act like I owned authority, even if I didn't. Juan Diego was a kind man, and he was in no power to deny the wife of Mexico's largest drug cartel access to her favorite flowers.

The flowers my mama used to put in my hair every Sunday.

He waved me through with a warm smile, and I returned in kind, acting a role, pretending I wasn't trembling on the inside. I slowly walked along the hedge, plucking the flowers, my hands filled with fragrant white petals. I eyed the cameras that were stationed around the outer edge, knowing I didn't look suspicious to Rico, the surveillance guy inside, but if Salvador caught sight of me on the cameras, outside the compound, he would lose his shit.

There was no time. It was now or never.

I had to run. I had to try.

So I did.

Where the hedge started to blend in to the surrounding jungle and the clipped front lawn became unruly and unkempt, I dropped the flowers at my feet and ran into the darkness. I had studied our land – his land, it was always his land – time and time again, and all I knew was to avoid the roads. If I headed down behind the house, I'd come across the river that was too deep and wide to cross, and if I went across the road I'd be heading into the backyards of our neighbors who were as guarded as we were. I had to keep running north, through the trees, through the twilight.

I just had to keep running.

I ran for a good twenty minutes straight, my body coasting on adrenaline and the endurance I had built while working out in the home gym every day. I fell a few times, my hands always taking the brunt of the fall before the ground could take out the rest of me. I always got back up. There was no time for pain. I felt it, but it was almost a relief to have. After what Salvador had done to me, I could take a lot.

I ran and ran and ran, tripping over roots, dodging the trees in the weak moonlight that filtered through the trees, until the river suddenly cut across in front of me. I had no idea where I was, and I could see a few more stars than usual without the city lights. Somewhere in the trees a bird called out.

I thought about my parents, the people I was most worried about. Actually, the only people on this earth who mattered to me. I worried about Salvador finding out that I had run, I worried that he would kill them. But as brash as he was, he wouldn't do anything until he knew the facts. At least, I hoped that would be the case. The plan was for me to call my friend Camila and get her to take care of them – before he could.

Looking around me, I made my way to the river's edge and contemplated going across. It wasn't as wide here and didn't look to be as deep, with the tops of a few boulders poking their way through the current. I wondered if Juan Diego had alerted Salvador about what happened. I wondered if Rico had been watching when I disappeared from the cameras. I wondered how much time I had before they found me.

A branch snapped behind me. Even though that was the only sound I heard, I knew it belonged to a person who was probably wincing very loudly at his mistake. You couldn't afford to make mistakes in Mexico.

I quickly jumped from the shore and into the river, the cold water coming up to my mid-thighs and catching me by surprise. I gasped loudly and was momentarily frozen from the shock. Then I heard a fervent rustling behind me and knew I had to keep going or I'd die.

Or worse. With Salvador there was always worse.

The current rushing up against me was strong, and my sneakers slid against the sand and pebbles under my feet, but I made myself move, made myself push through the river, the other side so close. I kept going, my legs turning to ice, my eyes focused on the dry land, my arms stretched out as if I could reach it that way.

I heard a splash behind me. I would not turn around. I would not give up.

I cried out in frustration, lunging forward to reach the sand, as if that would save me in the end. But there was no saving me.

Suddenly thick, rough arms went around my waist, lifting me up out of the water. I heard another splash, nearly drowned out by my cries, and everything went black as a bag was placed over my head. My arms were yanked back behind me so fast that I thought they were being pulled out of the sockets. I screamed in pain, my breath hot inside the bag that felt like it was already starting to drown me.

Another pair of hands went for my legs. I started kicking wildly, hoping that the current would catch the person off-balance, but within seconds my legs were wrapped with rope and I was being led out of the river like a pig on a stick, a man holding up either end of me.

"Two minutes," someone said, a man's voice that I didn't recognize. Despite the bag that made everything sound muffled, he sounded like he was from the east coast.

"Are you sure?" asked the other man, his voice low and baritone, and close to my ear, the one who gripped my hands behind my back.

"I'm never wrong, hey."

"All right, Este. Let's not go down this path again. We have the bitch, let's go."

I swallowed hard, my stomach sick, a swirling pool of knots. This wasn't Salvador. These weren't his men. This was someone else, and even though I was running away from him, it was always better with the devil you know.

I was suddenly jerked downward, my back arching, and I cried out again. I cried out for Salvador as a last resort.

"Salvador!" I screamed through the bag, the heat rising up to my cheeks. "Help me!"

A fist came down on my cheekbone, my face exploding in stars of pain.

"Easy now, Franco," said Este, and the fist didn't come again. My lips throbbed, my mouth filled with blood, and I knew better than to try and cry out once more.

The men, Este and Franco, carried me away, their pace

quickening. I only heard their breathing, fast and shallow, and the sound of the earth beneath their quiet feet. I could smell Franco's greasy breath, so close to my head. Every time I thought I might be able to move out of their hands and make an escape, their grip tightened around me even more.

I was going to die. There was no doubt about that now. Not at the hands of Salvador. In the hands of some unknown fate. These men, they were taking me somewhere. There was a reason I wasn't dead yet – death was the dessert.

I took in a deep breath, my mind beginning to swim laps in a dark pool. I wished these men had just killed me. My parents had money now because of my marriage. That was the whole point of it all. That was the point of everything – to give them a better life in their ailing years than I ever had growing up. If I died, I would die with peace in my heart knowing they were okay. It was the only thing that made my life worthwhile.

I must have lost consciousness due to lack of air because suddenly my head slammed back against something hard, and I fell over onto a cold slab. An engine whirred, the smell of exhaust seeping through. I was in a car – no, the back of a van – being taken somewhere. That dessert again.

I was in and out for the next while until the van jerked to a stop. I heard the back doors open, and before I could move, there were hands on me again, three pairs this time. They pulled me out of the van so fast that I cracked my head on the door frame. I heard Este apologize under his breath but that was it. Strong fingers seared into my arms and waist, and I was yanked forward across what felt like well-kept grass. For a split second I thought I wrong, and I was actually back at home. For that second I had hope, hope to just keep living, while before I only had the hope to live under my own terms. Now it was all about survival, instinct trumping reality.

The moment I heard a door open and I was shuffled down a staircase, the damp and musty smell permeating my nostrils, I knew I wasn't back at home. We didn't have a basement. Salvador had rooms for torture in other houses, but not ours. At least, no rooms that I could ever see.

My mind began to race, flipping through thoughts and images I had been subjected to ever since I married Salvador. Who had taken me? Salvador had the Sinaloa state military and the police at his command, so it wasn't them. It was another cartel or one of his old associates trying to usurp the boss. He had told me from the beginning that there were men out there who wanted me, who would do anything to have me – to take me, torture me, hold me for ransom, then torture me some more.

The wife of the jackal is the greatest card you can play in this game.

I was thrown down onto a chair, my hands and feet immediately unbound, and then tied back to the arms and legs before I could struggle. I thought about screaming again but the side of my face still throbbed with the violence. Este had warned Franco off, but I knew cartel men; I knew them too well, and I knew that courtesy never extended very far.

I started to shake uncontrollably and my whole body rocked with the spasm while hot tears pooled in my eyes. But I refused to let them fall. I knew what was coming next. The bag would come off my head. The bags would go on theirs. The camera would turn on.

I didn't want the world to see me afraid. I had been afraid for too long.

"Is everything ready?" Este asked.

"It's all set up," I heard someone say, another male voice, heavy footsteps coming toward me. I tensed up, sensing Franco and Este and some other figure on all sides of me, and the other person, the one who had just spoken, who stopped a few feet away. I wondered if there were more than four people in the room and decided there must be. I could almost *feel* someone else's eyes, hear their breath, read their silence.

"How drugged is she?" the unknown voice asked.

There was a pause. Then Este said, "Not badly. She's somewhat coherent."

"You didn't gag her?"

"No, but she shut up when she needed to."

"It's lucky she was out there."

"Yes. It was."

Who were these men? Which cartel? Salvador had so many enemies and so many alliances that harbored grudges, you could never be sure who was looking for some way to ground traction. But even though I knew my fate was most likely death, it all depended on who I was with. Who had me. Some men were more deplorable than others. Now that the famous gringo Travis Raines was dead, Salvador himself was probably the worst of them all.

Though there was one cartel, one man, who I'd been told could give my husband a run for his money. He was famous for slicing the heads, hands, and feet off of people and littering them in streets all over the country.

There was a strange moment of silence and I concentrated hard, trying to hear more than the obvious. They were all waiting. Waiting for the order. Waiting for the man in charge to speak.

He did.

It came from the left of me. His voice was cool, calm, and collected. I didn't have to see to know who had taken me. The man I'd heard so much about. The man I'd been taught to fear.

"Gentlemen," he said, and I could almost feel his infamous eyes on my body, "remove the bag."

There was a rustle and my face was immediately met with cool air that seized my lungs and bright lights that blinded me. I scrunched up my face, afraid to look, to see. Now it was all so real and I wanted to stay in the dark.

"Who did this?"

Suddenly, cool hands were at my swollen cheek and I flinched.

"Who did this?" my captor repeated, an edge to his level voice, his cigar-laced breath on my face.

"Sorry," Franco mumbled. "It was the only way to quiet her."

A heavy pause filled the room like dead weight. Finally the fingers came away from my skin, and my body relaxed momentarily. The man was in my face, the spicy scent of tea emanating off of him.

"Look at me, Luisa Reyes."

Chavez, I thought to myself. *I will always be Luisa Chavez.*

"Darling, aren't you curious to know where you are?"

"My name is Luisa *Chavez*," I said. I opened my eyes to see golden ones staring right back at me. It was like looking at an eagle. "And I know where I am. I know who you are. You are Javier Bernal."

He raised his brow in amusement and nodded. I'd seen his picture before, on the news. There was only one, and that was his mugshot, but even in that photo his eyes made an impression on you. They saw right into your depths and made you question yourself. He was one of the men that Salvador feared, even though Salvador had more power. He was the one I had been told to watch out for, the supposed reason why I'd always been locked in the compound or escorted by the local police to go shopping.

And yet here I was, tied to a chair in a cold, leaking basement with nothing in it except five cartel members, a video camera, and a knife that lay on top of a stool in front of me.

All of that for nothing. I could escape Salvador but I could never escape the cartels.

I had asked for this fate.

"You know why you're here," Javier said with deliberation, straightening up in his sharp black suit. He walked over to the stool, picked up the knife, and glanced at me over his shoulder. "Don't you?"

I could only breathe. I wanted to look at the others, at Este, at Franco, at the two other mystery men, but I was frozen in his gaze like a deer in headlights.

"What is the knife for?" I asked, my throat painfully dry.

"You'll find out after," he said. "It is for your husband. For your Salvador." He stepped to the side and waved his arm at the camera. "And this is also for him."

He eyed someone over my shoulder and gave a sharp nod. I heard a rip from behind and a piece of duct tape was placed over my mouth. I squirmed helplessly and the lights in the basement dimmed. The men stepped to the side while Javier went behind the video camera. A white light came off the front of it and bathed me in an eerie glow.

Javier cleared his throat, his face covered in shadow, and

said loudly, projecting to the camera, "This is Luisa Reyes, former beauty queen of the Baja State and property of Salvador Reyes. Salvador, we have your wife and we have a long list of demands, demands which I know you can meet. I expect full cooperation in this matter or she dies in the next seven days. If she's lucky. I'll give you some time to think about what you're willing to give up for her. Then we'll be contacting you. Goodbye."

The light on the camera switched off, but the rest of the room remained dim.

"I hope your husband checks his emails often. It would be a shame to have to put this on YouTube."

There was a smirk on his face at that as he slowly walked toward me, the knife glinting in his hand. His eyes burned through the shadows then grew somber.

He held up the knife. "I think it's only going to hurt the first time."

My eyes focused on the silver of the blade, but the terror inside me grew too strong, and my urge to breathe through the duct tape became too difficult. My lungs seized in panic, pulsing dots appearing in my vision. I felt a hand on my collarbone, gripping the edge of my blouse, and then everything went black.

CHAPTER ONE

Three months earlier

"Excuse me, miss?"

I sighed and took a moment to compose myself before I slowly turned around, reminding myself to respond in English.

"Yes?"

The man and his buddies were staring at me with that stupid ogling look they had the whole time they were here. I was happy when they finally asked for the bill, just wanting them out of the bar and back to their drunken tourist festivities or whatever the white men got up to in this damned city of Cabo San Lucas. But it seemed I wasn't free yet.

The guy who called me, the most obnoxious of the group, wagged his brows at me and nodded at a spot behind me.

"You dropped something."

I opened my mouth to say something but shut it. I looked down at my feet, then behind me. My pencil was on the ground. Not that I ever needed it to remember orders anymore.

"Thanks," I said, and bent down to pick it up. Immediately the guys snorted and I quickly snapped back up. Of course they'd wanted me to pick it up – my uniform at Cabo Cocktails consisted of the shortest skirt ever.

I ignored them, not even bothering to turn around again,

and made my way back to the bar. I slammed my bill holder on the counter and eyed the receipt. The little jerks hadn't even tipped me. Not that it was customary in Mexico, but with Americans in a tourist town, you always expected it.

"Stiffed again?" said Camila.

I looked over at her as she snapped the cap off of two bottles of beer. As usual, my colleague had an impish smirk on her pixie-like face. She always got the tips, maybe because she was always smiling.

"Yeah," I said, wiping the sweat off my brow. The fan beat overhead but it was always a bit too hot in the bar, didn't matter what time of the year it was. I turned around and eyed the boys who were still at the table, laughing and occasionally looking my way. "Those assholes over there."

"You know, if you just joke with them and smile sometimes, they'd probably tip you more," she said innocently, putting her beers on a tray.

I put my hand on my hip. "The minute I smile or play nice with them is the minute they take advantage of me. I don't want to give them the wrong idea."

"Luisa, I'm really starting to think you're afraid of men."

That bothered me a bit. "So? Aren't you?"

She rolled her eyes. "I'm a lesbian because I like pussy, not because men scare me." And with that she took the beers over to her waiting table.

I pressed my hand on the back of my neck, trying to alleviate the constant strain I felt there. It was nearly eleven o' clock at night, and I had been on my feet for twelve hours. I had three more hours of this before I could go home, which meant a forty-minute drive to San Jose del Cabo where I lived with my parents.

Which reminded me. My mother's birthday was tomorrow and I knew she deserved something special. We didn't have much money – I was the breadwinner at the house since my father suffered from early onset Alzheimer's and my mother was blind. She was healthy otherwise, but neither she nor my father could work, which meant everything fell on me. It was a lot for a twenty-three year old but I'd been working since I was a child; even when my father was able to hold a job it was never a high paying one. I was used to poverty and I was used to hard work.

I just could never get used to being treated like a piece of meat. I could never get used to the constant fear. And working at Cabo Cocktails, working for my boss, Bruno Corchado, meant I'd been dealing with those two things since I was twenty. And now, because the only way I could get my mother a gift tomorrow would be to ask for an advance on my paycheck, I was walking right into the lion's den.

I took a deep breath, looked around to see if any new patrons had come in, and when I saw they hadn't, I straightened my shirt, pulling it up around my cleavage, and walked around the corner to Bruno's office.

I gave three quick raps on it and stood back. I hadn't seen him much today so I wasn't sure what kind of mood he was in. I was hoping for generous and disinterested but knew that was pressing my luck a little bit. At this time of night he was usually drunk and a jackass. Or a lecherous pervert.

I swallowed hard as I heard him bark, "Come in!"

I opened the door and poked my head in. "Bruno?" I asked.

He was sitting at his desk, a row of empty beer bottles beside him, going over the ledger. He looked at me with red eyes, his head swaying from side to side, and I immediately knew I'd made a mistake. "Luisa. My beauty queen. Come on in." He nodded at the door. "And shut that behind you."

My heart rate started to pick up. I'd been in this exact situation too many times and knew this was going to end very badly. Still, I needed this favor. I did as he asked, the door shutting like a cell door, and walked two steps toward him, hoping I could keep my distance.

Bruno wasn't a bad looking guy. He was in his late thirties, an apparent family man, though he never wore his ring at work and told every waitress that his marriage was open. We'd never seen his wife, or his children for that matter – we weren't even sure if they lived in the city, and none of us cared enough to ask. Many men operated businesses elsewhere and only visited their families on the weekends.

But just because he wasn't bad looking, didn't mean he wasn't bad.

"What is it, Miss Los Cabos?" he asked, stroking his chin and looking me up and down with drunken eyes. "You know, I was Googling you the other night and I found a picture of you winning that beauty queen contest. What were you, eighteen? Your tits were higher back then."

I bit down on my tongue to stop me from saying something that would probably get me fired. Work in the waitressing industry in Cabo was hard these days and not easy to come by. Damned economy in America meant the tourists weren't coming here as much.

I ignored his remark and ignored that his eyes were still fixed on my breasts. I licked my lips quickly and said, "I was wondering if I could ask a favor."

He raised his brows and gave me a sloppy grin, teeth gleaming with opportunity. "Well, well, well. What is it this time? Time off to take your dad to the hospital again? Something wrong with your mother?"

I dug my nails into the palm of my hand. "No. But it does involve my mother. It's her birthday tomorrow and I would like to get her a gift. I was wondering if I could get an advance on my wages. Two hundred pesos."

He laughed. "What are you buying for your mother for two hundred pesos? She's blind, isn't she?"

It took everything I had to keep it together. "It's a Kobo. An e-reader. A used one. I can buy audiobooks for her on it. She doesn't like Braille so much anymore with her arthritis."

"Well aren't you just the perfect daughter. You must be the apple of her eye."

His choice of words wasn't lost on me. "They've given so much to me over the years just to keep food on the table. It's the least I can do in return."

He stared at me for a few heavy moments before picking up his beer and having a long swig of it. "And what will you do for me in return?"

This was what I feared. I looked him straight in the eye and said, "You can have my word that I'll pay you back. Dock it out of my paycheck."

He grinned, though there was only malice in his eyes. "Oh, you'll pay me back. I know you will. I will take it from you before you have a chance. But I mean, what are you going to do for me to thank me for being such a wonderful and generous boss?"

I took in a deep breath. I didn't have much choice but I still had a choice. "I don't know. What did you have in mind? An extra shift?"

Bruno snorted and got out of his chair. He wasn't a tall

man, but I was only 5'2" and he still towered over me. His eyes became lazy with lust and a bit of spittle dripped out of the corner of his mouth. "Not an extra shift. Tell me, Luisa, why is it that every single woman here, except for the dyke, has been with me and you haven't?"

It felt like a piece of dry toast was lodged in my throat. "Because you're not my type."

He raised his brow then nodded as if this whole thing was an elaborate joke. "I'm starting to think you don't have a type, Luisa. That you just like to be a tease. I see you every day, walking around in that outfit, flashing those legs and ass, showing those tits. You're fucking beautiful and you know it. But you don't fuck."

"This is the uniform you gave me."

"And yet you wear it better than any of those other girls. The men all come here to look at you. They want you. And you're such a stuck-up bitch that you can't even pretend to be nice. If you did, you wouldn't be here asking me for money. You'd be paying for everything with your tips. And your tits."

"This was a mistake," I said, feeling dizzy. I turned around, ready to leave. He reached out and grabbed my arm, his fingers digging into it.

"It is a mistake to leave," he said, pulling me close to him. He smelled like beer and chili, and it made my stomach roll. "I promise to give you your money, you just have to give me something." He read the fear on my face. "Don't worry, I'm not going to hurt you. I just want to see what others do not. I want to feel you."

I didn't know what to do. He dug his nails into mine and then he pushed me back. "Take off your shirt."

I opened my mouth to say no. I had to say no. In the past

he had grabbed my ass, rubbed his erection against me, had kissed me briefly on the mouth, and made an attempt to grope my breasts. But he'd never told me to take my shirt off. This was too much, and yet I thought, I felt, if I could just do it and go to some other place in my head, I would be okay. I wouldn't be a whore. I would still be a virgin. I would still be pure and intact.

I could be all that and be a good daughter. I could ease the guilt of my mother staying at home, essentially alone, because my father was often a million miles away and didn't know who she was.

So I pulled my low-cut T-shirt over my head and stood there before my boss, the fluorescent light flickering behind him and making everything look that much worse. I stared at him straight in the eyes while he leered at my thin cotton bra.

"Well," I said. "Now you're seeing what no one except for me and my parents and my doctor have seen. Is that all?"

He looked so dumbfounded that it was almost laughable. Granted, I knew I had a good body, but I worked hard at it by going for my 5K jogs every morning. But I wasn't any different from any other girl. My breasts were still breasts.

Bruno managed to close his mouth. "Your bra. Take off your bra."

I could tell this was non-negotiable.

You're not here, you're not here, you're not here, I chanted to myself while I reached around my back and undid the clasp. I took it off, my breasts free, and held the bra in my hands.

He whistled. "I feel privileged."

"Funny how I don't feel the same."

He gave me a sharp look. "You're not done yet."

I gulped while he walked up to me. I wanted to close my eyes, but I couldn't be afraid. I didn't want him to think he was winning. I looked straight at him while his greasy hands went to my breasts, cupping them. I sucked in my breath while he ran his thumbs over my nipples, and I felt relief that they were reluctant to harden. The last thing I needed him to think was that this was turning me on. The reality was that I wanted to vomit, and if it happened, I wanted it to be all over him, just so he'd know how disgusting I thought he was.

He leaned in close, and for a second I thought he was going to kiss me. But he whispered in my ear, "I should have asked for more."

I suppressed a shudder, holding my breath while I waited for his next move. To my utter relief, he took his hands away and stepped back.

"You may make yourself decent again," he said nonchalantly. "To be honest, I expected your breasts to be a little bit bigger. I guess the shirt makes it look like you have more than you have. Again, that would come in handy if you actually cared about tips."

I knew my breasts were just big enough for my frame, but I didn't dare say anything while he sat back down at his desk and started removing pesos from his wallet. I put on my bra and shirt in record speed and tried to remind myself that my loss of dignity was worth whatever happiness I could buy my mother.

He gave me the money, holding on to my hand for a little too long, before he said, "Don't say I don't do you any favors. But if you ever ask for one again, expect more involvement from your side. Nothing in life is free. You of all people should know this."

I nodded, thanking him curtly and yanked the money out of his slimy grasp. As I turned and left his office, back into the heat, satellite TV and drunken cries of the bar, I made a vow that at the first chance to leave this place, the first promise of a better life, I would take it.

I didn't even have to wait that long.

CHAPTER TWO

The next morning I woke up early and went for my jog around the neighborhood. The house I rented for me and my parents was just outside of the airport. All day long it was nothing but the unrelenting sun and the sound of airplanes. Dust coated everything, and I was convinced if anyone did a scan of my lungs they'd find a sandcastle in there. But it was cheap and cheap was all I could afford. Plus, we did have a lot of privacy which was great for when my father had one of his episodes, and the house was big enough so that there was a bedroom for each of us. That was more than we had when I was growing up.

I usually jogged just after dawn when the air was still relatively cool. After my shower I got breakfast ready and woke my parents. I was lucky that most mornings my father was still my father. He knew my name, he knew where we were, and he smoked his pipe with his left hand. It was during the day that he would falter. If I wasn't home, like I hadn't been yesterday, my mother had to deal with it all by herself. Her blindness wasn't even a disability at that point since she knew quite well how to handle herself. I just knew how hard it was to have to control Papa, to calm him, to make him understand he was loved and with loved ones. One day I could afford a nurse to take care of him, but that day always seemed so far away.

That morning I made breakfast with my special fried potatoes and peppers with goat cheese that I only brought out on special occasions, and brought the breakfast with a gardenia in a vase to my mother. She wouldn't see it, but the smell always lifted her spirits. When she and my father were both well fed and well caffeinated, I got in my car, a beat-up old Toyota with windows that didn't roll up, went out into the town of San Jose del Cabo and bought the Kobo device I'd had my eye on at one of the local pawnshops.

The woman who normally worked there wasn't on duty, but a young man was, and he tried to jack up the price at the last minute. I tried out what Camila had recommended – smiling more, acting flirty – and even though I felt a bit silly doing it, it actually worked. I got it for a lot less, leaving me enough cash left over to pay the library fees I owed and get a bottle of cheap sparkling wine for my mother.

"You shouldn't have," my mother said as I handed the e-reader over to her. Her mouth was set in a stern line, but I could tell from the way she was handling the device, like it was precious gold, that she already loved it more than she could say. She was a proud woman in every sense of the word, and if it wasn't for the empty look in her pupils, you wouldn't know she was blind. She always stood very tall, neck long, her dark hair pulled off her face with only a few strands of grey coming in at the corners.

"Well, Mama, it's your birthday and I have," I said, brushing back her hair. I looked over at my father who was watching us with a wry smile on his face, a few crumbs caught in his greying beard.

"You're a good woman, Luisa," Papa said. I gestured to his beard and he wiped the crumbs off. He continued, "But you shouldn't be spending so much on your mother and I."

"Are you jealous, Papa?" I asked wryly, getting up and pouring them both another cup of coffee. "I'm sure she will let you use it when she's not." He quickly put his warm hand over mine and looked at me with gentle eyes, the kind of look that made my heart bleed when I realized how close I was to losing this man.

"I always like it when you read to me," he said. "I am happy with that. When you were younger you used to make up stories. Crazy little stories about trolls and goblins and princesses with swords. Do you remember that?"

I couldn't recall any particular stories, but when I was younger and we didn't have enough money for toys, I would make up stories instead. I always liked the darker ones, the scarier ones, the ones with the villains and the ugliest crea- tures – those were the most like real life. Fairytales and happily-ever-afters were for people in other countries.

I kissed him on his forehead. "I remember you telling me to stop telling them, that I was scaring you."

Suddenly the Kobo started speaking and my mother jumped in her seat, letting out a nervous laugh. "Woo, *this* scared me."

I went over to her, picked it up, and pressed pause. Though the Baja state was often behind in the times, the local library did have an e-reader program where you could borrow e-books and audiobooks for free. Now that my library fees were all settled, I had borrowed a range of crime thrillers for her to listen to.

I left the house later feeling relatively happy. I hated the fact that I had to go back to work and face Bruno again, but knowing that my parents were full from lunch, my mom was listening to her books for the first time, and my father seemed stronger than normal, it was enough to get me by. Sometimes, when I took the car onto the highway that led me to Cabo San Lucas and the sea air came through the open windows just right, it was enough to bring a smile to my face. In those moments I always lived outside of my reality, outside my head, and was just a child of the earth, an element like the sun and water.

When I finally got to work – traffic being especially heavy today – I was relieved to find the bar half-empty and Bruno nowhere in sight.

"Where is everyone?" I asked Camila at the till before I headed to the washroom to change from my sundress to the dreaded uniform.

She shrugged, her long earrings rattling lightly. "Just one of those days. Bruno went out and I don't think he's coming back. Anita should be coming on the floor any minute. Dylan and Augustin are in the kitchen."

Thank god. I didn't want to see Bruno and remember his eyes on my body, his grimy hands on my breasts. I got changed and started my shift feeling a million times lighter.

For the first hour I only had two tables – one was an older gentleman with a bowtie who was more than content to sit alone in the corner and nurse his martini, while the other was three giggling girls. They looked to be around my age, maybe younger, but had the newest fashions and those care-free smiles that only belonged to girls who never knew what struggle was, who had the world at their fingertips and the appetite to make it work for them. Part of me hated them, my insides writhing with jealousy, even though I knew it was very wrong. I tried to be a good person, to do right, but sometimes it was hard not to feel how hopeless it all was.

But I was nice to the girls, and they tipped me quite well, and I made a note not to be so judgemental. I was filling up a bottle of hot sauce behind the bar when I heard someone clear their throat.

I turned to see a man staring at me. At least he looked like he was staring at me – he was wearing sunglasses inside.

"Can I help you?" I asked, remembering to smile.

The man didn't return the smile. With a deathly pale face and an all-black suit on his skinny, tall frame, he looked like an agent of death. "I'm here with a friend of mine," he said, voice completely monotone. "We would like you to be our server."

I looked over his shoulder to see a table nearest the patio occupied by a large man, his back to me. Camila was walking past him, giving me an I-don't-know look. "That's usually Camila's area . . ." I started.

"We don't care. My friend would like you to be our server. We will make sure you are treated justly and tipped generously."

I swallowed uneasily. Why was this guy wearing shades now anyway?

"All right," I said carefully. "I'll be with you in a minute. Will you be having food?"

The man nodded and then went back to the table. I quickly waved Camila over while their backs were turned to me.

"Who are they?" I whispered, pulling her close.

"I don't know. They just sat down and said they wanted you to serve them. I said they'd have to ask you."

"He's weird. He's wearing shades inside. And it's night-time."

"The other guy is too," she said. "In fact, the other guy looks familiar and not in a good way."

The skin at the back of my neck prickled. "Familiar like he comes in here sometimes?"

Camila looked me dead in the eyes. "Familiar like I've seen his face on the news. But with the glasses, it's hard to tell."

I straightened up and looked back at them. The man who had spoken to me was watching me with an impassive look on his face, his hands folded in front of him like he'd been waiting awhile. The other man, the one that Camila said looked familiar, was sitting there rigidly, but I still couldn't see his face.

I grabbed the menus and Camila squeezed my hand for good luck. I walked carefully over to them, reminding myself that these men probably just wanted a hot waitress to attend to them, that they didn't have to want anything else, and that I would be tipped for my efforts.

I stopped in front of the table and smiled. "Hello, my name is Luisa. I'll be your server tonight."

The other man looked up at me and my breath caught in my throat. Camila was right. He did look familiar. Though his wide aviator sunglasses covered up his eyes, there was no mistaking the overly thick mustache peppered with grey or the mullet-like swoop of hair on his head. His face was scarred in places, with both scratches and pockmarks, and had that slightly bloated look that middle-aged men got. Though his clothes were simple – faded blue jeans and a western shirt over his beer paunch – they didn't hide the immense power and notoriety this man had.

He was none other than Salvador Reyes, one of the most feared and well-documented cartel leaders in the country. And he was sitting in my bar, asking me to serve him.

I kept the smile plastered on my face while invisible fingers trailed ice down my back. This could not be a good thing. This wasn't even his area; he controlled most of Sinaloa. Aside from Tijuana, most of the Baja Peninsula was relatively untouched by the cartels and the impending drug violence.

Untouched until now.

I was vaguely aware that both men were staring at me through their sunglasses, their faces grave and unmoving. I quickly placed the menus down on the table like they were hot to touch and launched into my specials. "Nachos are half price as are the buckets of Tecate," I said, nervously tripping over the words.

The man I thought was Salvador picked up the menu and glanced at it briefly. The other man didn't even look.

Finally Salvador smiled. It was nothing if not creepy. "Top shelf tequila, two shots. And the nachos. Please, Luisa."

I nodded and quickly trotted back to the kitchen to place my order with Dylan. I felt something at my back and whirled around to see Camila staring at me expectantly.

"Well? Do you know what I mean?"

I nodded, trying to stay calm. "He does look familiar. But I don't know how. They seem harmless."

The funny thing was that I felt like if I told Camila it was Salvador, the infamous drug lord, things would take a turn for the worse. Right now he was in the bar, with his friend, probably his right hand man – *the one who lives with the jackal* – and no one seemed to notice him or care. This was good. This man had the power to murder everyone in here if he wanted to and completely get away with it. To him and to many others, he had a right to rape me in the back room and I could never press charges, or he could rape me in front of everyone, and no one – not even Camila – would ever dare say anything. This man was above the law, as so many men in Mexico were, and the less attention that was brought to that fact, the better.

For my sake and the sake of everyone around me, I had to pretend that I didn't know who this man was.

I went over to the bar and poured a special edition of Patron that we only had for high rollers, my hands shaking so badly that the tequila spilled over the edges and I had to mop it up with a washcloth, then took the shots over to the table. I thanked Jesus that I had worn my ballet flats to work today instead of the ridiculous heels that Bruno often made us wear.

The men were conversing with each other, voices low, and I stood back for a few moments to let them finish before I placed the shots in front of them.

"Here is a special edition of Patron." *For the patron*, I finished in my head.

"You didn't get one for yourself," Salvador said, smiling again. He did have very white teeth, probably all fake. Even though I had seen his picture on the news and in the paper on occasion, I'd always imagined his teeth would be gold.

"I can't drink at work," I told him, forcing confidence into my voice and trying out that smile again.

"That is nonsense. What do you think this is, America? Of course you can drink at work," he said. "I don't see your boss anywhere and I promise I won't tell." There was a teasing quality to his voice, the kind that people used when they were flirting, but the concept of Salvador flirting was a hard thing to swallow. I was reminded about how wrong this situation was.

"I'll go have a shot for you after work," I said.

"And when is that?" he asked. He still hadn't had the drink yet. "When do you get off work?"

Damn it.

"When the bar closes, at three a.m." I tried to sound nonchalant, adding an extra hour.

"Then we shall wait here until you are done with your shift. And we will have the shot then. Isn't that right, friend?" he said, looking across the table. The pale man nodded but didn't say anything.

"I don't think that sounds like a lot of fun," I said, the words coming out of my mouth before I could stop them. Salvador stared at me, his thick greying brows knitted together but I still continued. "I mean, there are better bars here in Cabo. This one is pretty boring – I should know, I work here." I attempted a smile again. I felt like I was slipping. "Are you two just here on business or . . .?"

Salvador stared at me for a few long moments – moments that had me cursing in my head – before running his stubby fingers over his mustache, his gold rings glinting. "We are not here on business. We are here to relax. Have a little fun. Enjoy the beach." He picked up the glass of Patron. "And we're here to get drunk. And I don't think you have any right to tell us where we can do that. If we want to get drunk here, if we want to wait until three in the morning for you to get off your shift, we can do that. And we will do that."

At that, both he and the other man slammed back their shots.

I gulped and squeaked out a "sorry" and then turned to leave.

"Oh, Luisa," Salvador called, stopping me in mid-step. "Do come back here. We aren't finished with you."

I closed my eyes, trying to find my inner strength, willing myself to stay calm, before I went back to him.

"Yes?" I asked.

"I have a few questions for you. If you answer them truthfully, I will not wait for you until you are done with your shift. I will leave now and leave you a lovely tip for your cooperation. If you lie to me, I will not tip you. I will instead wait for you. And then hopefully you will learn to be honest with me – at three in the morning. You understand?"

"Yes," I said, barely audible. My knees started to shake.

"Good," he said. He rubbed again at his mustache, seemingly in thought, then asked, "Where do you live?"

"In San Jose del Cabo."

Please, please, please don't ask for my address, I thought.

"Ah. And who do you live with?"

"M-my mother and father."

"No husband."

"No."

"Children?"

I shook my head.

"Boyfriend?"

"No, just my mother and father. I don't have a boyfriend."

I knew that's what he wanted to hear. His smile became very sly.

"Good girl. Boyfriends are useless. You need a husband – a man, not a boy."

I didn't say anything to that. My mouth was drying up.

He went on, looking around, "Is this your only job?"

"Yes."

"How long have you been working here?"

"Three years."

"How old are you?"

"Twenty-three."

"Are you happy?"

I frowned at him, taken off-guard. "What?"

"I asked if you were happy. Are you happy?"

"Are *you* happy?" I retorted.

He raised his brows. "Yes. Of course. I have everything I could ever want . . . almost."

He wanted me to comment on the *almost* part, I could tell. But I steeled myself against curiosity.

"How nice. Well, I am poor and I work this job to take care of my parents, who are sick. I have always been poor and I have always worked hard. I am not happy." I was slightly amazed at the honesty that was coming out of my mouth, things I didn't even admit to myself.

"Do you ever get in trouble for talking back?" he asked, and for a moment I thought I was in big trouble. Then he shook his head. "It doesn't matter, you can be trained out of that. So you're not happy. But you're so beautiful, Luisa. Beautiful enough to bring me in here, to make me want to talk to you, to make me want to know more about you."

"Beauty means nothing," I said.

"Ah, but you've won pageants before, prizes that have given you money."

My heart jump-started. "How did you know that?"

"I know many things," he went on, "and I want *many* things. Final question: are you a virgin?"

My cheeks immediately grew hot. "That is none of your business."

He grinned like a crocodile. "I'm afraid it is my business. Whether you like it or not, you are my business now. You can tell me the truth or I can wait until three in the morning and I'll find out for myself. Oh, and don't act like you're going to call the police over this. You know exactly who I am and you know exactly what I can do."

I felt like I was seconds away from fainting, the fear was so great. But somehow I managed to say, "Yes, I am a virgin."

He nodded in sleazy satisfaction. "I thought as much. Perhaps that is why you're so unhappy."

He looked to the other man who brought out his wallet. He placed $500 on the table.

My mouth dropped open at the wad of money just sitting there while Salvador and the man got out of the booth. I quickly backed out of the way.

"You can eat the nachos," Salvador said, hiking up his jeans and looking me over. "You look like you could use a bit more weight in those thighs. I wouldn't want to hurt you . . . much."

Then Salvador and the man left the bar. One moment they were here and I was caught in the most frightening conversation of my life, the next minute they were gone. I stood there for a long time, trying to wrap my head around what had happened. Then I realized that they had gone, for real, and there was a huge amount of money on the table waiting for me.

I quickly scooped it up and stuffed it down my shirt before anyone could see. Then I tried to go back to work, but every hour I was looking over my shoulder in fear that the drug lord would come back.

He didn't come back that night. Not even when I finished my shift.

But he did come back the next day.

And the next.

And the next.

And the next.

Until I learned not to fear him as much.

Until he made me an offer I couldn't refuse.

CHAPTER THREE

"Luisa you've barely touched your food," my mother said. I looked up from my plate to her blank stare, always wondering how she could sense such things. It must have been motherly instinct.

"I'm just not very hungry," I admitted, pushing the chicken around on my plate, my head and heart heavy as if someone had opened my mouth and poured sand inside me.

She slowly placed her fork down and sighed. "You haven't been yourself for the last few weeks. Is there something you need to talk about? Is it work?"

I glanced at my father. He was eating away, apparently content. I knew he wasn't really here right now – when my father was one hundred per cent himself, he was very intuitive and a straight shooter. I could rarely keep things from him either.

"It's not work," I said slowly, knowing that I was going to have to tell them. I just didn't know how. They wouldn't see it the way I saw it. I wondered how much I could hide from them.

"Mama, Papa," I said. I cleared my throat and straightened up in my chair. Even though my mother couldn't see me, I felt her looking. Only my dad remained lost in thought, and for once I was okay that he would have no reaction. "I met a man."

"Oh?" my mother asked, her interest piqued by the foreign subject. "Who is he? Where did you meet him? Do you like him?"

"I met him at work," I said, skirting the other questions and shoving a piece of stewed tomato in my mouth. I chewed slowly, planning my words. "He took an interest in me. He is very wealthy and has promised me the world."

Her face fell slightly. "I see." She paused, pushing her plate away from her. "I am not surprised, Luisa. You are a beautiful, intelligent woman. I am only surprised that this is the first man you have talked about to us."

Here it came. "That is because it is serious. He has asked to marry me."

The room stilled, choking on silence and the oppressive heat. My heart throbbed with fear from just hearing those words out loud.

It was the cold, hard truth; Salvador Reyes had asked me to marry him.

I couldn't read my mother's expression at all. She was in shock, that was for sure, but whether she was happy, sad, angry or suspicious, I didn't know. Finally she said, "When did this happen?"

"A few days ago," I told her. He had come into the bar every day, sometimes with David, that creepy crony of his who always wore his shades inside. A few times, though, it was just Salvador. I never had any doubt that there was an army of people stationed all around, so we were never really alone, but it was during those times that he would ask me to have dinner with him, even if I was in the middle of the shift. At this point, Bruno knew who he was and what was going on, and he had to allow me as many breaks as I wanted.

Salvador controlled the entire bar from the moment he stepped into it until the moment he left.

And he controlled me.

The curious thing, however, was that each day I grew more comfortable with his presence. It wasn't that I was less scared or intimidated by him. It was just that I got used to the fear. The fear of Salvador, of what he wanted from me, of what he would do next, became as soft and easy as my favorite blanket. And because he was the scariest of them all, I no longer feared anyone else but him. Bruno, he was nothing in comparison. My terrors had become consolidated into one greasy, mustached man with a beer gut and bad hair. A man who ruled such a violent part of the world and who would now rule mine.

Because, when he asked me the other day, when I had finished my shift early and he insisted I walk down to the marina with him, I knew I had to say yes.

If I was being honest with myself, there was a part of me that could have swooned at the proposal. When Salvador got down on one knee and took my hand in his, his palms sweaty, his fingers large and fat, I tricked my mind and heart into momentarily believing that Salvador knew me, cared for me, loved me. Of course, he only wanted me to look good at his side and that was it. Well, that and be in his bed. What else could there be after just a few weeks?

So I said yes and tried to believe I meant it. If I said no, I would be killed. There was no doubt about that. No woman turned down Salvador Reyes, not for a date, not for marriage.

"I will treat you like a princess," he had said to me, a stupid, lopsided grin on his pockmarked face. "And you will have everything you ever wanted. You'll be richer than the President."

And that's when I found the tiny shred of hope to cling to. By marrying the country's most notorious drug lord, a man who had politicians and police under his thumb, a man with more money than he probably knew what to do with, I would be buying myself safety from everyone but him, and I would be buying me and my parents a life we would never get to experience otherwise. I would no longer have to work for Bruno. I could have my mother and father taken care of and their every whim catered to.

It was at that thought that I was finally able to give Salvador a genuine smile. He responded by kissing me for the first time, his mustache tickling my upper lip. I wished it could have meant something to me, but all I could do was concentrate on the two competing feelings in my chest: relief.

And dread.

"Did you say yes?" my mother asked quietly, snapping me back to reality, to the kitchen table with the one wobbly leg, to the overhead fan that did nothing to disperse the hot air, to my father's kind but desolate eyes as he stared curiously at my mother, perhaps seeing her for the first time today.

I nodded and dabbed at my mouth with the napkin. "I did. It is for the best, Mama, you will see."

She gave me a funny look. "You act as if marriage is a bargain you have to make." When I didn't say anything, she went on. "So what is the bargain here?"

"He has a lot of money, I told you. He will take care of me and I can take proper care of you." I quickly reached across the table and put my hand on hers. "Mama, please, this is a good thing."

"Then why can't I hear it in your voice? You are anything but happy."

"I am happy," I said. "I will be happy. In time. It's all so new and . . ."

"And so who is this man who you suddenly agreed to marry?"

"You don't really know him," I said carefully. "But he has a lot of power and a lot of influence."

"And what does he do?" she asked, her voice taking on a strange steely quality. She knew that no wealth in our country came honestly.

There was nothing for me to do but tell the truth. The truth would hurt her, but it would also keep her safe.

"His name is Salvador," I said. "And he is in charge of a cartel."

My mother's mouth dropped open while my father muttered the first words I'd heard from him all evening. "Salvador Reyes," he said, musing over it. "He is a bad, bad man." Of course he could forget his own wife and daughter sometimes, but a notorious drug lord lived in every memory.

"Luisa," she said breathlessly. "You can't be serious."

I gave her a tight smile. "Unfortunately, I am."

"Salvador Reyes. The Sal? The drug lord? The jackal?" She shook her head and folded her hands in her lap. "No. No, I refuse to believe this."

"But it is the truth."

"But why? Why here? Why *you*?"

"I wish I could say, Mama. I don't know. He thinks I am beautiful and worthy of a better life." *He thinks I am worthy of his bed.*

She snorted caustically. "A better life? Who does he think

he is? Has he been here? We are not living in squalor, Luisa. We have everything that we need right here."

"No, we don't!" I yelled, surprised by the ferocity in my voice. "Every day I struggle to get by, for you, for Papa. And it's still not enough."

She rubbed her lips together, taken aback. I could see the wash of shame on her face and I immediately regretted losing my temper.

"I'm sorry," I said quickly. "You know I've done everything to take care of the both of you and I'll do whatever I can to keep doing so. This is an opportunity—"

"This is a death sentence," she muttered.

Her words sent cold waves down my spine. I swallowed hard. "No," I said, though I didn't believe it myself. "He can protect me. I will go and live with him in a mansion in Culiacán. I will be safe, safer than anyone in the country. And you will be safe too. I will make sure that you and Papa are taken care of, you can live with us on the compound or stay here, in some place really nice. I will do whatever it takes. I am doing this for you."

She just shook her head, a few strands of her greying hair coming loose around her face. "This is wrong. You deserve to marry a man for love, not money."

"Maybe I can learn to love him. Maybe he can learn to love me."

Her mouth twisted into a sad smile. "Oh, Luisa, I know you are not that naïve! He is a drug lord. They do not know how to love a fellow human being. They only love money and they only love death. He will never love you. He will have other women on the side. You will never be able to leave. You will become a prisoner of his life."

Is it any different than being a prisoner to this life? I thought to myself. I sighed. "You know I have no choice. Whether I'll love him or not, whether he'll love me or not, you know I can't say no."

"There are always choices, my daughter. God gave you free will to make them."

"Then I am choosing to die later instead of dying now."

I thought my mother would admonish me for talking so fatalistically, but she understood. There was nothing easy or right about this situation, so there was nothing left for me to do but try and make the best of it.

"You deserve so much more," she finally said, staring at nothing.

I looked pointedly at her and my father. "As do the both of you. And now, we shall have more. Let's just ignore the cost for now."

She nodded and went back to her food, picking aimlessly at the chicken that had grown cold. Now that she knew of the weight on my shoulders, she didn't have an appetite either.

The next day I had my final shift at the bar. My mother thought I was crazy, but Papa had instilled such a good work ethic in me that it was hard to shake. Despite everything Bruno had done to me over the years, he had provided me with a job and the means to take care of my parents, and I couldn't just leave without warning. The moment Salvador had asked me to marry him and told me he would be taking care of me from now on, I gave Bruno one week's notice.

I have to admit, it was a bit sad to say goodbye. As I stood behind the bar and looked over the people in the booths, laughing over drinks, I forgot about all the times I was treated like dirt by customers and forgot about being afraid of Bruno's advances. I only remembered the comfort and security, as false as it had been. Faced with the infinite unknown of my new life, the job had seemed so simple and safe.

"I'm going to miss you," Camila said after she'd hugged me for the millionth time that day. She held me by my shoulders and leaned in, her eyes inquisitive as they searched mine. "And I'm going to worry about you, you know."

I nodded, trying to keep my posture straight, my face falsely confident. "Don't worry about me. I am better off."

She frowned, and her eyes flitted over to Bruno who was standing by the entrance and hitting on the hostess. "Perhaps so. But as obnoxious and disgusting as Bruno can be, he is not Salvador Reyes."

"Don't worry about me," I repeated, looking her hard in the eyes.

She smiled softly and squeezed my shoulders before letting go. "Then I won't."

The rest of the shift went smoothly, with the staff and Bruno giving me a small slice of cake at the end. We all did shots to honor my departure, and Bruno gave me a very proper, very professional handshake, wishing me well in the future. As much as I wanted to spit in his face and take advantage of his newfound respect for me, I played polite and silently hoped that one day karma would come knocking at his door.

It was around nine o' clock when my last day was finally over. I walked out the door and made it about halfway down the block, squeezing through throngs of slow tourists, before a black town car pulled up to the curb.

"Miss Chavez." David stepped out of the passenger side and gestured to the back door, those sunglasses ever present on his skinny face. "Would you get in the car, please?"

My heart thumped loudly. "Of course," I said, trying to keep my voice steady. I hadn't planned on seeing him or Salvador today.

I opened the door and got in the backseat. To my surprise it was empty. My limbs were heavy with dread.

"Where are we going?" I asked David as he quickly sped away from the curb.

"To see Salvador," he said simply.

"I parked just around the corner from work," I said feebly, looking behind me as it all got lost in the traffic.

"I will return you to your car after," he said, not looking at me in the mirror. "Salvador has a few things he needs to discuss with you."

He could have added, "Don't be afraid," but he didn't. I'd probably always be afraid when Salvador wanted to talk with me whether we were married or not.

After about twenty minutes, we were coasting up the dry, cactus-strewn hills outside of the city. David pulled the car over, and in a minute the door opened and Salvador stepped in. He was wearing jeans and a grey, sweat-stained T-shirt that was covered in a layer of dust.

"Turn up the air conditioning," he barked at David as he closed the door and the car pulled onto the road.

Salvador sat across from me and pushed his shades to the top of his head. He was sweaty and his eyes were extra puffy, perhaps from drinking too much. For a split second I wondered if I could marry this man, let alone share his bed. There was just nothing to attract me to him. If he had a good personality, it might have been different. But he didn't have that, not even when he was faking it.

"I am sorry, princess," he said, still overly polite with me. "I'm afraid I cannot stick around Los Cabos any longer. It is no longer safe."

Well, you were kind of flaunting that you were here, I thought to myself but didn't dare say.

He reached into the back of his pants and pulled out a small, cloth wallet. He took my hands in his and placed it in them. "Here. This is one thousand American dollars. It's enough to take care of you for the next month, just as I promised. But it's not enough to buy you a new life, if that's what you're thinking."

I opened my mouth to protest, fear coursing through me.

He shook his head. "I am only joking," he said, though I could tell from the cold, wicked glint to his eyes that he wasn't. "But in one month, I will be back for you. We will have our wedding less than a week after that. Don't worry about the dress, I will pick that out for you as well."

I could only stare dumbly at him. "We'll be getting married in a month . . ."

"More or less," he said. "I thought you'd be happier."

I forced a smile on my face and leaned over, placing my hand on his clammy arm. I swallowed my revulsion. I played my part. "I am happy. Very happy. I am just surprised and sad that you are leaving me for so long."

He smiled at that, his bushy mustache twitching up, droplets of sweat gathering in it. "You will survive. You have until now. And after we are married, you will always be at my side. You will never be alone again."

Those words rang through my head as I later drove back home, toward my mother and father, the fat wallet on the seat beside me. I had one month to enjoy my life as it was before it would change for good.

CHAPTER FOUR

Javier

The whore was beautiful.

Then again, Este usually did have good taste in women, if not in fashion. I watched as she walked uneasily down the cobblestone driveway, heading toward the guards at the gate, heading toward freedom. She reminded me of a spindly-legged fawn, her high heels a poor match for the uneven ground, and for one brief moment I felt sorry for her. Pity, even. Such a pretty thing selling her body for riches that never came. She only got money, but that was never what the whore really wanted. What she really wanted, she would never, ever get.

She was better off dead.

And at that thought, the twinge of pity was gone.

I watched as she approached the gate. Though the two guards were facing forward, their eyes hidden by sunglasses, I could tell they were exchanging a look, wondering who was going to kill her first. Orders were orders.

They didn't need to debate for long. A shot rang out, a bullet to the back of her head, and the whore fell to the ground slowly, as if she had just grown too tired to stand. Blood began to flow from her head.

I craned my neck, mildly curious to see who had done it.

I couldn't see anyone but the guards, which meant it had to have been Franco. It had turned into a hobby for him lately, as if he discovered he had a taste for being a sniper, but it was better the whores than anyone else at the compound.

Somewhere I knew my gardener, Carlos, was cursing himself. Franco never disposed of the bodies, and it would be Carlos's job once again to do something with her, wash away the red mess from the hot stones. Naturally, he would never complain to me, or someone else would have to clean up his own blood.

There was a knock at the door behind me. I kept my hands behind my back, my eyes glued to the blood that was pouring out of her head, a hypnotic, moving painting.

"Come in," I said. I didn't have to turn around to know it was Este. "What was the whore's name?" I asked, still staring at the growing crimson pond.

The door clicked softly and I felt him step into the room. "Laura," he said. "She could fuck like no one's business, hey. You should have tried her. You know I don't mind sharing."

I ignored him. "Don't you think it's a bit, oh, I don't know . . . crude, to have the whores leave this way?" I asked him. "Wouldn't it be better to kill them in bed?"

I heard him snort. "No, *that* would be crude. We might as well let them have that bit of hope that they'll make it out alive, don't you think? Besides, this is more sporting. It's hunting. Hunting is elegant."

I nodded. I supposed he was right. It wasn't very sporting otherwise. I watched as Carlos came scurrying toward the body and started to drag Laura away. I never asked what he did with the bodies, but as long as I never saw them again, it didn't really matter. Out of sight, out of mind.

I turned around and eyed Este. "I suppose in a perfect world, we wouldn't have to kill them at all."

He smirked and leaned on my desk. "Well, look at you getting all soft."

I raised my brow. "It's just a shame that you can't buy silence anymore."

He shrugged. "One whore talks and then you get fuckers at your door. We all need to get laid, well at least I do." A wry look came across his face at that. "There really is no other solution."

"I suppose not," I said, and sat down at my desk. I adjusted my watch and stared up at him expectantly. "So, why are you here? Showing off your terrible taste in shoes? Are those made of cardboard?"

He peered down at his feet. As usual the man looked like he'd rolled out of the California surf with his T-shirt, board shorts, and terrible Birkenstocks. Not the image the cartel had at all, but there was no talking style into him. Believe me, I had tried.

He placed a large envelope down on the desk. "Got the email from Martin just a few minutes ago and had these printed out for you."

I stared at the envelope for a beat before laying my fingers on it and sliding it toward me. A quiver of anticipation ran up my arms and I did my best to quell it.

"I didn't respond," Este went on. "He mentioned that the location of the wedding changed at the last minute yesterday, but he was still able to get everything done. I printed out the email. It's in there too."

I nodded and slowly opened the flap.

"Should I get anything more from him?"

I shook my head and slid the papers out of the envelope and onto the desk. "No, it doesn't matter. Martin is dead."

I glanced up to see Este staring at me with a stunned expression. "So soon?"

"Yes," I said absently, looking back to the paper in my hands. I skimmed the printed out email.

"What a shame, I liked the guy."

"I didn't," I said. "But he got the job done and that's all that matters."

"Kind of like the whores."

I pursed my lips. "Mmmm," I conceded. From the email, Martin had done the job well. He had observed Salvador Reyes and his bride from a few days before the wedding and gotten photographs during the ceremony. "But killing women is always so ugly, isn't it?"

"You see," Este said, crossing his arms, "right there, that sort of shit surprises me. You know, considering your issues with women and all that."

I shot him a piercing look. "I don't have issues."

"No," he said slowly with an easy smile on his lips, knowing all too much. "Of course not."

It was those moments that I hated Esteban Mendoza. Hated that he was my right hand man, hated that he was the closest person to me, even though that never amounted to much. I hated that it would hurt me so to kill him.

"Martin would have talked," I said to him. "Much like the whores. He did well. Don't worry, his wife and children will be taken care of."

Este raised his brows.

"With money," I supplied quickly. "They will be fine without their father, who was stupid enough to get involved with us to begin with. I'm not cruel."

"Well, you're not shooting whores," he said. "And I'm not worried. You know I rarely worry about you."

"How touching," I said wryly.

He walked around the desk and stood behind me, looking over my shoulder. I hated when he did that. "I'm interested in what you think," he said.

"About what?"

"About *her*," he said while I slid a photograph out of the pile. "Mrs. Reyes."

It was black and white and printed on paper, making it less sharp than a photograph, but it did the job. It was a picture of a woman in a white strapless wedding dress, very fluffy and extravagant from the waist down. Her hands were clasped demurely at her front, her face caught in a nervous smile.

She was extremely beautiful but that was to be expected. The country's most flagrant excuse for a drug kingpin would never marry anyone less than stunning, and this woman, Luisa, fit the bill. But despite her body, with her round, perky tits and elegant neck, her long dark hair and classic face, there was another layer to her that immediately got me hard. It was this look in her eyes. They were so pure and soft, giving her radiance that seemed to leap off the page.

I wanted nothing more than to have her on her knees, have her fix those round, angelic eyes on me and watch as I pinned her down and came right into them. I would take her purity and make her see the world for what it really was – a hot, sticky mess at the end of my dick.

"I bet she'd be a tight little fuck," Este leered over my shoulder.

I shot him a disgusted look. "She's not a whore, Este," I chided him.

"Not to you," he said, as I looked at the next picture of her, now with Salvador at her side.

"I mean it," I said, my eyes drawn to her again and again. "No one is touching her. Not you, not Franco."

"I give you my promise," Este said. "But Franco can barely control himself around the whores."

"No one is touching her," I repeated. "She will be our hostage. She is collateral. No one is laying a hand on her."

"Except for you, I assume."

She almost seemed too good to even touch. I couldn't wait to break her down. "She is very valuable," I admitted.

I flipped through a couple more photographs and grew harder at each one. I wished Este would just fucking leave so I could deal with it. I almost wished Laura was still alive so I could flip her over and come all over her back. I never fucked the women around here, but that didn't mean I didn't use them.

"You know," Este said, his lazy voice starting to grate on me. "If Martin had been there close enough to spy on them, close enough to photograph, why didn't you just get him to put a bullet in Salvador's head? Especially if Martin was going to die anyway."

I eyed him warily, disappointed that he could be so rash. "Because life is a game and we're all just trading cards. We play the right hand to get ahead." I studied the smiling, ignorant face of Sal as he stared at his bride. "Death stops the game. It's too final, too inflexible. Death is viciously stubborn."

When Este didn't say anything, I looked up to see a dull gleam in his eyes. I sighed and pinched the bridge of my nose, annoyed at his ineptitude. "What good would killing Salvador do? Right? David Guirez or whoever, anyone, someone, they would step in and take over faster than you can shit after your coffee, and nothing will have changed. Look at Travis Raines. The moment he died, I was able to slither on through to the top, to right here, right now."

"Only because you killed Travis," he noted. "More or less."

"We killed Travis," I corrected him. "Anyway, the point is that the dead make lousy deals. If we want the shipping lane, we have to force him to give it to us. Killing him does nothing. Taking his new bride, now that will do something."

"You sound so sure," Este said, walking around the desk.

"I have no reason not to be sure," I said. "They are newly-weds. He needs her, he wants her. We will get her soon, before he gets bored of her cherry ass. Sal has pride. We all do. It is our weakness. I know that enough about myself to know it about others."

He smoothed his hand over the scruff on his chin and gave me a smooth nod. "All right."

I stared at a photo of them at the altar, a lavish outdoor ceremony. He was staring at her with that pride I was talking about. And she was staring at him with a look that was all too familiar to me.

"She doesn't love him, though," I commented, almost to myself.

"How can you tell?" he asked, taking a step closer and peering at the photos again.

I shrugged. "I just can. She doesn't."

"So is she marrying him for money then?"

I took the papers and sorted them until they were neat and evenly stacked before slipping them back into the envelope. "Probably. Does it matter?"

"No. So when do we act?"

"Soon," I said, putting the envelope in the first drawer. I knew I'd be taking it out again after he left. "But we'll do it slowly. Start with recon first, perhaps see if we can track down Derek to help us with this."

Este gave me an odd look. "Derek . . . we haven't talked to him since he . . . I'm not sure he's even in Mexico anymore."

"Perhaps not," I said. I wasn't too worried. Derek Conway was an American ex-military man, an assassin for hire. He had been contracted to us during some of our more important moments. In fact, the last time I saw him was three years ago. He'd put a bullet through Travis Raines' head. Ordered by me, of course. Then he screwed us over, but I couldn't fault him for that. He would be loyal to whoever paid him the most.

But he wasn't the only man at my disposal. Since I had taken over the cartel, I had a whole legion of men to do my dirty work, the best of the best. For the next month or so, I wanted someone who would be sleek and loyal. Kidnapping the wife of Mexico's largest drug lord wasn't going to be a walk in the park, but with the right people, it wouldn't be impossible.

Perhaps I was just being overconfident, but it had only served me well in the past.

I gave Este a levelling stare. "I'm putting this in your hands. Can you handle it?"

"When haven't I?"

"Oh, I don't know. I sent you to Hawaii once to finish a job but you ended up fucking some suicidal surfer chick instead."

"I still got the job done. What's the difference if I get action at the same time?"

I rolled my eyes at his crassness and gave him a slight, dismissive wave. "Go put this all together. And don't disappoint me."

"Funny," he mused. "I'm not sure what it's like to *not* disappoint you." Then he turned and left the office, shutting the door behind him.

I got up and walked over to the window. The driveway was wet where Carlos must have watered it down, and the body of Laura was gone, the blood all washed away. It was like nothing ugly ever happened. I took in the mountains, the violently green foliage that stretched beyond the property and melded into the cliffs of The Devil's Backbone. Sometimes I wondered if there was someone out there plotting something in the way I was plotting for Salvador. I usually decided there was. You didn't run a cartel without having an army of people out there wanting to kill you. After all, I used to be a soldier in that very army. I just never dwelled on it – I moved through each day thinking that I was better off alive, a card that kept the game going.

I also clung to the archaic, and perhaps slightly naïve belief that everything happened for a reason. I hadn't cheated death so many times, I hadn't had my heart ripped out, my soul lost, my family murdered, my future trampled all for nothing. I was put away in an American prison for three months, and thanks to the grace of God and friends in high places, I miraculously walked away and back into Mexico where I was able to jump back in to the cartel that had rightfully become mine. All of that, all of those miracles, all of that grace, hadn't happened for no reason.

My destiny was constantly being rewritten and it would continue to be until it was fulfilled. Until I was at the top of the world and I had everything I'd ever wanted at my feet. Until I could crush everything with none of the mercy that was bestowed upon me.

I went over to the wet bar, and with some pleasure, pushed back the curved top of the old-fashioned globe that revealed the bottles of alcohol beneath. The bar used to be Travis's, something he had picked up at an antique store in Mississippi where I had worked for him back in the simple times. I'd always admired it, the vintage elegance, of a time when men were really men and when they got up in the morning they showed up for the world.

I poured myself a glass of old Scotch, opting for that instead of my usual tequila, and went back over to the desk. I sat down and gently brought the photographs of Luisa out of the drawer. I felt a foreign pang of indignity as I looked them over again, as if someone was watching me, judging me, for something I shouldn't have been doing. But I needed to look at her. I needed to study her. I needed to know the exquisite creature I would be bringing into this house. I needed to know the woman I would destroy through and through before I handed her back to Salvador.

I needed to ask her soft, radiant, pixelated face for forgiveness for what I was about to do.

She would soon be sorry she ever married Salvador Reyes.

CHAPTER FIVE

Luisa

"You look nervous," the makeup artist said to me as she dusted a light coating of glimmering blush across my cheekbones. "Don't be. You look beautiful."

She had a singsong quality to her voice that would have soothed any bride-to-be, but there was no soothing me. If I got up and looked out the window, I would have seen the plaza below absolutely filled with people here to see me and Salvador get married. I would have also felt, though not seen, the countless snipers that were lined up to take out anyone who might have . . . interfered. That should have made me feel better, safer, but it didn't. I felt I was only safe until the moment I said "I do." After that, I was just a rat scurrying through the desert, the hawk biding its time from above.

"And you said your parents are here," she went on, her voice quicker now, trying to get me to talk, to say something. I'd been more or less silent the whole time. Perhaps she was nervous too. She knew who I was marrying, after all.

"Yes, they are here," I said, my throat feeling strangely raw.

"They must be so proud," she said, tilting my chin up with her fingers in order to line my lips with precision.

"They don't normally travel," I said by way of explanation,

barely moving my lips. My parents weren't so much proud as they were scared out of their minds. My father hadn't been himself for days now, and it was only by luck that he was calm and under control. Luck, or perhaps some medication my mother borrowed from a friend of hers. My mother herself was rigid and unyielding, trying hard to be happy for me but failing at it. For the first time in my life, I could hardly stand to be around her. She only reminded me of what I was giving up and giving in to.

"Where do they live?" she asked.

"In San Jose del Cabo," I said.

"They won't be joining you with your husband?"

I shook my head and then smiled apologetically when I realized it messed up her work. "They wanted to stay where their friends were. It's too . . . inconvenient for them to be living with me and Salvador." Not to mention that with Salvador's help, I was able to buy them a beautiful new home close to a retirement center and hospital. Both my parents had a full-time caregiver now, a tough but lovely woman named Penelope, and they had their activities and their friends. It happened fast, and we were all still adjusting to the change. I did what I could to ease the guilt since I couldn't live with them anymore, but it was so much better than them risking their lives to live with us in Culiacán. Though they were out of my reach, I felt they were much safer in the Baja.

"Well, perhaps that is for the best," she said, giving me a quiet smile. "Nothing ruins a marriage like in-laws."

I returned the look, and to my relief, she finished up my face in silence.

The wedding ceremony itself went a lot smoother than I

thought. The three glasses of champagne I nicked off a waiter certainly helped. It was quite elaborate with the priest and our vows and the endless sea of people watching our every move. But I did my part, acted in the play, and did my best to pretend I was the blushing bride eager to be wedded to her powerful husband. I could only hope that my face would not betray me and show the world just how terrified I was.

The moment he slipped the ring on my finger – a big, blinding diamond that cost more than most people would earn in their life – and we said our vows, I knew I should have wept with power. I was the wife of the jackal, nearly the most powerful man in the country. But while others would see power resting on my shoulders, I knew deep down the cape was an illusion.

And it didn't take very long to find out how fake it was.

For our honeymoon, Salvador and I headed to the coast to a quiet little village that was completely under his jurisdiction, where he had a massive beachfront property. I barely had any time to say goodbye to my mother and father, my hands still clasping theirs, holding on for dear life, as I was ushered away from the ceremony, flowers in my hair, and into the waiting limousine.

It was bulletproof. But I was not.

Salvador and I sat in the back, the only inhabitants, while I craned my neck around and watched as my parents disappeared from sight, two frail frames against the relentless sun.

"That was rude of me," I said, even though I knew it was best to keep my mouth shut. I wished my voice wasn't shaking. "To just leave them like that." It was more than rude; it frightened me more than anything else to have them out of my reach, so fast and so soon.

Salvador turned in his seat to face me. He looked almost handsome in his tuxedo, his hair slicked back, his mustache trimmed. His eyes though, they always betrayed him. They were frazzled, sparking, like bad wiring.

"You're my wife now," he said with a grin that was far too wicked to be genuine. "You no longer answer to your parents, you answer to me."

I swallowed uneasily, trying to decide on whether to wear defiance or pleading compliance on my face. It was a split-second decision and defiance won out.

It got me a smack across the face.

I took a few moments, my newly ringed hand on my cheek, trying to soothe the throbbing. I stared at Salvador in dumb shock. I knew that everything had been for show so far, I just had no idea it would turn to the truth so fast.

"You answer to me," he repeated, his eyes growing thinner and hard as steel. "That means no talking back."

I opened my mouth and he immediately backhanded me again, harder this time, enough that I saw lights flashing behind my eyes, my teeth biting down on my tongue as the back of my head hit the seat rest. I tried not to panic, tried my hardest to remain composed, all while wanting to cry out from the pain. The fear was greater than I'd ever known.

After a moment, I straightened up in my seat, inching away from him. He only leered at me, as if the whole thing was one giant joke. Perhaps it was.

"When I say no talking back," he said, running his fingers over his mustache, "I mean it, like I mean everything I say. We can have a nice, happy marriage if you learn to behave.

I will still give you the world and you will want for nothing. But there are rules that you will have to follow. Nothing is free in this life, do you understand?"

I nodded, not daring to speak.

Suddenly he shot forward and was in my face, a vein throbbing at his temple. "I said, do you understand!?" he screamed, spittle flying onto me.

I shut my eyes tight, as if it would make him go away. I felt like the life was being drained out of me with every second that I spent in that limo, that this was the start of a slow and painful death. And I had willingly walked into it.

You're doing this for your parents, I told myself, trying to draw myself inward to where it was dark, warm, and safe. *Remember that. Remember whose happiness you are buying.*

"Look at me," Salvador said, his voice quiet now, though I could feel his hot breath on my skin. "You have to look at me when I'm talking to you. That is one of the rules." He grabbed my chin and squeezed hard enough to make my eyes flutter open. I stared at him blankly, not wanting to really see him. My husband.

"The other rule," he went on, softer now, "is that you will not talk back. You will also be loyal and you will not stray. You will not even look at other men. For your own protection, you will not be allowed to have any friends that I do not choose for you. You will not be able to leave the house on your own. You will always stay thin and beautiful, with a big smile for everyone you meet. And you will not deny me my rights as a husband." He licked his lips as he said that. "Now. Do. You. Under. Stand?"

I did understand. The life of Luisa Chavez was really and truly over.

There was only Luisa Reyes now.

And she was about to live a life of pain.

Salvador took my virginity in the back of that limo, minutes before we even reached the beach house. It happened quickly, and for that I was glad. It didn't lessen the pain – the horrible, ripping pain – but it meant I didn't have to suffer the humiliation of my first time for too long.

He wasn't kind, he wasn't gentle, he wasn't generous. If that's what sex was, I wondered how anyone could enjoy it. He treated my body like a piece of meat, a slice of property. I had no claim to it, and that's what he wanted to show me, again and again and again. I had no say, no rights. I was his, whether I wanted to be or not, and he would have me anytime he wanted. My own feelings and desires didn't matter.

I didn't want to the second time. I was sore, oh so sore, and trying to sleep in, afraid to face him and my first morning as his wife. But Salvador didn't believe in the word *no*. It didn't matter how many times I said it, if I struggled . . . in fact, he liked it when I did. He'd strip his bloated, ugly body naked and force himself on me and into me with a grin on his face that not even his mother could love.

If he even *had* a mother. I couldn't imagine anyone ever raising him. When I tried to picture him as a young boy, I knew there would have been no innocence in his heart. He'd have been the one to put firecrackers in dogs' mouths, to take the fights in the playground too far, to spit in his grandmother's food. I tried to think about these things, trying to figure out how one becomes such a vile, hateful thing, while he violated me from the inside out.

It wasn't enough that I was clearly in pain and vulnerable while this happened – if I struggled in the least, he would assert his dominance in other ways.

"Mrs. Reyes," the housekeeper called out from the balcony behind me. I was sitting on the beach, the warm Pacific lapping at my feet and soaking the ends of my dress. I'd been sitting there for hours, and I knew she was calling me in for lunch. But I couldn't eat even if I tried.

I ignored her and stared down at my arms, at the marks and bruises up and down them, ugly purples and yellows from the last few days, so bright in the daylight. For a split second there was so much terror filling up my chest like ice water that I thought about running straight into the ocean and trying to swim until I drowned.

But that would be nearly impossible. To the left of me, standing half-hidden in the palms, was one set of guards, watching the property and watching me. I couldn't see who was to my right, further down the beach, but I did know that they wouldn't let me drown.

They wouldn't let me escape.

We'd been on our honeymoon for one week. I never once got the opportunity to speak to my parents on the phone. I never once got to leave the property, not even if I was escorted. Salvador was only around at night and in the mornings when he would systematically beat me and rape me. One time, he made me perform a lewd act on David, his second in command, and when I didn't want to do it, he put a gun to my head. Part of me was tempted to keep refusing, just so he could pull the trigger, but I knew he never would. I'd only been his wife for a few days, and there was a lifetime of enjoyment still left for him.

"Mrs. Reyes," the housekeeper repeated. "Lunch is served. Mr. Reyes would like to eat with you."

So he was in the house today. Lucky me. It took all of my strength not to yell back at her and tell her that I was Luisa Chavez first and Luisa Reyes second, and that Salvador could go fuck himself. But now I was learning how to play the game. I got punished either way, but the safer I played it, the smaller the punishment I got. I'd learned not to talk back to Salvador after the limo ride, I'd learned not to refuse him the morning after, and I'd learned never to question him after what he made me do to David. I'd learned a lot in such a short time.

The reluctant education of the narco-wife.

I sighed and got to my feet, absently brushing the sand off my dress. My hair billowed around me like a dark scarf, caught in the cool breeze off the ocean. I closed my eyes and imagined, just for one moment, what it would be like not to live in fear. To actually feel happiness and love from a man. My heart practically shuddered from the realization that I'd never, ever have that for as long as Salvador Reyes lived.

As I walked back to the beach house with a heavy heart, I tried to think about my parents and how they were better off. I tried to think about how I was better off, not having to slave every day for someone like Bruno, how I'd never have to worry about how to make ends meet.

The fact was, I wasn't better off at all, and neither were my parents. I'd take Bruno and his busy hands, the long hours on my feet, the fear of never being able to give my parents what they deserved – I'd take all of that and hang on to it tight if I could. If only I could have realized that what I had wasn't so bad after all and if I could have gone back in time to take it back, I would. I gave everything I had away, just for a shot to have more.

Of course, there was the fact that I never really had a choice. That I could not have said no to Salvador. But as my mother said, we always have choices. And I was starting to think that in the grand scheme of things, perhaps I had made the wrong one.

The lesser of two evils was actually the greatest.

CHAPTER SIX

Javier

"So finally I meet *the* Javier Bernal." The man sat down across from me, a cigarette bobbing out of his lazy mouth. I wasted no time in snapping it out of his lips and breaking it in half, tossing it to the ground beside us.

He stared at me, dumbfounded for only a second, which I appreciated. A man who can get over things quickly is a man you want on your side.

"No smoking," I said, my eyes boring into his as I jerked my chin at the sign on the wall. The bar couldn't give two shits if people smoked or not, the sign was only there for legal reasons. But that wasn't the point. The man needed to know the score. I'd heard a lot about this Juanito, though there was no point in committing his name to memory. I only needed him for his intel, and the less I had to know, the better.

He nodded, that easy smile still there, if not faltering. That was good too. You needed to bounce back, but you also needed to stay afraid of the ones in charge.

He needed to stay afraid of me.

"Can I still drink?" he asked, raising his bottle of beer.

Ah, and he had a sense of humor. This made him easier to deal with, even like – too bad a sense of humor wouldn't

save him in the end. I've killed some of the funniest fuckers
I've ever met. They had me laughing even with their heads
on the ground.

"Of course," I said to him and raised my glass of tequila.
"To new beginnings."

We drank as some ballad from a Mexican pop idol played
in the background. This bar was one of the few bars in the
area where I could go and relax and not have to worry about
watered down booze or uncouth patrons. The owners were
paid handsomely by me, as were all law officials in the town
and the state of Durango. I had no fear of a rival cartel coming
in and blowing my head off, and I had no fear of the Mexican
Attorney General coming in and trying to take me away. As
much as I hated to admit it, without siphoning Salvador Reyes'
Ephedra shipping lane and adding more routes for opium,
cocaine, and marijuana, I really wasn't the guy they were
after. Naturally, with more power and influence came the
danger of being public enemy number one. Right now,
Salvador Reyes was the most wanted criminal and drug lord
in the country. Not that the police or anyone were doing
anything to stop him.

As for me, I had more to fear from rivals than from authori-
ties. I wasn't clean by any means – I couldn't ever step foot
in the United States again, for example. The last time I was
there, I was arrested for drug trafficking. It was a minor mix-up,
I wasn't actually trafficking any drugs, just trying to trade a
hostage to get ahead, but there was bloodshed and the feds
got involved. Apparently they have nothing better to do up
there than to worry about us Mexicans.

However, having enough money and knowing enough
people who work for the DEA gets you a free ride in the

states, so long as you promise to send them information on your enemies from time to time and swear to never set foot in the country again. And so that's what I did. Paid the right people and made my promises, and I was free to go, three months later.

Those three months though (while Esteban was taking care of my affairs and the cartel I had taken from Travis Raines) had cost me a lot. I should have been on my home soil and expanding; instead I was behind bars. The prisons in America were nothing like the ones in Mexico. It could have been a vacation for some, though perhaps I was treated so well because my dollar went further in the cells. There is so much power and influence in money and drugs that it makes me wonder why anyone would bother going straight. To save face? No, that is ludicrous. Your face never looks better than when you've got a gun in your hand and money under your ass.

I suppose I should have been grateful that I was only in prison for such a short time and I walked away unharmed with only a new smoking habit to add to my regrets.

At that thought, I fished a cigarette from my slim gold case and placed it in my mouth.

Juanito frowned at me. "The rules . . ." he said feebly.

I struck the match along the side of the wood table, then lit the cigarette and slowly blew smoke in his face. "The rules don't apply to me. Never have, never will." I placated him with a smile. "Now, let's talk business, shall we?"

He nodded and relaxed a bit on his stool, eager to get started. Another good sign. It said he was confident in his job.

"What I need from you, Juanito," I said, continuing to stare at him, "is to perform your job like it's the last job you'll ever do."

His smile went crooked. "Will it be the last job I ever do?"

I suppose my reputation preceded me. I puffed on the cigarette, in no hurry to answer him, until he had to look away from my stare. "You'll be paid enough so you never need to work again, if that is what you mean."

He swallowed hard, and I could sense his leg bouncing restlessly under the table. "There are rumors, you know."

"About me?" I asked simply.

More nervous gestures. "Yes."

"Are they about how large my dick is?"

Relief washed over his face, and he managed a laugh. "Not really."

"Too bad. It's true, you know. About my dick."

He didn't seem too impressed. He spun the bottle of beer around in his hands. "They say you end up killing most people who do jobs for you."

I shrugged. "So?"

"Is it true?"

I tapped the cigarette and let ash fall onto the floor. "It's not a lie. Look, if I promise not to kill you, will that ease your worries?"

His forehead scrunched up, unsure of what way to take me.

"I keep my promises," I added. "Just so you know."

"Well, that will help," he said.

"Then it's settled. You do your job, I'll pay you a lot of money and I won't kill you either." I signalled the bartender to pour me another drink, then went back to staring Juanito down. "So, before you start jacking up my bar tab, tell me your plans."

Now that his worries were eased, he was able to clearly explain exactly what he had to offer. Juanito had done some work with Esteban while I was in prison. Este was the technical guy who could hack into accounts, security systems – hell I think he'd even done some fucked up wizardry with satellite cameras before. But Este was needed at my side, for counsel and for my own protection. Juanito would infiltrate the Reyes compound as best he could, spying on Salvador and Luisa's routine for a week or two before reporting back with concrete intel. I had no doubt that Salvador had his new wife watched, but as the days went on, I also had no doubt that one of them would slip up. When that happened, we would make sure it happened again.

Then we would take her.

Juanito, at first glance, didn't look like the kind of man best suited for the job. Aside from his nervous mannerisms, he had a wiry build and a young face with round cheeks. But I knew better than to judge a book by its cover. All you needed to know about a man was in his eyes, and in Juanito's I could see the confidence in his skill. That sold me.

It also made me stop regretting my promise not to kill him – perhaps he would come in handy in the future.

"When will you start?" I asked as I nodded my thanks to the bartender who placed another glass of tequila in front of me.

"Tomorrow," he said matter-of-factly. "I can be in Culiacán by noon. By tomorrow evening, I promise you I'll know what house they are staying at and where. I've got connections there."

I raised my brows. "Who doesn't," I muttered, and then swallowed my drink. I cleared my throat. "Well, Juanito. I guess that's it."

"And you're not going to kill me?"

"My promise is my promise," I told him solemnly as I made the sign of the cross over my heart. He probably didn't believe me, but when he realized he wasn't dead yet, he would. I gestured to the door with a flick of my wrist. "You better be on your way. Este will pay you your deposit tonight. You'll get the rest after you deliver Luisa Reyes."

He licked his lips eagerly and got off the stool. "Fifty thousand American dollars."

I nodded with a tight smile. The longer I was in the business, the less I liked spending money. People like Salvador and other narcos, they wasted it on lavish bullshit. I liked the finest things in life, but anything better than the finest was just gratuitous.

But in order to get ahead, you needed a loss leader. Luisa was my loss leader.

I stuck my hand out and Juanito stared at it in surprise before he shook it. Call me old-fashioned but a deal was not a deal unless you shook on it. There was still a code among men in this business.

His eyes widened as I squeezed his hand and pulled him slightly towards me. I lowered my voice, my eyes fixed on his, and said, "But just so we're clear, if you fail, if you do not bring me the girl, I will hunt you down and skin you alive. I have a couple of pigs that get fat on human jerky, and I make *them* promises, too. Do you understand me?"

He blinked a few times, nodding quickly.

I let go of him and leaned back, raising my glass in the air. "Well then, cheers."

"Right. Cheers." He awkwardly took a sip of his beer, then wiped his hands on his shirt, and took off out of the bar and into the black night.

I sighed and finished my drink before pulling out another cigarette. At least Juanito would be putting in one hundred and ten percent now. Any boss worth their salt knew how to best motivate their employees and I was no different.

We had good news from Juanito a week later. He'd located the Reyes compound and had started infiltrating their security system, taking it slowly, so that no one would even know something was amiss. He did nothing but observe Luisa day in and day out, not exactly the toughest part of the job. At least it wasn't when you had something as easy on the eyes as she was.

A week later, he suggested we start getting ready to move. The perfect opportunity would eventually present itself, but we couldn't do a thing unless we were set up and primed for action. That meant a lot of waiting in the trees, scouring neighboring houses, and hiding in unmarked vans. It all took patience, but luckily I had grown to be a very patient man. I could chase something for years before I felt the need to catch up with it.

While Este and Franco went to Culiacán to join Juanito in the operation, I used two of my bodyguards, Tito and Toni, to help me set up the safe house. We needed the location to make our demands and to keep Luisa for the first few days or at least until Salvador gave in. When we were all done, I'd return to The Devil's Backbone a smarter man, and Luisa would return to her husband, perhaps a bit more broken than when she'd left.

I'd also included The Doctor as part of my arsenal. The Doctor was, yes, an actual physician and very shrewd. Though nearing his late sixties, he had been an integral part of Travis Raines' cartel and now he was a key figure in mine. He knew a lot, especially about the kidnapping side of the business. In Mexico, taking hostages and demanding ransom was as ordinary a job as operating a food cart. The Doctor had been involved in many of them over his lifetime and was the best of the best.

He was also supremely skilled at torture – another good reason to have him around. In some ways, with his knowledge and his groomed, elegant appearance, The Doctor would have made a superior assistant instead of Este. But as much as I respected The Doctor, there was something about him that reminded me of my father, and for that reason I didn't want him around me all day long. The dead were better off dead.

It wasn't long after we headed off to the safe house that I got the call from our driver, The Chicken. He reported that Este and Franco had captured "the girl," and they, Juanito included, were heading right back to us.

I hung up the phone and grinned stupidly at The Doctor, who had been standing beside me in the modest kitchen where he had been frying shrimp and rice for our dinner. There was something kind of nice about operating out of the safe house – it was basic and simple, like camping for kingpins.

I immediately smoked a cigar, both in celebration and in anticipation. I hadn't been this excited and anxious about something since . . . well, since a very long time ago. But that memory needed to stay in the deserts of California, where it belonged. The new memory was upon me, and I could practically smell it. I could practically smell *her*.

Luisa Reyes.

She was mine.

After we made quick work of the cigar and the meal, The Doctor and I headed down into the basement to get everything set up for her arrival. We had the chair and the ropes, and chains if we needed them. We had the digital camera set up and ready to record our ransom note which would then be uploaded and emailed directly to Salvador's account, thanks to Este's expertise. We even had bottles of water and carafes of hot tea and coffee – for us, of course. I liked for my men to be hydrated and have a clear head at our most crucial times, and this was most definitely one of those times.

With the safe house being much closer to Salvador's compound, The Doctor and I only had to wait a few hours for them to arrive. We drank our tea and discussed local politics to pass the time and smoked another cigar – anything to calm the nerves. I didn't even know why I was so nervous; it was very unlike me. If things went wrong with our hostage, it wasn't that big of a deal. She'd die and that would be that. There would always be another card to play.

I suppose, if I was being honest with myself, I wanted more than just to get the shipping lane into the Baja, the one Salvador controlled. I wanted to humiliate him, to prove that I was as big of a player as he was. All my life I struggled to get ahead and be the best, but my personal best no longer mattered. Each step I took, the higher and higher I went, the more power I had, it never satisfied me. I wanted more, always more.

I wanted Salvador to fear me, to be looking over his shoulder for me. Perhaps he already did – I'd been known to commit some unsavory and highly publicized acts over the years – but

I wanted him to feel that fear first-hand. And what fear is greater than the fear of feeling stupid?

I got up from my seat and picked up a knife I had placed on the table earlier.

"Is that for show?" The Doctor asked, raising a neatly trimmed white eyebrow. He sipped his tea carefully.

I shook my head. "No. It will be put to use. Every day."

"On the girl?"

I nodded. "Yes. On her. One letter a day. When she goes back to Salvador in a week, I want him to see my name on her back."

He crossed his legs and gave me a small smile. "You're getting more twisted and snarled the older you get. Like a root over the years. Are you sure you're only thirty-five?"

I managed a grin. "I'll take that as a compliment. And I'm only thirty-two."

"Wouldn't know it." He shrugged with one shoulder. "Guess Salvador might not want his wife after you give her back with your name carved into her. Ever think of that?"

I let my fingers slide around the blade. "That's not my problem, is it?" I picked up a nearby stool and placed it in front of Luisa's empty chair. I put the knife on top of it with reverence. "As long as I get what I want, what Salvador does with his wife afterward is none of my business."

"And your indifference is what will get you far in this world."

"Indifference," I said with a dry laugh. "I've heard worse."

At that I heard the faint sound of a car door slamming shut. There were two ways into the basement – one from inside the house and the other leading to the driveway. My eyes flew over to the latter just as the door opened. Feet appeared first on the steps, followed by long legs. Este. Behind him were Juanito and Franco, holding on to the girl.

In person, Luisa Reyes was a lot smaller and more delicate than I imagined. She looked like I could pick her up and carry her in the palm of my hand, the same hand that I could so easily crush her with. Her legs were bare, short, and splattered in mud, but they had soft curves that I wanted to run my hands over. Her hips were full, her waist tiny, even in a loose blouse that was achingly low-cut over her perfect breasts. I couldn't see her face because of the black canvas bag they had placed over her head, so I focused instead on her collarbone. I wanted to nip it with my teeth.

I bit down on my lip instead.

I needed a moment to get back in the game.

They took her over to the chair and immediately bound her hands behind it. I watched, trying to steady my breathing, and took in every detail of her that I could. The more I could deduce about her character, the better. Her shorts were jean cut-offs, her shoes were Adidas runners. She had on no jewelry. She wasn't at all what a typical narco-wife looked like. She looked . . . normal.

I had to make sure that wouldn't be a problem for me.

I nodded at The Doctor who got the ball rolling. He walked over to the video camera on the tripod and lined it up with Luisa's hooded figure.

"Is everything ready?" Este asked him.

"It's all set up," he said, and walked toward Luisa, peering down at her. "How drugged is she?"

"Not badly," Este said, shooting me a nervous glance. I didn't like that glance. "She's somewhat coherent."

"You didn't gag her?"

"No, but she shut up when she needed to."

"It's lucky she was out there."

"Yes. It was," The Doctor said. There was a pause and everyone looked at me.

Waiting.

I took in a deep breath through my nose.

"Gentlemen," I announced as I slowly walked toward her, "remove the bag."

Este leaned over her and quickly pulled it off her head.

She immediately put her face to the side, her eyes shut tight, trying to avoid my gaze or perhaps the overhead light. All it did was highlight a red and purple bruise that marred her beautiful cheek.

A curious bit of rage simmered in my stomach. "Who did this?" I asked, my hands going for her ruined face while my eyes immediately went to Franco. "Who did this?" I repeated. Luisa flinched under my touch, perhaps from pain, perhaps from revulsion. She still didn't look at me.

"Sorry," Franco mumbled, not sorry at all. "It was the only way to quiet her."

I sucked in my breath and tried to bury the fire inside. The man was such a sorry excuse for a human being. He got the job done, but he often went overboard while doing it. He was a messy, sloppy fuck with beady eyes that showed what little intelligence he had in his thick skull. If Luisa was going to suffer any pain – and she would – it would not be at the hands of this brute, a man who had no finesse in his actions, no respect for violence. It would be from me. I was the one in charge of her.

When I was calm and air was flowing through my lungs with ease, I took my hands off her soft, swollen skin and bent down in front of her. Now I wanted her to see me. She couldn't avoid this forever.

"Look at me, Luisa Reyes." She didn't move, didn't open her eyes. Her chest heaved, but I kept my eyes on hers. "Darling, aren't you curious as to where you are?"

For a moment there I started to wonder if I had the wrong girl. With the bruise and the pain in her wincing expression, I wondered if I'd captured a woman who was already broken. There was no challenge in that, only pity.

"My name is Luisa *Chavez*," she said. She straightened her head and her eyes flew open, staring right at me. "And I know where I am. I know who you are. You are Javier Bernal."

I had nothing to worry about. She was not broken at all. Those deep brown eyes burned with strength.

I raised my brow and nodded, exceedingly pleased and terribly turned on. The fact that she knew my name made my dick twitch.

"You know why you're here," I said, straightening up. I walked over to the stool, eager to begin, and glanced at her over my shoulder. "Don't you?"

She was staring at me, a bit of fear coming off of her, making her look even younger. My god her lips looked so full and juicy as they quivered before me.

"What is the knife for?" she croaked.

"You'll find out after," I said. "It is for your husband. For your Salvador." I stepped to the side and waved my arm at the camera. "And this is also for him."

I eyed The Doctor who was standing behind her now, duct tape in hand. He quickly ripped off a piece and placed it over those lips while Este dimmed the lights in the room. I went behind the video camera and focused the light on her. She looked like a ghost, lit up against the darkness. So hauntingly dramatic.

I cleared my throat and hit record on the camera. "This is Luisa Reyes," I said, making sure my words were clear enough for the recording. "Former beauty queen of the Baja State and property of Salvador Reyes. Salvador, we have your wife, and we have a long list of demands – demands which I know you can meet. I expect full cooperation in this matter or she dies in the next seven days. If she's lucky. I'll give you some time to think about what you're willing to give up for her. Then we'll be contacting you. Goodbye."

At that, I switched off the camera light and hit stop. The room remained dim. It was romantic.

"I hope your husband checks his emails often," I told her, picking up the knife. "It would be a shame to have to put this on YouTube."

I walked over to her and then held up the knife, making sure she could see it well. "I think it's only going to hurt the first time," I said truthfully, hoping that would make her feel better about what was going to happen. It was the only courtesy I could offer.

While Franco held her still, I ordered Este to rip apart her blouse and push her down, exposing her back. That's when she passed out, her chin down to her chest, her shoulders slumping.

In an instant, The Doctor had a syringe in his hand, filled with lidocaine, ready to be injected into her heart. "Shall I keep her awake?"

I quickly shook my head. "No. I'll grant her this mercy." After all, she never asked for this. I guess it wouldn't hurt the first time after all.

Only the second.

With careful precision I carved the letter J into her shoulder blade. It bled, bright crimson on her creamy skin, but only a little – the cut was deep enough to leave a light scar but not so deep to cause damage.

I wasn't a savage.

CHAPTER SEVEN

Luisa

When I woke up, I could have sworn for one moment I was back at my old house in San Jose del Cabo. Something about the way the light slanted in through the window and onto my face.

For that one little moment I was happy again.

It only took me a second though to realize that I couldn't have been farther from home. The events from last night came flooding into my mind like rancid garbage. I'd finally done it. I'd finally escaped.

And I'd only gotten a few minutes away before I was captured.

By Javier Bernal.

I groaned quietly, afraid that I wasn't alone, and opened my eyes wider, trying to take in what I could. To my surprise, I wasn't locked up in some cage in the dingy basement. Instead I was lying under the thin covers of a soft bed in what looked like a bedroom. There was one bare window from which the light streamed through, and through a door I got a glimpse of a dark bathroom. The rest of the room was empty, the walls covered with faded, yellowing wallpaper.

Once I realized I was alone, I slowly sat up in the bed. I

was wearing a man's linen shirt that smelled like spicy tea. The smell hit me like a hammer and I suddenly wished I was naked. To be undressed was one thing, but the fact that I was dressed again was another, something far more intimate than I wanted to think about.

Suddenly the image of a blade flashed through my mind. I gasped, and in a panic, started feeling over every inch of my body, making sure everything was intact.

As far as I could tell, I was in one piece. But when I moved, the shirt stretched over my back and made my skin sting. I felt along my shoulder blade and winced. There was a curved cut there, just in that one spot. Why? What were they trying to do?

I stared down at my hands, turning them over, studying them. I needed to ground myself, to bring myself into this new reality. These were my hands and I was still Luisa Chavez. I was free from Salvador but imprisoned by another danger.

And yet, as I sat there on that bed in that small room with the sunlit walls, in some house in some location I'd probably never learn, I didn't feel any fear. I had no idea what they were going to do to me. Perhaps I should have been more afraid. I was just . . . sad. Sad that my life had to go this way, sad that I could never catch a break. Sad that I'd probably never see my parents again.

I swallowed painfully. I knew Javier would kill me. That was what he did, just as it was what Sal did. There was no difference between the men in that regard. I knew that Sal would never do what Javier was going to ask of him; I wasn't important enough to negotiate for. He'd just find another woman to rape, another woman to hit, to kick, to beat on a daily basis.

The last seven weeks had been pure, unadulterated hell. Now I was in another hell, but this time around I couldn't find the energy to dance with fear.

But, perhaps I could find the energy to escape once again. I looked around the room, searching for cameras. Salvador had cameras in every room of our house, and I had no doubt that Javier or one of his men were watching my every move. Still, I couldn't see them, though that didn't mean they weren't there.

I carefully got out of bed, feeling sore all over, and checked out the bathroom. It was plain, just a toilet and sink and one roll of toilet paper. I walked over to the window. There wasn't anything except forest for miles. It looked a lot like the woods surrounding Salvador's, which made me wonder if we were still in the Sierra Madre Occidental. Though it was blindingly sunny, there were dark grey clouds hanging above distant green peaks.

There was a knock at the door and I quickly spun around. My instincts told me to cover myself up – the linen shirt barely covered my underwear – and to grab the nearest weapon. There was nothing I could do for either of those. I was practically indecent and completely defenseless.

The knock came again, followed by the sound of the door being unlocked. Why didn't they just come inside the room, why put up the faux-polite pretenses? If they were doing it to confuse me, it was working.

I waited, my breath in my mouth, and watched the doorknob. When nothing happened, I swallowed my courage and walked toward the door. With my hand on the knob I waited a beat before flinging the door open.

Standing on the other side was a man holding a tray of

food and a pot of coffee. I recognized him from last night, I think his name was Esteban. The one who didn't hit me in the face, though possibly the one who carved something into my back.

He smiled at me, a lopsided grin that made him look innocent even though he was anything but. His hair had a bit of a curl to it, brown with lighter streaks, which reminded me of some of the surfer hippies we had in Los Cabos. He was even dressed like them – board shorts and a wife-beater tank top that showed off his muscles. The only thing that reminded me of his line of business was the scarring on the side of his face. However, it didn't make him ugly, just dangerous. It kept me on my toes.

I eyed the tray in his hand with suspicion. "What is this?"

"Your breakfast," he said, nodding down at it. "Tortilla, eggs, salsa, fresh mango juice. Coffee."

"All laced with drugs to knock me out," I said, not trusting him for a second.

His smile straightened out, looking playfully amused. "You're free to do whatever you want with the food. Eat it, don't eat, we really don't care. We just want to make sure we're a good host."

I could have laughed until I realized he was serious. "You want to be a good host? Let me go free then." I looked down the hallway and noticed a man stationed at the end of it, standing guard. For a moment I thought I could throw the food in Este's face, perhaps smash the coffee pot into the other cheek and scar that one up too. But I wouldn't get far. Where there was one guard there were more guards.

"I'm afraid we can't let you go until Salvador pays the ransom," Esteban said. "That's how these things work."

"Too bad for you he'll never pay any amount for me," I told him.

At that Esteban looked completely surprised. The look vanished when he said, "It's not money we are after. We have more than enough. We want a certain shipping lane going into the Baja."

I gave him an incredulous look and shook my head slightly. Was he for real? They had absolutely no idea about my and Salvador's relationship. They were going to have a rude awakening when they realized he wasn't going to give them anything. And I was going to die.

When I didn't say anything he gestured to the room behind me. "May I come in?"

"If I say no, will you do something about it?"

He frowned. "You're a bit of a feisty one, aren't you? You do realize what has happened to you, don't you? Javier Bernal is not a nice man and you're his prisoner."

"I'm being treated fairly well for a prisoner," I countered.

He raised his brows. "We like to extend some courtesies when we can. So I take it you don't want your food?"

"You and your food can go fuck yourself," I said, feeling a rush of hot blood go through me. I wasn't used to swearing or talking back. If it was possible, my newfound fearlessness scared me.

I was so certain that Esteban was going to throw the coffee in my face or strike me, force me into the room and brutalize me. But that never came.

He only gave me a stiff smile. "I'm only trying to make things more comfortable for you. The others aren't as nice as me." His look darkened. "But I can be the bad guy if you want me to."

I believed him. Underneath the boyish demeanour I saw depth that held anger and malicious intent, a bitterness that marred his true nature. Perhaps the darkness wasn't for me, but it was there. I had seen that same look on Salvador, only he wore his depravity on the surface. While I had no doubt that Esteban was probably considered the good guy in this whole operation, I told myself to never think he was on my side.

Without taking my eyes off of his, I slowly stepped back into the room and shut the door in his face. I stood there, waiting on the other side of it, until I heard a shuffle and the door being locked.

I breathed out a long sigh of relief that rocked through me until I felt like I was too heavy to stand. I leaned back against the door and slowly slid down it until I was sitting on the floor. I rested my head back and stared at the window, at the sun that was still shining through.

I was going to spend my last days in this room unless Salvador came through. But even that would mean a return to a horrible life. There was no winning this game.

The only thing I had to hold on to was my sense of self. I had let Sal ruin me, day by day, piece by piece. I wouldn't let that happen here. They could try and carve me up, they could rape me, torture me, try and confuse me with hospitality, but they would not get to me. They would not break my soul. They would not see my pain.

And at that, a single tear leaked out and ran down my cheek. I swallowed and willed myself to stop. That was for my father and mother who I tried so hard to do right by.

That was the only time I would cry from now until my death.

They would never reach the deepest parts of me.

I woke up to the sound of the door being unlocked. I had fallen asleep sitting on the floor, my head slumped to the side, my neck aching. It was twilight now and the sun was long gone.

The door suddenly opened, pushing against my back. Whoever this was, the whole knocking courtesy didn't extend to them. I quickly rolled out of the way and got to a crouch just as someone stepped in.

In the dim light, I couldn't make out who it was, but I knew right away. He stared down at me, and I could see his eyes glinting against his shadowy face.

"What are you doing down there?" Javier asked in a silky smooth voice.

I didn't say anything, I didn't move.

He shut the door behind him and cocked his head at me. Even in the low light I could feel his eyes, feel him studying me. "I heard you weren't too interested in eating today. Este says you told him to go fuck himself. I wish I could have seen that."

When I didn't say anything, he took a step toward me and held out his hand. "Get up," he said, waiting. His posture stiffened and his voice lowered. "I said get up. I don't like to repeat myself."

It was only then that I noticed he was holding something in his other hand. Two things, it looked like. A folded-up rope and a knife. I waited for the pang of fear to hit me. It was subtle and I didn't let it show. I also didn't obey him.

He quickly reached down and grabbed me by the arm, yanking me up to him until I was pressed against his chest, crushing the front of his suit jacket.

"You're a light little thing, aren't you?" he asked in a bemused voice, his breath smelling faintly of cinnamon and tobacco. "Delicate and easy to break."

We'd see about that.

I acted instinctually. With my free hand I jabbed my palm into his nose. He yelped in surprise, maybe even in pain, and momentarily let go of me. That's all I needed.

I pushed past him and went for the door. I put my hands on the knob and turned, pulling it toward me. There was a wonderful feeling of freedom for just that one moment where the door opened and the light from the hallway spilled in. The feeling of power that came from fighting back.

Nothing in my life had felt as good as my hand connecting with his face.

But the feeling was fleeting. All at once the door slammed shut and Javier was behind me, the rope going around my chest. He hauled me backward into him so that he was holding me tight from behind.

"Don't you know it turns me on when you fight back?" he whispered in my ear, his voice ragged. "Though it turns me on when you don't fight back, too. I guess you can't win." He sniffed. "I think you bloodied my nose."

"Then I guess you'll have to bloody my face," I taunted him, my veins on fire with the strange adrenaline that was running through me.

He sucked in his breath. "No, my darling. I would never do that to your face. Just your back. I have a lot of respect for beautiful things, you know. They are usually the most dangerous."

Oh, how I wished I could be dangerous to him, to anyone.

"You know, Luisa," he said, holding me tighter now. I could feel his erection pressing into my ass. "We're going to be doing this dance with each other until we give you back to your husband. You could make things easier on yourself. I don't like to play rough with you."

"No," I said quietly. "You just want to cut me up."

"I'm merely branding you," he said. "Don't make it sound so ugly." He lifted his arm so that the knife was shining in front of my face. I could almost see my warped reflection staring back at me. "My penmanship with a knife is very delicate. A hard-earned skill. If your husband's name was Javier, I think you would be quite pleased with the finished result."

The man was completely crazy. He planned to carve his name in my back, as if he was doing me a favor.

"Come on," he said, and quickly wrapped the rope around me so my arms were held tight to my sides. He made a few knots and then shuffled me over to the bed before he pushed me onto it, face down. I turned my head to breathe and he pressed down on the side of it, to keep me in place. "Now stay."

He straddled me, legs on either side of my waist, and his hands stroked softly along the back of my neck until he grabbed my collar. "My shirt looks good on you," he commented. "But it looks better off." He reached underneath me, grabbing me by my collarbone, and ripped the shirt open before pushing it to the side and sliding most of it off until one shoulder was bare.

"He's not going to want me when he sees what you've done," I managed to say.

"He's not going to see what I've done until I have what I want. What your marriage can and cannot handle is not my problem and none of my business."

"You're disgusting."

"I'm many things but disgusting isn't one of them."

"You're sick."

"Well, there's no argument there. Good or bad, there is great power in knowing who you are and owning it. So, tell me, my beauty queen . . . who are you?"

He leaned down so those blazing eyes of his were visible to mine.

"No one you will ever know," I told him, relieved at how strong I sounded.

"We shall see about that."

He adjusted himself on my back, and I felt him press the dull side of the blade into my shoulder. The cold threatened to make me shiver, but I suppressed it.

"You know what I am going to do to you and yet you are not afraid. Why is that?" His voice was lower now, wispy like smoke.

He wouldn't be interested in the truth. "Why do you want me to be afraid?"

Silence thickened the room. He didn't answer. I knew now that I had spurred him on to try and do his worst. It would hurt me dearly, but as long as I never showed it, never gave in, I would be the one who would win in the end. I could beat Javier Bernal at his own twisted game.

"There are some things in life you should be afraid of," he finally said.

"Like you?"

His eyes burned into me but I didn't look away. He straightened up and turned the knife over. He dug the blade in, and it pierced me with a sharp, nauseating blast of pain. "Like me," he said quietly.

I bit down on my lip as he carved the A right beside the still tender J. I didn't know what his penmanship looked like, nor did I care, but he was very quick, I had to give him that. He could have drawn it out a lot longer. The pain was sharp but brief.

"Now that that's done for today," he said, his voice still soft as he removed the knife, "can I get you anything?"

It was as if my back wasn't bleeding from his torture. I didn't even know what to say so I didn't say anything. I just pressed my teeth together and prayed he would go away.

"You really should eat something," he said, still straddling me. "I happen to be a good cook." He waited, and when he didn't get a response, he leaned down and gently blew on my fresh wound. "I can get you fresh clothes, I have a whole selection put aside for you. Perhaps they will be a bit long, I had no idea how short you were."

I kept my mouth shut and my face emotionless, giving him nothing. But inside, I couldn't quite comprehend what a psychopath this man was. He and Salvador were so much the same and yet so different.

"All right," he said, straightening up. "If you wish to be stubborn, then I'll leave you." He gracefully eased himself off of me, and I heard him walk over to the door and open it. "I'll see you tomorrow, Luisa Reyes."

The door shut behind him and I could hear it being locked.

It was only then that I realized he'd left me on the bed, still tied up and unable to move my arms.

   I spent all of two seconds trying to figure out how to free myself before the pain and exhaustion overtook me and pulled me off to sleep.

CHAPTER EIGHT

Javier

"Need a sparring partner?"

I hadn't even noticed that Este was behind me, but my right hook never faltered and it delivered the blow head on. The heavyweight bag swung and I stepped out of the way, wiping the sweat from my brow as I looked to him standing in the doorway. They all called me self-indulgent when I insisted all the safe houses be equipped with a small gym and heavyweight bags, but if I wasn't staying in shape by boxing, I wasn't myself.

"Do you remember the last time I sparred with you?" I asked him, grabbing a bottle of water and having a sip.

He shrugged, trying to act like he wasn't embarrassed. Este always had this way of trying to prove something to me, to one-up me. The last time we had a sparring session, he turned it into a full-fledged fight. Naturally, I knocked him down with just a blow. All my training hadn't been for nothing. I had hoped I knocked his ego down, too, but that wasn't the case.

He pointed at me and wiggled his fingers. "Were you sparring with someone else? Your nose looks more crooked than normal."

I raised my brow. "You were right about her being feisty."

He smiled. "I see. But I guess you still got your way."

"When don't I?"

He casually jammed his hands in the pockets of his cargo shorts. "Oh, I can think of a few times."

That was enough. "What do you want, Este?" I asked pointedly.

He nodded, smiling to himself, knowing he got to me for just that one second. "I was going to go check on the girl, bring her some breakfast. Just letting you know that Doc's cooked up a feast. Do you think it's too soon to let her eat with us?"

I grabbed a towel and started wiping the sweat off my arms and chest. "I'd like to see if you can convince her to eat, let alone eat with us. But you never know – I did leave her in a rather vulnerable position."

He frowned and sighed, leaning against the doorway. "I don't think she realizes what a vulnerable position she's actually in."

"I was being literal, but I agree," I told him, stretching my arms above my head. "So she really thinks that Salvador won't give a shit about her life?"

"I've been checking my phone, my emails all morning," he said. "There's nothing from him yet."

"Maybe he hasn't seen the video yet." I went over to the bench and picked up my watch that I removed only for boxing. I didn't like the way my wrist looked without it. I quickly strapped it on and felt an immediate sense of relief when it covered up the tattoo that resided on my veins.

"Javi, he's seen it. I can tell."

"Then he's waiting for us to tell him what we want. He's not a stupid man, not entirely. He won't act rash right away."

"I hope you're right," he said. "Otherwise, this was a lot of effort for nothing."

I glared at him. "That's not for you to ever question or worry about."

He raised his palm at me. "It's all cool, hey."

I gave him a disgusted look. Everything was always so fucking cool to him, like the cartel was one big frat party where he could coast along, screwing chicks and trying to be the big man on campus. He took all the wrong things seriously.

I watched as he left the room, and then I turned back to the bag. Despite the watch being on my wrist, I started punching again, harder. I hated to admit it, but there was this tiny thread of doubt that Este had placed in my head, wriggling around like a maggot.

Even if Salvador didn't love his wife, he still had pride, and that was what I was banking on. I could only hope that his pride was worth part of his empire. I had built my own empire – or siphoned it, depending on who you asked – and I knew how much it was worth to me. But my pride, my image, was worth just as much.

Then there was the other piece in the game, the lovely, stubborn Luisa who so bravely dared to defy me last night. After I had left her tied on the bed, it took all my willpower not to go in there and make her see how serious I was. She hadn't been afraid – she didn't even make a sound when the blade cut her beautiful skin – and it was driving me mad. I couldn't tell if she just didn't realize the danger she was in, or she just didn't care. If it was the latter, that made her more dangerous than I wanted to admit. She needed to appreciate the art of violence, the beauty in fear, the fragility of her own life.

I had to make her care. If all went well, I only had her for four more days, and in that time I would make her care, make her cry, make her realize just who I was and what I could do to her.

Luisa

I'm not sure how I slept the whole night through with my arms bound to my sides, face down on the bed, but I did. I didn't wake until I heard knocking at my door. I knew who it was — Esteban knocked, Javier didn't — and hoped that he would just go away. But I guess his politeness didn't extend that far.

The door opened and I heard Esteban say, "Wow, he wasn't kidding."

It closed behind him and he walked over until I felt him hovering over me. I stiffened, wondering what would come next.

Esteban placed his hand on the small of my back. "Would you like me to untie you?"

Again, I didn't answer. I didn't want to beg or ask for anything.

"Well, I'm going to," he said. He started undoing the rope and soon it loosened, my arms falling beside me, my muscles screaming from the pain.

"You know I'm not going to hurt you," he murmured. "Let me help you up."

He reached for me, but with what strength I had, I sat up and swatted him away.

"Don't you touch me," I scowled.

He raised his palms at me. "All right. Just trying to help."

"Somehow I doubt that," I said, sliding the shirt back to normal and making sure I was decent.

He nodded at it. "I have something here for you."

I looked down at his hands and noticed him carrying a piece of fabric in hot pink.

"It's a dress," he said. "You know, if you don't feel like wearing Javier's shirt for the rest of the week. Or, you know, you can go naked. If you want." He gave me a cocky grin and I wished I could do the same to his face as I had done to Javier's. I just wasn't sure I had the strength. My arms felt weak from being tied all night and I was absolutely starving.

When I didn't move or say anything, he threw the dress on my lap. "Put it on," he said. "I promise to turn around. I won't look."

"I don't care if you do look," I told him, raising my chin. I didn't want to do a single thing Esteban or anyone told me to do, but I also wanted to get out of this shirt.

He raised his brows but slowly turned around anyway.

I quickly slipped off the shirt, wincing as it brushed against the cuts on my back, and pulled on the dress. It was strapless and had a smocked bust and waist that conformed to my body perfectly. To what little credit Esteban had, he didn't turn around for quite some time.

"You look very fresh," he commented, looking me over. There was a strange look in his eyes that I couldn't quite place. It was as if he were devious, but at the same time, it wasn't lustful or sexual. "Are you ready to eat, or do you still want to be stubborn about it?"

I wanted to say yes to both those questions. "I'm fine."

"I'm afraid you don't have a choice, hey," he said. Before I could move, he reached over and grabbed my arm, yanking me straight out of bed. My wrist twisted painfully, and his fingers pressed into me with startling ferocity; enough that I couldn't help the yelp that escaped from my lips.

"You're hurting me," I managed to say, staring up at him, at the highlighted hair that fell in his hazel eyes.

"You're being an idiot," he said back, smiling, the scars looking unsettling on his face. "Now come on. You're having breakfast with us and you're going to behave. A big smile for the boss."

He let go and grabbed my upper arm, not as tightly as before, but I obviously wouldn't be escaping. He led me out of the room and down the carpeted hallway to a set of stairs where a guard was standing watch. I stared at the guard while he took me past. He winked at me in response.

Downstairs the house was a bit more modern. Light pierced through the slats in the blinds. I noticed all the windows were covered, and the furniture in the living room was bare yet still tastefully decorated. I'd never been in Salvador's torture houses, but I assumed they weren't as nice as this. It could almost be a middle-class home if only I didn't know its purpose.

"Right in here," Este said, leading me through a doorway and into a black-and-white tiled kitchen that smelled of fried pork. At a round table sat an older man with grey, slicked back hair and a mustache. He was dressed all in white and was wearing small round glasses as he looked over the newspaper. He didn't even glance up at me.

Beside him, sipping on a mug of tea and staring at me

with vague surprise, was Javier. This was the first time I was able to get a good look at him in daylight. He was wearing a white dress shirt with the top few buttons undone. A gold watch glinted from his wrist while his elbows rested on the table.

In some ways Javier was an unusual looking man. He wasn't movie star handsome – or even *Telemundo* handsome. His mouth was a little too wide, his nose was a bit crooked, perhaps a tad puffy from last night. He wasn't terribly tall, and his body was sleek with an athletic build, not as muscled as Esteban. But he had sensual lips, dark, expressive brows, and high cheekbones. His hair was dark, shiny and thick enough to make any man or woman envious, a shaggy and slightly long cut. Then there were his eyes, that stark, golden gaze that cut you from the inside out. You couldn't help but get sucked into them, swirling into whatever darkness lurked below. They were relentless, terrifying, and oddly beautiful, just like the man himself.

Javier took his eyes off of me and fixed them on Esteban. "I wasn't expecting her."

Esteban let go of my arm and nudged me toward the table. "She wanted to come. I told you I could convince her."

I swallowed hard as Javier looked back at me, searching my face. I wasn't sure why Esteban lied – he had certainly not convinced me of anything – but I wasn't about to call attention to it either.

"Well then," Javier said, nodding at the empty seat across from him. "Sit down. Eat Este's breakfast."

I didn't want to move, but Esteban nudged me again, harder this time, until I practically fell into the chair. The mugs and glasses of juice on the table rattled, spilling over slightly, and Javier briefly shot Esteban a deadly look, though I couldn't tell if it was for my unceremonious treatment or the spilled drinks. Most likely the latter.

"I got her to wear the dress too," Este added, standing behind me and resting his hands on the back of my chair.

Javier's gaze slid over my body before resting on my face, looking remotely suspicious. "So I see. I hope you like it, Luisa. If you don't, there's more where it came from."

I could only stare blankly at him, too overwhelmed by the situation.

"Oh, and where are my manners?" He looked over at the grey-haired man. "Luisa, this is The Doctor. Doc, this is our dear houseguest, Luisa Reyes."

The Doctor eyed me dryly before turning back to the paper. "Yes, I met her the other night."

"Ah, but the other night was so . . . chaotic, don't you think?" Javier folded his hands in front of him. "Perhaps proper introductions are still needed. You know who I am, so you say. The man behind you is Esteban Mendoza. Another partner of ours, Franco, is running errands. I'm afraid you don't want to get on his bad side – again." He gestured to my cheek which was still tender, thanks to the hit it took the other night. I'd made a note not to look at my reflection in the bathroom mirror, but I knew it was deeply bruised.

"There are a few more people you'll see milling about, but their names aren't important. They won't have much to do with you unless you make trouble for yourself. It seems as if that's something you like to do – I recommend you don't. We don't want to do any harm to you. That said, we're not completely against it either."

I snorted and gave him the most disgusted look I could muster.

It made him smile, cunning and cruel. "So you know how to find humor in life. That will go a long way, my darling. But you should also know when I'm serious. We've given the demands to your husband. The ball is in his court."

I couldn't help the smirk that sneaked angrily across my face. "He'll never make a deal with you. You'll see."

"I think you underestimate your worth," Javier said earnestly.

"And I think you overestimate my husband," I said. "You would have been better off just killing him instead of taking me. That was your biggest mistake."

His jaw flexed very lightly, as if he were biting something back.

"There was no mistake," he said carefully. He paused. "So you would have preferred we kill your dear Salvador?"

"If you killed him, I wouldn't be here right now, wearing a whore's dress and being forced to eat your shitty food."

A genuine smile spread across Javier's face, lighting his eyes up like citron stones. There was a beauty to it that shocked me, making me momentarily forget who I was dealing with.

He laughed, nodding his head. "You are something, aren't you? You know, by the time you leave, I think the two of us will get to know each other very well. I might even end up liking you."

I didn't return the smile. *No, you won't,* I thought. *Because I won't give you what you want.*

It was all for show now, all of this, the banter, the pretenses that this could be a cordial experience. It didn't fool me for a second. After all, there was a V that needed to be carved into my back.

"I'll have you know," The Doctor said, slowly getting to his feet, "that the food is only shitty when Este is cooking."

"Hey," Este said from behind me, sounding hurt.

The smile suddenly departed Javier's face. He looked to Este and The Doctor. "Do you mind giving us some privacy? Luisa and I need to talk. Alone."

I felt Esteban hesitate at my back, but he and The Doctor left the room by way of the kitchen door. Sunlight, heat, and birdsong streamed inside for a moment. I breathed in deeply, trying both to find my courage to face Javier alone again and to take in the smell of the surrounding mountains. It smelled clean, like sunbaked leaves and dry air. It reminded me that life was going on outside this house, and that it could be beautiful.

"What are you thinking?" Javier asked me in a low voice, sounding genuinely interested.

I would not let him in. I looked at him point blank. "About how you're going to kill me."

He raised his brow. "And how do you think I'm going to kill you?"

I shrugged, pretending that even talking about it didn't scare me. "You'll probably slice my head off. That's what Salvador does . . . when he's in a good mood."

He stared at me intently. "It wouldn't be the first time for me. But the blood is starting to be a real pain to clean up."

"Then how will you do it?"

His brow furrowed. "You really think I'm going to kill you?"

"If Salvador doesn't give you want you want, then yes. But

before that, you'll start sending him my body parts. My fingers and toes first. Perhaps my ears. A tit."

He leaned back in his chair and shook his head, looking disturbed. "You are a morbid little woman."

"I didn't used to be. Then I became the wife of a drug lord."

He licked his lips, looking me over. "You're very good at pretending not to be afraid. But I am very good at seeking the truth in people. You can't go far in this business without becoming somewhat of a mind reader." He folded his hands behind his head, looking utterly casual. "And I can sense your fear, buried beneath all your bravado. I can smell it."

I ignored him and looked up at his wrist. His watch had moved over an inch and I could see the word "wish" tattooed beneath it in English.

"What does your tattoo mean?" I asked.

His face froze for a moment then relaxed. "It's English."

"I know how to read English," I told him. "I worked at a bar in Cabo San Lucas for the last three years."

Oh damn, big mistake. He didn't need to know anything else about me.

"So I heard," he said. When he noted my expression he added, "Don't look so surprised. I had people researching you for some time. I know a lot of things about you, Luisa Reyes."

"I'd rather you call me Chavez," I told him. "The Reyes name means nothing to me."

"Apparently. So why did you marry him then? Money?"

"What does the tattoo mean? You tell me something, I'll tell you something."

He pursed his lips for a moment and then nodded sharply.

"All right. The tattoo is for a Nine Inch Nails' song. I got it when I was young and stupid and living in America."

That couldn't be all there was to the story, but his face was completely unreadable.

"So you married him for money?" he asked.

"Yes." I nodded. There was no chance of me telling him the real reason. As long as my parents were alive, this monster would never know about them. "He took an interest in me, and of course I said yes to him."

"Of course," he said slowly, a hint of disappointment on his brow. "Well, Luisa, I hope it was worth your life."

My heart thumped uncomfortably. "I thought you said you weren't going to kill me."

He gave me a small smile. "I never said that. I only asked why you thought I was. If Salvador does not comply, we probably will have to start sending him little pieces of you. Or we may just chop your head right off and send him that."

It was hard to ignore the fear now. I don't know why it suddenly felt so real. I guess sitting across from him, looking at Javier Bernal, made it hard to ignore. Still, I straightened up in my seat. "You'll have all that blood to clean up."

He shrugged lazily. "True, but that's what Este is for, after all." Suddenly the look in his eyes darkened. "You like him, don't you?"

I frowned, totally confused. "Like him?"

He gave me a dismissive wave and got out of his chair. I could see now he had on dark blue jeans with a hand-tooled leather belt. That, combined with his pristine white shirt, made him seem so elegantly casual.

So elegantly dangerous.

"It doesn't matter," he said, coming around the table. "Get up. Take off your dress."

I blinked at him. "What?"

He kicked at the leg of the chair, moving me back a few inches. "Do it. Please. Or I will do it for you. Would you like that?" He reached out for me and I balked from his touch. "Because I think I would."

I didn't know what to do. I felt frozen, stuck to the chair, unable to move.

He didn't wait for me. He quickly reached down and put his hands around my waist, lifting me straight out of the chair. He was deceptively strong, and he placed me on my feet with grace, as if we were a figure skating pair.

He held me close to him, hands still cupped around my waist, staring down at me like he was trying to hypnotize me with his eyes. "You are my enigma," he said gruffly. "But I never leave anything unsolved."

Before I could say anything to that, he pulled the dress right over my head and tossed it on the ground behind him. There I was, standing stark naked in his kitchen, still dirty from my escape. I felt like the dirt was in every corner of my soul while I stood there and he looked me over with an unmeasurable smile.

He stepped back and I did what I could to cover myself. He quickly swatted my arms away. "No, no, Luisa. You just stand right there until I tell you otherwise." He slowly walked to the side of me, pushing the table out of the way. "You were a beauty queen, this should be nothing but second nature to you."

"I was never a whore," I managed to say, keeping my eyes focused on a blank spot on the wall. I wondered if Esteban and The Doctor knew what was going on, wondered if one of Javier's guards would come sauntering in here. I tried to push the memories of Salvador and the humiliating things he had made me do out of my head. It was all I could do to stay strong.

"You're right," he said softly, stopping behind me. "I can see you were never a whore. Your purity shines through you. It's intoxicating." I felt him step closer, his breath at the back of my neck. He breathed in. "More intoxicating than the finest liquor." He breathed out, slowly, blowing a few strands of hair. "And this is why I refuse to believe that Salvador won't give me what I want, not for as long as I have you."

I closed my eyes, knowing I couldn't change his mind, not now.

He pressed close to me.

"I will break you," he whispered in my ear, his breath hot. He ran his hands down my sides, then reached around my breasts, finding the nipples. I steeled myself against him, not allowing myself to feel anything. Though his touch was soft and gentle, his intentions were not. The intentions of men never were.

I swallowed hard and said as steadily as I could muster, "Then do your worst. And you will see that the worst has already been done."

He sucked in his breath, just for a moment. Then he said, "Is that so?"

"You've only stripped me naked."

"Are you asking for more?" he asked softly, his lips now at my other ear, my nipples finally starting to pucker under the rhythmic teasing of his thumbs. My body was responding in a way it shouldn't, in a way I never thought possible. "I'm not done with your back, you know. There are more letters in my name."

One of his hands traced the letters J and A. I winced from even that light pressure on the wounds but quickly buried the pain. Thankfully, his fingers didn't linger there. His hands began to drift down my bare back. They swept over my ass, sliding his finger underneath my cheeks, in the soft spot where they met the thigh. It nearly tickled me and brought out a low groan from him.

I'm not here, I'm not here, I'm not here, I chanted to myself.

Javier walked around me, keeping his hands at my waist, until his face was right in front of mine. I opened my eyes to see that perpetual smirk twisting the ends of his lips. "I am far from done with you, Miss Chavez, the beauty queen."

He then crouched down, his hands sliding down my hips, the sides of my ·thighs. His touch was so gentle and so deceiving. I sucked in my breath, doing what I could to ignore the goose bumps of pleasure.

"You're doing this for revenge," I said, staring down at him, refusing to look away, refusing my body's betrayal.

He smirked and started running his hands up my inner thighs. "On Salvador? Well, I suppose that is pretty obvious, my beauty."

"No," I told him. "This is your revenge on women." His hands paused at that, gripping my skin. "Because a woman broke *you.*"

His eyes slowly trailed up to mine, simmering in a golden fury that belied his cold exterior. He straightened up, and that look of anger, of pain . . . was gone. The hypnotizing, handsome mask was back.

"I don't know what you are referring to," he said with ease.

I couldn't help but smirk right back at him. I had found his sore spot. Someone had broken his heart. "No. Perhaps you don't." The tattoo had tipped me off. If it really had just been about a band, I would never have seen that look of fear pass through his eyes. Now I was thrilled I had something to go on, some way to get to him. "Perhaps you don't want to talk about it."

"There is nothing to talk about." This time he said it a little too easily. His voice grew husky. "Now, give me your hands."

He grasped both my wrists and brought them behind my back. Before I could look over my shoulder, I felt them being bound together with rope. Did he keep a length of rope on him at all times? Probably. That and a knife.

"Get on your knees," he commanded.

"Here?" I asked, my breath catching in my throat.

"Yes," he said. He leaned in and said into my ear, "Here. Now."

I wondered what would happen if I refused. One moment he acted as if he would never hurt me, the next moment there was this dark malice in his soul, the part of him that chopped people's heads off.

Either way, the only choice I had was to be as unaffected as possible. So I did as he said. I dropped to my knees, carefully, with my hands bound behind me.

"Good. Now put your face on the floor. Keep your gorgeous ass in the air."

I complied, leaning over until my cheek was pressed against the cold tiles. I couldn't have felt more vulnerable, more humiliated, if I tried.

And it seemed like Javier was a person to try. I heard him

unzip his jeans, the sound seeming to echo off the kitchen walls, so simple and so terrifying.

I squeezed my eyes shut and braced myself. As I had done with Salvador or whatever man he'd made me have sex with, I removed a part of myself from the situation. I swallowed the fear and the feelings, and I became a blank slate, a void that wouldn't feel any pain, wouldn't process any emotion.

Javier could do his worst. I was ready for him. Ready to feel nothing.

But the pain never came. I didn't know if this was part of the game, but he never touched me. Was he waiting to pounce when I least expected it? Was he taking his time?

I opened my eyes, and though I didn't dare look over my shoulder, I caught sight of him in my peripheral. He was standing there, right behind me. But he wasn't just standing there. He was moving ever so slightly.

I heard a small moan escape from his lips and finally realized what he was doing – he was pleasuring himself.

I felt a jolt of revulsion mingled with perverse curiosity. A part of me wanted a better look, wanted to see him in the act. Another part of me – the better part – wanted to pretend none of this was happening.

So I closed my eyes again and tried to pretend I wasn't there, but I could hear his palm sliding up and down on himself, skin on skin, his breath as it hitched in pleasure. I couldn't shut it out of my mind. The more worked up he got, the more it teased me, taunting me to look. I could barely imagine a man like Javier wrapped up in the vulnerability of release, and yet it was happening right behind me. It was happening because of me.

And yet he hadn't laid a finger on me, not yet. He was

getting off on just the sight of me, the bare sight of me before him. I didn't know whether to feel humiliated or flattered.

He is only making fun of you, I told myself. *Just because he's not forcing himself on you doesn't make him any different from Salvador.*

Then how come I was tricking myself into thinking this was . . . better?

"You're so complicit," I heard him moan from behind me, his voice low, rough, caught up in his own passion. "So good. Why do I feel there's a bad girl in you that needs to come out?"

I didn't say anything. The sound of his breathing, his stroking, intensified.

"Perhaps if I come all over your beautiful back," he whispered, pausing to catch his breath. "Come onto my letters. Rub myself into your skin, into your blood. Will the bad girl come out? Will I awaken the true Luisa?" He let out a deep groan that reverberated into my bones. "We'll see, won't we, my darling?"

At that he sucked in his breath and groaned even louder. "Fuck," he cried out, gasping over the words. "Fuck."

Hot fluid spurted onto my back, making me flinch, catching me by surprise. For a moment I could only hear his heavy breathing and I waited, not knowing how literal he was going to be.

I heard his zipper go back up and felt his shadow looming over me.

"I look good on your skin," he murmured. He pressed his hands on my back and began to rub the sticky fluid into my back, into the wound. I bit my lip and held back a cry as it stung like crazy, making my eyes water.

"Finally," he whispered, and I could feel his yellow eyes observing me closely. But he didn't say anything else. He kept rubbing until my skin had absorbed all of him, just as he wanted. He then undid the rope around my wrists and stepped back.

I put my hands on the ground, and he walked around so I was facing his leather boots. He crouched down until we were almost eye to eye and he held up my dress in his hands.

"Thank you," he said with a small smile, his eyes glazed with lazy exaltation. Then he grabbed me by my arms and hoisted me to my feet. Quickly, he slipped the dress on over my head and pulled it down until I was covered again. "You're free to go," he said.

I stared at him in surprise which brought out another smile from him.

"To your room, of course," he said. Suddenly, he was turning around and snapping his fingers. "Tito," he barked, and the guard who had winked at me earlier appeared in the kitchen doorway. "Take her to her room."

I felt my cheeks flare from embarrassment – had the man seen the whole thing? If he had, Javier definitely didn't care who saw him come all over me.

Javier reached down to the table and handed me the plate of uneaten food that had been for Esteban. "Almost forgot your breakfast."

And at that he turned around and walked down the hall, disappearing into one of the rooms.

I stared at him, bewildered, clutching the plate of food in my hand.

Tito pointed the way toward the staircase, gesturing as if he were being polite. I barely took in his youthful but menacing appearance before I walked numbly up the stairs and back into my room. He shut the door behind me, locking it, and I was left alone again, with food that I didn't want but needed, and thoughts that I didn't need but wanted.

CHAPTER NINE

Luisa

When the sun rose the next morning, I was so tired I felt like I'd been drugged. I hadn't been – I just hadn't slept at all. The fact that I couldn't be on my back, on the fresh V that Javier had carved on it late last night, didn't help either. But mainly it was the nightmares that plagued me at every turn.

I'd never been the type of girl to fear the dark – when I was young, I loved for my father to tell me scary and thrilling stories. But now they were no longer stories, they were real, and every time I woke up from a nightmare, I was faced with a reality that was no better.

In some strange way, being alone made it worse. It's not that I wanted Javier's company, but I had to admit that when he was in the room with me, even when he was branding me and inflicting pain, it took my thoughts away from their darkest places. He distracted me. Even when he asked me questions about my past, questions I tried to dance around, it was still a distraction.

I would have thought that having someone nightmare-inducing with me would have made things worse, but it didn't. Because my nightmares weren't about Javier. They weren't about what he was going to do to me. They weren't about the fact that I could die in a few days at his hands.

My nightmares were about Salvador. They were not about what happened if he told Javier they had no deal – they were about what happened if he traded for me back.

What would happen to me if at the end of the week, I was set free and picked up by Salvador's men? If I was brought back to the house? If Salvador saw how Javier had claimed me as his? I knew what the man was capable of, and it scared me to think of what else could happen – not only to me, but to my parents. Salvador was sick beyond comprehension, and I had a feeling that I had only seen the tip of the iceberg.

I think Javier even sensed that I didn't want him to leave. When he was done carving the V, I started asking him questions. About his family, about his own past. He waited in the dark, thinking, perhaps about my angle. Why I was curious. Then he told me that I could have answers at another time.

Then he left, locking me in the room, locking me in with the nightmares that would never end.

I suppose the lack of sleep showed on my face, because when Esteban came into the room in the morning, he did a double take as I lay there on the bed, staring dumbly at the wall.

"Rough night?" he asked, a careful tone to his voice.

I didn't have the energy to be amused at his apparent concern.

He put the breakfast tray down beside him and walked to the end of the bed. He playfully grabbed my foot. It made me jump, withdrawing my knees to my chest as my attention snapped to him.

"So you are alive," he said, taking his hand back. "Glad to see it. I brought you breakfast."

I glared at him. I'd refused dinner last night and thought

I could pretend not to be hungry, but my stomach growled in protest.

"Tell you what," Esteban said, noting my expression. "How about we make today a little bit better for you?"

"Better for me," I spat out. "How about you stop pretending that you're doing me favors? Don't think for one second that I haven't forgotten why I'm here."

"Just eat your breakfast. I'll come back with some new clothes for you. I think you've earned it. Then we'll go for a walk. Doesn't that sound nice, hey." He grinned at me and then left the room, locking the door behind him.

I waited a bit, trying to ignore the food, but my resolve could not overpower my stomach. I scarfed down the tortilla and eggs and a large cup of coffee. I never knew when I'd need my strength.

I'd just finished when Esteban came back into the room, carrying a woven bag full of clothes. He tossed it on the bed. "For you," he said, bending down to pick up the empty plate. "Take a shower, get dressed. I'll be back here in thirty minutes whether you're ready or not."

I eyed the clothes spilling out of the bag. "Where did these come from?"

"Long story," he said. "Let's just say Javier can be sentimental."

I wanted to hear this story – I had no idea that someone like Javier could possess that emotion. When he'd gone again, I pulled out an aqua skirt that was so long on my short frame it would fit me as a dress instead. I went into the bathroom and ran the shower. As the room filled up with steam, I couldn't remember the last time I had been clean. It had to have been at Salvador's, the night I ran away, yet I never felt clean when I was his wife. He filled my life with dirt.

Of course, I technically still was his wife. But the word had never meant anything to me.

I stayed in the shower for so long, letting the hot water strip me down, wishing for my worries and nightmares to be carried down the drain, that I was surprised when there was a knock at my door. I could hear Esteban in my room, and I quickly dried myself and slipped into the dress, my wet hair cascading down my back.

I paused in the doorway of the bathroom as Esteban looked at me and smiled.

"You look ravishing," he said.

His compliment bounced right off me. I didn't understand how I could look ravishing with no makeup and wet hair and a bruised face, and I wasn't falling for it. Men thought women were so easy, that they could tell us how beautiful and thin we were, and we'd excuse them for whatever they'd done or were about to do. Until I met a man that saw past all of that, saw me for me, compliments meant nothing.

I nearly smirked to myself. There was no chance of that happening anymore. I'd either die here, surrounded by drug lords, or live with Salvador. All my chances of love and happiness with a man had gone out the window the moment Salvador stepped into Cabo Cocktails.

"Care to join me?" he asked, holding his arm out, as if he were some gentleman.

I stared at it and then at him. "Where?"

He shrugged. "I told you. A walk. I thought it might be good for you to get some fresh air."

"Oh, and you're so concerned about my well-being?"

Another shrug. "I'm not a monster," he said.

"No. Just a chump."

He frowned and I knew I was pushing my luck with him. I stifled a wave of apprehension that coursed through me.

"You know," he said slowly, his gaze intensifying, "I may be the only friend you have here. I might be the difference between life and death for you . . . or losing your little toe or your whole leg."

I wasn't sure if I believed that. Even though Esteban was Javier's right-hand man and business partner, I don't think he had the power he thought he did. It seemed that he constantly wanted to call the shots with Javier but wasn't quite there. If I were Javier, I'd keep a close eye on him.

"Friends don't threaten each other," I told him.

The darkness on his brow eased up. "I guess not. Well. Come on then."

He gestured for me to grab his arm again. I ignored him but slipped on my running shoes just the same. The truth was, I wanted, needed, to get outside and breathe fresh air and feel the world again. I felt like I was losing perspective of the value of life.

We walked out into the hallway, me in front of him, and were just about to head down the stairs when the guard who was stationed at the end of the hall stepped out in front of us. At least, I thought he was a guard, at first. But from the way he blocked the stairs, arms crossed, with a menacing twitch to his face, I could tell he was more than just a guard.

He leered at me in a way that made my skin feel sick.

This was Franco, the man responsible for the bruise on my face. I could just tell.

"Where are you going?" Franco asked Esteban, though he was staring at me.

"None of your business, Franco," he said. He gestured for him to get out of the way but Franco wouldn't budge.

"Planning on running away with the hostage?" he asked. He had a stupid look in his eyes, but in this world, it was the stupid people you had to fear. Too much testosterone and too little brains were a dangerous combination. I had no doubt that if Esteban wasn't there, I would be in big trouble. It didn't help that Franco was a huge guy with muscles that pulsed grotesquely.

"I just want to feel her hair," he said, licking his lips as if I was a steak. "The whores have such rough hair."

He reached out and made a fist in it. I gasped but couldn't move or else his grip would yank a huge chunk out.

"So you've felt it now," Esteban said, sounding tired. "Kindly move out of the way. We're just going for a walk."

Franco gave my hair a small tug, enough to make me gasp again. Then he grinned and let go.

"Sure thing," he said, chuckling to himself and moved aside to let us pass.

Esteban quickly led me past him. We were halfway down the stairs when I heard Franco whisper after me, "Much better than a whore's."

I shivered even as Esteban took me out of the house and into the bright sunshine.

"Don't pay any attention to Franco," he said to me. "He's a bit messed up in the head."

"I can see that," I said, my heart rate returning to normal as the fresh air filled my lungs and the heat hit my skin. The house was located at the end of a rocky road. There was a

simple dirt driveway leading out and long, overgrown grass
that stretched toward a decrepit wooden fence and miles of
forest beyond that. No neighbors, no nothing.

"You shouldn't be afraid of him," he went on as we walked
together. "Or maybe you should."

I swallowed. "I'm not afraid."

"You know, I met a girl like you once," he told me as we
walked down the driveway, ochre dirt rising up in the still
air. I was barely listening to him. I was taking in every sight,
every opportunity. There were no guards out here which I
thought was curious. Franco, thank god, had decided not to
trail us, and all the rest of the guards seemed to be inside
the house, perhaps with Javier.

"You met a girl like me once," I repeated absently. "How
nice."

"Yes," he said. "About a year ago. I was in Hawaii. I saved
her from drowning. I saved her from a lot of things, including
herself."

"What a hero," I said dryly. "You must think you're such
a nice guy."

He nodded. "I do. For the most part. But she was like you
because she no longer cared about life. She was more or less
suicidal."

I stopped and glared at him. "I am not suicidal," I hissed.

He shrugged. "You don't seem to care much about anything.
Javier is right . . . he thinks you're unbreakable."

"Just because he can't break me doesn't mean I'm suicidal,"
I told him. "What kind of sick man wants to break a woman
anyway?"

"I don't know. You married one of them, didn't you?"

"I married a demon, not a man."

"Well, I guess Javier's not exactly a demon."

"No such thing as a sentimental demon?" I asked. "Tell me about the clothes. This skirt, this dress . . . whose is it?"

He gave me an inquisitive look. Our path continued down the rough road, birds calling from the towering lush trees. "Why are you so interested?"

Now it was my turn to shrug. I didn't know why. I guess I felt that the little bit of information I could get about Javier, the more I'd have to work with, to use against him when needed.

"I'm making conversation," I said.

"Right. Well, if you care so much, the clothes belong to an ex-girlfriend of his."

I snorted lightly out my nose. "Girlfriend? I would have thought Javier only used whores. Who else could be interested in him?"

I felt Esteban studying me closely. Of course on the outside I could see why any woman would be interested in Javier Bernal. He was beautiful to look at, and I was sure he could be charming when he wanted to be. He also had money and power. But any woman worth her salt would run once she realized what kind of a depraved psychopath he was. The idea of him having an ex-girlfriend, one to get sentimental over, confused me.

"*She* was interested in him," he said, "a very long time ago. When they were young and stupid, I guess. But she was also a con artist."

I nodded. "I see." She was just as bad as he was, then. That explained some. "What was her name?"

He frowned. "Ellie. Why?"

"Just curious. Mexican?"

"American."

"And she broke his heart? Or did he break hers?"

He pursed his lips. "Both. He broke hers and she broke his. And then she broke his again."

"So she won."

"Something like that."

I smiled to myself. "Good." I hoped the bastard suffered.

"It was good," Esteban admitted. "I liked the woman, but she never would have joined his side, never would have had the confidence you need in this business."

We slowed and he turned me around so we were walking back to the house again.

"You need confidence to be a good torturer, kidnapper, murderer?"

"You need confidence in yourself, to never question who you are."

I nodded. "Maybe you all need to question yourselves more often."

He gave me a funny look, as if I were the one who was crazy.

I stopped, noticing my shoe was untied. We were almost back at the yard, and I could see Javier stepping out of the house with Franco milling around in the doorway. Javier was staring in our direction.

Bending down, I tied my shoe and eyed the pile of rocks we were beside, the result of someone clearing this road a very long time ago. Javier and the guards were far off. It was only Esteban and I out here. I made a split-second decision.

I tied my shoelaces then quickly grabbed the nearest rock. I swivelled and leaped up, my arm overextending, as I smashed the rock into Esteban's face. Because I was so much shorter, I got more of his jaw instead of his temple, but it was enough to make him yelp, holding on to his face as he staggered backward, barely able to stand up.

I didn't check to see if he was going down. I turned on my heel and started bolting toward the trees. I didn't know what the rest of my plan was, but I knew I had to get away while I could. Esteban said I was suicidal, just because I didn't show fear. But I was the opposite of suicidal. I loved the life – the free life I once had – and I would do anything to get that back.

I was almost at the trees, at the freedom they represented, when I heard a small pop, like a gun going off. The next thing I knew my body was stiffening, and I lost all function to move as my nerves fired in a burst of strange, buzzing pain. I fell straight down to the ground, I think I was screaming, as my muscles vibrated nonstop.

I heard someone, Javier I think, yell, "What the fuck are you doing?" and then the vibrations and pain stopped. Just like that. And then I was out cold.

CHAPTER TEN

Javier

"What the fuck are you doing?" I bellowed at Este and started sprinting down the driveway toward them.

One moment I was about to berate Este for taking Luisa out of the house, the next moment she had bashed his face in and was making a run for it before he took out a motherfucking Taser gun and fired on her. I don't even know when the fuck he got the Taser, I thought I left that back home.

He looked over at me in surprise though he was still firing the gun, the wires connected to Luisa's fallen, twitching body twenty feet away. I yanked it out of his hands and immediately the electricity stopped jolting through the wires.

"She tried to get away," Este said unapologetically.

"I can see that," I sniped at him. I looked at her, now motionless on the ground. "Jesus Christ."

I ran over to her, dislodging the cartridge from the gun and tossing it to the ground. I crouched down beside her and gently put my hand on her neck, shaking her back and forth. "Luisa?" I said.

There was no answer or movement from her, but I could see her breathing in and out, which was a relief. I removed the darts from her back, blood trickling out of the holes. It looked so cheap and brutal below my letters.

I turned and glared over at Esteban who was watching me from a distance. "You're a fuck, you know that? What if you accidently killed her? The Taser isn't supposed to knock her out, just bring her down. And why the fuck did you put yourself in this position in the first place? You were supposed to give her breakfast, give her clothes, and that was it."

He shrugged. "I wasn't worried, Javi. I figured she may try something but thought I'd let her see who she's dealing with here. If she ran, I'd Tase her. She'd learn not to do it again."

"*I'm* who she's dealing with here," I said, the anger simmering in my blood. "Not you. She's not yours to touch, not yours to go on walks with, and not yours to fucking brutalize."

He laughed. "I think Luisa was right. Maybe you should question yourself more often. You should hear the shit that comes out of your mouth."

I wished I could reuse Taser cartridges because there's no doubt I'd be delivering all those volts right to his miniscule balls. I sucked in a deep breath and tried to regain my cool. There was no point losing it here and now.

"Why don't you get the fuck out of here," I told him. "Go check on Juanito. Perhaps he has word from Salvador."

Esteban hesitated, as if he was going to argue with me, but his brain kicked into gear and he turned and walked back toward the house with his wide-legged, frat boy stroll. Fucking degenerate.

I looked down at Luisa, realizing she was wearing the skirt I gave her as a dress. The color was stunning on her smooth, tan skin; her long hair was extra shiny in the sunshine, cascading into the earth around her. I reached over and ran a strand through my fingers – soft and wet, probably just out of the shower. Now she was dirty again.

The sight of her lying unconscious and broken should have made me smile. It should have soothed something inside of me. After all, this was what I wanted. But it wasn't the same. This was unplanned and without merit. She may have looked weak, but I still did nothing to break her. If she were conscious, she'd be fighting me with her body and heart and mind.

I'd come to appreciate the fight in her.

I picked her up under her arms and hauled her to her feet, her head hanging down, creating a curtain of hair that masked her face. It took little effort to scoop her up, one arm under her arms, the other under her knees. I carried her back toward the house, and her head rolled back, exposing her fine collarbone, her fragile neck, her beautiful, sleeping features.

She really was light as air in my arms, just this helpless, submissive creature. As I approached the door where Franco was standing watch, I felt a pulse of possessiveness run through me. It wasn't just that while she was here, I thought she was mine. I also felt like I needed to protect her. If I didn't, no one would. Esteban had Tasered her without care, and Franco was staring at her with such ugly lust that I made a mental note to never let her near him. I knew his appetite for destruction was large and unceremonious.

"What happened to her?" Franco said, licking his lips as he looked her over. "Este looked pissed off."

He reached over and grabbed a few strands of her hair. I automatically stopped walking and shot him a steady, deadly look.

"Don't touch her," I said, my tone both hard and calm. "Don't you *ever* touch her. Do you understand?"

Franco slowly brought his eyes to mine. They were mildly defiant for a moment as a snarl appeared on his face. Then it melted into a sloppy smile. "Sure thing, boss."

I went inside and took her to her room, kicking the door shut behind us, and laid her down on the bed on her back. I wasn't about to leave her, not with her being unconscious. I had never been Tasered before, but I knew that sometimes there were complications. Sometimes people died. I had the Taser gun for torture, for the purpose of pain. After all, we shoot to kill in Mexico, and if we want to stop someone, a bullet works pretty well. A Taser though, that doesn't kill . . . that *prolongs*. But I had no idea of the effects of a Taser on a woman.

The morning light was streaming in through the window, illuminating her like an angel, but a dirty one. Feeling strangely remorseful, I brushed some of the dust off of her. I ran my hands over her legs, her hips, across her stomach, her breasts, her chest, her arms. I rubbed the earth from her face, carefully running my thumb along her cheekbones, her skin so devastatingly soft. Though I needed to wake her up to make sure she was okay, I also wanted her to keep sleeping. I went to the end of the bed and pulled off her shoes, letting them fall to the floor, then put a pillow under her head. I stood there for a few minutes, just taking in the sight of her, my sleeping beauty.

The impulses that sporadically ran through me were hard to fight. I wanted to keep feeling her, that effortless glide of my palms against her skin. I wanted to caress her breasts, lick at her nipples, make her wet with my fingers. I wanted to take out my cock and rub the head against her slightly open lips. Then I wanted to flip her over and finish carving my name. Today I would do the I.

But I wanted her awake for all of it. It would be wrong otherwise.

I must have stood there for an hour, having this fight between my body and my mind, before she finally stirred. Her head moved to the side and she let out a small moan, stretching her limbs for a second. I sucked in my breath in anticipation as her eyes slowly blinked open, staring at the ceiling.

She carefully lifted her head and looked straight at me, having sensed I was there. Disappointment was etched into her face.

"You didn't quite get away," I said in a low voice.

She stared at me for a beat or two before looking down at her body in alarm, her hands smoothing over the dress.

"I didn't touch you," I told her, examining my fingernails, making sure they were clean. "Don't worry."

"Then what are you doing?"

"Watching you sleep."

"I wasn't sleeping," she said. "I was knocked out."

I grimaced. "Yes. That was Este. He had a Taser. But you tried to run." I flicked my eyes to her. "Sorry."

"Sorry? You're actually sorry I was Tasered?" There was a bite to her voice. The fight was back, and it was making me hard.

I gave her a soothing smile. "I am. I had no wish to see that happen." I paused. "What did it feel like?"

She glared at me. "Like when you hit your funny bone, but more intense and all over your body until you think you're going to die."

"That sounds terrible."

"It was," she seethed.

I took steps closer so I was leaning right over her, my eyes fixed on hers. They were so impossibly lush and dark, I nearly felt a little lost. I cleared my throat. "So next time, maybe don't try to run. At least not around Este."

She stared up at me and swallowed – I could see her throat bobbing. So delicate. "What if I try and run from you?"

"You won't want to run from me. You don't want to know what happens when I catch up with you."

I watched her closely, waiting for fear, waiting for ambivalence, waiting for apathy. But I saw nothing in her except this fire that burned deep within her eyes. I wanted to taste that fire on my lips, I wanted to fuck it with my dick. I wanted to feel it in every way I could. I wanted to bring the fire out of her.

But she kept it inside, out of reach. She was utterly fascinating because she was not broken and refused to break. No matter how hard I tried, she refused to break.

Though I wasn't done with her yet.

"I'll come back for you later," I said to her, and turned to leave the room. I heard her breathe a sigh of relief in my wake and I couldn't help but smile. At least the sight of me leaving meant something to her.

For the rest of the day, Este acted like he had this giant chip on his shoulder. Of course he did. He always did. He was usually better at hiding it under that surfer boy persona. It was enough that I hesitated after dinner when he asked if I wanted him to bring Luisa her food. At least he did ask – his manners hadn't all gone to shit.

When he'd come back to the kitchen, The Doctor and I had lit up our cigars. We kept the kitchen door open, the screen keeping out the mosquitoes, and watched the breeze pull our smoke outside. It was a hot night, sticky, and I was feeling all out of sorts. I felt as if I was starting to lose my control of the situation.

The fact was, we hadn't heard from Salvador. Juanito had left earlier in the day, on a mission to Culiacán to gather information. People talked. He'd know right away if Luisa's disappearance was gossip or not. Este had been scanning websites for any mention of Luisa being taken, in either casual blogs or newspapers, but so far there had been nothing. It was as if she wasn't upstairs in that room and we weren't here figuring out what to do with her.

"How did it go?" I asked Este between puffs. I let the smoke fall out of my mouth and watched it drift away to the door.

"She's eating," he said. "She's kind of being a bitch."

The Doctor snorted with mild amusement.

I narrowed my eyes briefly at Este. "She has every right to be a bitch."

Este grinned at me and pulled out a chair and sat down. "Well, look at Mr. Bernal empathizing with his own captive."

"Don't mistake understanding for empathy, my friend," I replied.

"Don't mistake collateral for something you can keep," he said. "Once Sal does the deal, back she goes."

"Javier is not an idiot," The Doctor said thoughtfully as he blew smoke through his nose. "She goes back when Sal comes through. If he doesn't come through, she dies. Slowly. And painfully. Until our point has been made." He gave me a pointed glance. "Isn't that right?"

"Of course." I nodded quickly. "Of course."

"Anything less than that," The Doctor went on, "and well, news travels fast, doesn't it? No cartel that has gotten this far has ever shown that kind of weakness. We're all about preserving the empire. Javier's empire." He gave me a kind smile, the type that an elder would bestow on someone younger that they were proud of. Only I knew the type of man The Doctor was. He didn't have a lot of kindness for me, just tolerance. I doubted you could become so revered in the art of torture and negotiations and still have a kind bone in your body.

It was at that moment that I realized what we all must have looked like. A bunch of sharks sitting around a table, giving each other our razorblade grins and winking with black eyes. If we stopped eating, stopped swimming, we died.

"There is no question of what will happen to Luisa if Salvador doesn't come through," I said, leaning back in my chair. "But I do believe Salvador will come through."

"Why don't we make another video?" Este suggested with a wag of his eyebrows. "A warning."

"Yes," said The Doctor. "That couldn't hurt, could it?"

It wouldn't hurt us, no.

I gave him a quick smile and tapped my fingers on the table. "I thought standard procedure was to do that if the ransom was being negotiated or the kidnappers weren't being taken seriously. Not if he just hasn't responded."

"Oh, Javier," he said. "You're an odd duck with this code of honor and following procedures. You're a fucking drug lord. You can do whatever the hell you want to do, there is no rulebook. There is no honor. Not here." He looked at Este. "Tomorrow would work."

"It has to be tomorrow," Este said. "Or we're running out of time. Tonight would be best."

I felt as if the room had started to tilt. I placed both my palms flat on the table and pressed down, trying to steady myself. "Hold on. Let's not rush into this. We have to plan this perfectly."

"You and your planning," Este scoffed. "I say we go upstairs and smack her around a bit."

"Losing an appendage is always more effective," The Doctor added. "I know the right cuts to make."

My chest tightened. I wasn't sure why my body was reacting this way. "No," I said. "No one is doing anything to her except for me. This is my operation and she is my prisoner."

"So, then you do it," Este said. "But we have to act fast. Why not start tonight? I can get everything set up in a minute." He stood up, pushing back his chair and stared down at me. "Or are empathy and understanding confusing themselves again?"

"Sit the fuck down," I sneered at him, pointing at his seat. "Or have you forgotten your place?"

Our eyes locked in a deadly stare until he finally looked away. He always looked away. He sat back down but his attitude never cleared up. "Have you forgotten *your* place?"

I was fast with a knife. Always was. Before Este could register it, I pulled the knife out of my boot under the table and threw it at him with an easy flick of my wrist. I heard him scream and knew it had lodged itself into his shin.

He kept yelling and fell off his chair to the floor. I got up and walked over to him. The knife hadn't gone in very far. I tapped the end of the knife with my boot, driving it a bit further into his leg. Este let out a bloodcurdling scream that only made me grin.

"You're a fuck," I said as I leaned over him. His face was contorted in pain but his eyes could see me. "This is your place, right here on the fucking floor. I'd piss on you if I could, but I'm a bit too turned on at the moment." I straightened up and gave The Doctor a warning look. I was about to turn around, but then I reached down and plucked the knife out of his leg. "Forgot, I'll be needing this," I said over his scream.

I took it over to the sink, rinsed it off, and dried it on a faded washcloth and looked back at The Doctor. "Let's leave Este out of this one, shall we? Though I'm sure his screaming would come in handy. What a fucking pussy."

He nodded, his brows frozen on his forehead. Seemed I had the ability to surprise him, too. I think I showed them to not ever question how the fuck I did my job.

Together we left Este writhing on the floor and went to get the video camera before bringing it up to Luisa's room. I don't know why I felt the need to knock, but I did. She would be expecting me, but not the camera, and not The Doctor.

Good thing she wasn't in a position where she should ever expect anything.

I unlocked the door and flicked on the lights when I entered.

Luisa was sitting on the bed, her knees drawn to her chest, hands wrapped around her legs. She was in a pair of jeans and a grey tank top that had belonged to someone else, looking like any young woman out there. Except she wasn't just any young woman. She was beautiful. She was mine. And she was going to bleed for her husband.

"We're mixing things up," I told her, raising the knife in

the air as The Doctor shut the door behind him. "The Doctor is going to set up the video and film our little nightly interlude."

"Why?" she asked softly. "Did Sal not want to negotiate?"

"Your husband hasn't responded at all. We hope this will be seen. And I'll come join you in the video, just so he can see who has you, in case he hasn't realized how fucking serious I am."

Was that fear I saw in her eyes, or was the light playing tricks on me? I walked over to her and pointed at the bed with the knife. "Lie on your stomach."

She didn't move. "Are you going to let him see what you're carving into me?"

I shook my head. "On the off chance that my name would forever taint you for him, no, I won't let him see. All he will see is that you will be in a lot of pain."

She smiled at me, wicked, her eyes smug. "We'll see about that."

I wanted to ignore that, but the fact was, she had never given me any reaction before. I needed her to react this time. Otherwise it looked like I wasn't doing anything to her. I would have to drive the knife in deeper, and as much as I hated to admit it, I wasn't looking forward to that.

I gestured to the bed again. "Lie down, *now*."

She did as she was told, and I winced inwardly at the crusted marks on her back where the Taser probes had gone in. She had a hell of a day and it was about to get worse.

I looked to The Doctor. He was watching me, bemused. "Are you ready?" I asked, annoyed by his look.

"Yes," he said, getting behind the camera. "The light

isn't very good but it's all ready to go. Aren't you going to tie her up?"

I looked at her. "She's not going anywhere."

"No," he conceded. "But if you don't, it looks like she's complying with you. Letting you. Not exactly the kind of message you want to send to Salvador. She also doesn't look the slightest bit afraid. I think you need to fix that."

I didn't like being told what to do, but he was right. She looked at me, waiting. I smiled back, wolfish, as I took the rope out of my pocket. There was just enough for her wrists, and it wasn't very strong, but it would do for this situation.

Grabbing her hands, I quickly tied them behind her back. Then I got on the bed and straddled her.

I leaned down so my lips were at her ear. "I'm going to hurt you more than normal," I told her. "You'll react this time. If not for me, for the camera."

She fixed her eye on me, head to the side. "Why? So Salvador will trade with you? I don't want to go back. It's a worse hell than here."

Something in my gut sunk like a stone. I inhaled sharply and said, "This isn't about what you want." I looked up at The Doctor who was watching her curiously.

"Interesting," he said in that slow voice of his. "But Luisa, he is right. It's not about you. It's about us. And it's about other people you may care about."

At that her head lifted up to look at him.

The corner of his lips twitched at her attention. "You do have parents. They were at your wedding. If Salvador doesn't think you're in danger, if he thinks you'd rather die at the hands of a rival cartel than come home, what do you think he's going to do to your parents?"

I felt her body stiffen beneath me, as if it had just crossed her mind. So this was what she cared most about. Her parents. It killed me that The Doctor knew this and I didn't.

"Just something to think about, anyway," The Doctor finished. "I'm about to hit record. Are you speaking to the camera, Javier?"

I nodded, shaking myself into the role, and pressed the knife down on her back, ready to make the slash for the I. I waited for The Doctor's cue, then looked up at the camera.

"Salvador, we're a bit disappointed that you haven't reached out to negotiate the safe return of your wife. My suggestion to you is to at least respond to us, otherwise you won't be getting Luisa back in one piece." I grabbed her hair and yanked her head back so he could see her face. To my surprise, she let out a cry of pain. I really had hurt her.

The Doctor was smiling behind the camera at her reaction, and I had no choice but to smile as well. Only difference was, mine was fake.

"You have a very lovely wife," I went on to say. "Very beautiful. It would be a shame to ignore this because you didn't think we were serious. I am very serious. You have two days to contact us. After that, she becomes property of my cartel. And I'm sure you know what that means. This is just the start." I pressed the tip of the blade into her skin. Instead of feeling the thrill I normally felt, I felt my guts twist. But I persevered through the frivolous sentiment and dug the knife in sharply, an inch deep.

She let out a scream. I didn't know if it was because of the pain or the thought of losing her parents. It was what we wanted though. I slowly dragged the blade down, rivers of crimson pooling around the metal and spilling down her back and onto the bedspread. She screamed again until The Doctor told us we were done.

Then her screaming stopped. She was breathing heavily beneath me, the blood pouring freely, but she wasn't even whimpering.

The Doctor shook his head slightly and said, "I'll go upload this and check on Este. There's been too much blood tonight, even for someone like me."

He gathered up the camera and left the room. Once we were alone, I felt completely flustered, a feeling that was foreign and terrible. I untied her wrists then got off of her and stared at the blood for a moment before going and getting a towel from the bathroom. I pressed it down on her back and she flinched under my touch.

"Are you okay?" I asked.

She didn't say anything.

I kept pressure on the towel and watched as the red monopolized the white. "It is a fairly deep cut this time. Ugly. I don't like to make ugly marks."

I expected her to tell me off. I wanted her to tell me off. But she gave me nothing, as usual. It was frustrating beyond belief.

"Interesting thing about your parents," I told her, searching for that spark.

Her muscles tightened beneath my hand and she looked like she was holding her breath.

My heart danced. There it was. "I had no idea they meant so much to you," I went on. "Of course, I don't know anything about them at all, but I'm sure I could find out their names and addresses tomorrow if I wanted to. I'm assuming they weren't living with you and Salvador. No, my guess is they are back in Los Cabos, completely unprotected." I leaned in closer. "You know, my darling, most daughters don't leave their parents behind to go off and marry a drug lord."

She suddenly sat up, hair in her face, her eyes blazing with fury. I kept the towel pressed against her wound, keeping her close to me. Fuck me, I wanted to put my tongue in her mouth and feel that anger. I wanted to take her fury right here on the bed, let the blood wash over the both of us.

"You don't know anything about me and my parents," she hissed at me. "So don't even try."

I grabbed her arm and pulled her even closer so she was almost pressed up against me. "Oh, I'll try. Tell me then how it went? Girl ditches her proud mama and papa for a chance to marry the man of her dreams and become a narco-wife? Bet you regret that little fancy of yours, don't you?"

She raised her other hand to smack me, but I was quick. I dropped the towel and snatched her by the wrist. I forced her down on her back, holding her hands above her head and pinning her to the bed. She struggled but not for long as I climbed on top of her.

I stared down at her and couldn't help but smile. She'd be so easy to fuck right now, but I wanted to fuck that pretty little head of hers even more, see what was inside.

"You don't know anything!" she said. "I was a good daughter. I did this all for them. This was all for them. If I married Salvador, I could pay for someone to take care of them. They're ill and I struggled every fucking day to provide for them, to make sure they were fed and happy, and it was never a guarantee. I did everything I could to give them the best life I could. We grew up poor but they made sacrifices for me. I had to make sacrifices for them. My life was the biggest sacrifice. So I married him because he asked me, and I knew I could give my parents the life that they deserved. I never expected love, I never expected anything good except knowing that they were going to be okay."

She wasn't quite crying, but her eyes were wet. I frowned, a strain of compassion running through me for this strong little woman. She didn't feel sorry for herself, she rarely got angry, and yet she'd been handed the shit card in life, just as I had.

"You care that much about your parents?" I asked, aware that I was crushing her. "You'd marry Sal just for their happiness? Though I don't see how any parent could be happy with you marrying *that* man."

Her brows knitted together as she stared up at me. "Don't you care about your parents?"

"My parents are dead," I said simply.

"Oh. I'm sorry." And the curious thing, I could see she was.

"I'm not," I said, not wanting her pity. "Family gets you killed."

She shook her head. "That is not the Mexican way. Family is everything."

"Then perhaps that is what is wrong with Mexico."

"That's a terrible thing to say."

True. "And I am a terrible person," I told her glibly.

"Yes," she agreed. "You are. But that is nothing to be proud of."

"And yet here I am, lying on top of you, full of pride for all the terrible things I do. I worked hard to be this way. It's not easy to have confidence in who you are, to say fuck it, the world thinks I am a monster because I *am* a monster. And I don't care."

She bit her lip and I wanted to do the same. "You're not a monster."

"Just a terrible person, then."

"Yes. There is a difference. I lived with a monster. I know what that feels like."

I gave her a wry grin and lowered my face so it was just inches away from hers. This close, I could see flecks of gold in the mahogany of her eyes. "Does it feel like a knife in your back?"

She blinked, taken aback, realizing the truth. Monster, terrible person, it didn't matter. I wasn't so different from her husband. I was just another man playing the game.

And it had to stay that way.

I got off of her and pulled her to the edge of the bed so she was in a sitting position. I turned her back so I could see the wound. The pressure of being pressed against the bedspread had stifled the bleeding a bit, but now her bed was soaked with blood. "I'll get you new sheets."

She stared at me with a dull expression. "Don't bother. I kind of like it."

I raised my brow at her. She was nothing if not always keeping me on my toes. "I think the bleeding has stopped. The Doctor may have to give you stitches tomorrow."

She gave her head a nearly imperceptible shake. "You're giving a hostage stitches because of the torture you inflicted on them?"

She had a point. A good one.

I couldn't care about that. I couldn't care about her pain

or her well-being or her past or her feelings. I was holding her for ransom, using her body and life to get what I wanted. I couldn't care about any of that.

And yet, I think I did.

CHAPTER ELEVEN

Luisa

I woke up in incredible pain, my back feeling like it was on fire. Memories from the night before came flooding into my brain, first a trickle, then a dam unleashed. My attempted escape from Esteban, the Taser shocking me, waking up with Javier watching over me with an unpredictable look in his eyes, Esteban's half-hearted apology with dinner, then Javier coming back with The Doctor and filming his branding for Salvador.

Javier had hurt me, really hurt me this time, but I did whatever I could to keep that hurt buried. That was until my parents were brought into it and the whole reality came smashing down on me. This was no longer about me – my parents' lives were at stake. It was a cold desolate feeling knowing that what I wanted – freedom – I could never have. When I was with Salvador, my parents were safe. When I wasn't with him . . . they would be cut off or worse. As much as every instinct in my body was telling me to never go back, to be glad that Salvador wasn't giving in to their demands, I knew that my selfishness would cost everything.

So when Javier told me to react for the camera, I was reacting to more than just the brutal, deep cut he carved into my back. I was reacting to the fact that I would never ever win, no matter what I did. I was reacting to the unfairness of it all, of my very existence.

And somewhere on that bed, as a drug lord knifed his name into my back, I found the thread of anger that I'd hidden from for so long. It was starting to unravel, slowly, like a snake. I nearly welcomed it. I almost invited it to stay. I suppose it was enough to just know it was there, to know I had a wicked part of me that was mad, that wanted more than what was given to me and everything that was taken away.

That morning, I spent the hours locked in my head. Every time there was a knock at the door, I was both relieved and disappointed that it wasn't Javier. In some ways, I wanted to talk to him. He had made me open up about my family, about my life, and now I was itching to get the same kind of information from him. There was something so traumatic about the night before that I felt even he was affected by it. That was a silly thing to think, of course. He was a man used to torture on a much worse, much larger scale. But even so, some part of me felt like last night was a first for him, in whatever way that was. Maybe because as he dug that blade in on the side of my spine, I could feel the hesitation in it, like he didn't want to hurt me to that extreme. I wanted to know why.

Why would this man hesitate for even a second when he had so much at stake?

I know what my mind wanted to think. It wanted to think that perhaps this man found me special, that he would change his ways because he saw me for me. But I knew that wasn't true, and every time the thought entered my head, I felt sick because of it, because something in me wanted to entertain it. But I'd given up those fantastical notions a very long time ago. Fantasies were for young girls who had no idea how the real world worked.

The last time I remember thinking that perhaps I was special and interesting and would one day capture the attention of a man was right after I had won my first pageant. There was a boy who worked at the restaurant, a line cook, who was only there for a few months. I could tell he liked and wanted me, and I wanted the same, but I was too afraid. So I locked myself in my mind, in daydreams about a better life, and I did that until he left. After that, there was no one else. There was nothing else. Because the truth was, as beautiful as some people said I was, it had done nothing for me but bring me pain. It didn't end the threat of poverty and the constant struggle, and it didn't prevent my father from losing himself.

You're an idiot, I told myself after Esteban left, the lunch tray lying on the floor. *Get your head back in the game, this is about survival.*

And I was right. But even though it was a game, I wondered if I was playing it right. Javier was drawn to me in some form, and though I couldn't figure out what form that was, he still seemed to take special interest in me. I needed to figure out how to make that work to my advantage. Javier was my only way out of here, I knew that much. Forget Esteban, his power seemed weak at best, and the others seemed ready to throw me to the dogs at first chance. As much as I hated to think it, Javier was the one person who could save me.

I just didn't know how.

Javier

"Good news," Este said, limping into the makeshift office I had at the safe house. The door didn't close properly, which cut my privacy down to zero and apparently other people's manners as well.

I sighed and snapped my laptop shut, looking up at him with dry interest. I'd been having a hard time believing in good news lately. Luisa had become this ticking time bomb in my life, her presence and predicament penetrating my thoughts, whether I was away from her or not. No matter where I was in this house, I couldn't escape her.

"Don't look so happy," Este said, and flashed me that cheesy dumbfuck grin of his.

"Give me a reason to be happy, then," I said, gesturing to the worn office chair on the other side of the desk. It didn't help me get into the right frame of mind when I felt like I was setting up camp in a derelict's house. Este had assured me the furnishings in the safe house were classy, but then again, he wouldn't know classy if it took a shit right in front of him.

He sat down and I exhaled hard through my nose. He was complying, which was good. It meant there were no hard feelings about the knife. Well, I'm sure he hated me as he usually did, but at least he was showing respect now. Sometimes subtle violence is all you needed to keep a man in line.

"I just heard from Juanito. He says that though everything is being kept from the media, Salvador knows we have Luisa, has seen both videos, and is currently thinking of a strategy."

I raised my brow. "Strategy?" I wasn't sure if that was good or bad. A year ago we had tried to strike a deal with an informant for the Tijuana Cartel. He tried to strategize. We turned our assassin – *sicario* – on him instead of the narco we were after. That's what happened to people who tried to out-think us.

Unfortunately, I was no longer so sure that we were holding all the cards. We only had one, a queen, and I was starting to think she was worth more to me than to Salvador.

Este shrugged. "I wasn't sure. My call with him was brief. But it seems to me like Salvador is ready to make a deal. Perhaps we can't get the Ephedra coming in from China, but maybe he'll give us coke from Colombia."

A pang of anger ran through me. "We already have that. We want *more*."

He didn't look too concerned when he tried to cross his legs; instead he winced from the pain in his shin. Good. "Well then we'll have more coke. It's better than nothing."

He was right, but it did nothing to make me happy. If I wanted more coke shipments, we could have easily gone east, after the Gulf Cartel in Veracruz. I just didn't like the idea of returning to that city, what used to be the disputed territory of Travis Raines, a city that held filthy memories. I took Luisa because I wanted something I never had – an opportunity for new power from a new source.

"Come on, Javi," Este said. "If it makes you feel any better, I'm in a lot of pain."

I frowned. "You don't seem like it."

"Well, what good is The Doctor if he can't get you high all the time? Poppies, Javi, from the very mountains we're in, possibly from the very farms owned by Salvador. When in Rome . . ."

I could tell Este wasn't that high on morphine, otherwise he'd be floating, but I made a note to speak with The Doctor after this. Pain was a lesson, and besides that, we all needed to have clear heads. That was why I had such a low tolerance for drug use. I'm sure it was ironic to many, considering my empire was built on the drug trade, but I'd been burned too many times by past employees whose addiction not only fucked them up but made them mutinous.

As for me, I almost never partook in it. After prison there was a period where I understood how drugs made a preferable reality for some people. It was one of my few moments of weakness, but even then I found strength in it. Discovering how dependent people got, how the right drugs could bury every broken heart and heal shattered pride, made me realize that in some ways, the cartels were doing the world a favor. We were giving people an escape from their sorry existences.

I tapped my fingers on the desk, my gaze directed out the window and at the sunlight trying to break through the clouds. "I suppose the bright side is that we'll hear from him in two days."

"How many letters do you have left?" Este asked.

"Today is E. Tomorrow is R."

"And then we say goodbye."

"Yes." I cleared my throat. "Then this is all over."

"I can't tell if you're sad it's ending because you're enjoying the torture, or . . . other reasons."

I shot him a sharp look. "What do you think?"

He smiled and got up carefully. "I don't think anything. You could say I've learned."

"Keep it that way."

I glared, and he nodded his head, leaving the room while trying to stifle his limp. Once he was gone and I was left in peace, I flipped my laptop open and stared at it. It was a picture of Luisa, the ones that Martin had taken at the wedding. It felt so much safer for me now to admire her from afar, even though I knew she was in the room above my head, even though I knew I would have to return tonight, knife in hand and face her once again.

After dinner, I decided to be the one to take up Luisa's food. I told The Doctor to ease up on the morphine for Este, and I volunteered to make dinner. I'd always been somewhat of a good cook, and was curious to see if Luisa would notice. Franco had even been sent into the local village to buy tomatillos, lime, and corn.

I paused at her door, taking in a deep breath. Out of the corner of my eye, I could see the guard down by the stairs trying not to watch me, and I automatically stood up straighter. I quickly knocked and waited for a few seconds before I knocked again.

I heard nothing from her, not a "fuck off" or a cry to go away. It was dark out, evening, and she must have known it was me and what I was there to do. Her silence compelled me to open the door.

The room was dark, and from what I could see, she wasn't in the bed. I quickly shut the door behind me and switched on the light, ready to be ambushed. She wasn't anywhere, but the bathroom door was closed. I couldn't hear her which made my heart pulse with worry. I racked my brain, trying to think if there was anything around here that she could hurt herself with.

But there was only me.

I slowly placed the tray on the bedside table. "Luisa?" I asked softly.

No answer.

I walked over to the bathroom door and rapped on it with my knuckles, saying her name again, hiding the urgency in my voice. Knowing the door had no lock, I turned the knob and slowly opened it.

The bathroom mirror was fogged up with steam, obscuring my reflection. Luisa's clothes were scattered on the ground. She was in the bathtub, lying there, fully naked and exposed. Her hair pooled around her like octopus ink.

I expected her to cover up, to glare at me, but she did nothing but stare forward, her eyes fixed on the beads of condensation that ran down the edge of the tub. I could do nothing but stare at her naked form, the way her nipples poked above the still water, how beautifully vulnerable she looked. I liked that. Naturally, so did my dick. It strained against my zipper, and for once I tried to ignore it.

"I brought you dinner," I said, once I was able to gather some of my wits.

"You sounded concerned," she said, her voice chilled on ice, her eyes avoiding mine.

"I was," I admitted as I stepped closer to her. I crouched down so I was at her level, one of my hands on the rim of the bathtub. "I was afraid something had happened to my greatest asset. Without you, I have nothing to trade."

A small smile tugged at the corner of her lips. "Right. Well I'm alive, as you can see."

I noticed the way she was laying there, her head taking off most of the pressure from her back. "Are you in pain?"

The smile vanished but she said nothing. I knew she was. "Lean forward," I told her.

"Why?"

"I want to admire my handiwork."

She finally looked over at me and my eyes locked with hers. "You'd rather admire your handiwork than admire my body?"

I swallowed hard but managed to give her an easy smile. "I can do both. Your back is just as beautiful as the rest of you. Perhaps even more so."

But that was a lie. I knew it as soon as she leaned forward. I reached over and lifted her dark, heavy wet hair from her back, placing it over one shoulder. Her back looked ugly now, the Taser wounds plus that deep gash of the I all ragged and crude, her flesh flayed and puffy from the water.

She looked so small and pure and helpless in the bath, those letters such a contrast, that I was hit with an unwelcome jolt of shame. It nearly knocked me off balance and I found myself gripping the edge of the bathtub harder than I wanted to.

Unfortunately, she noticed that too. Her eyes flew to my hand.

I had to remedy this right away. She was just a woman, a woman of no consequence. I didn't know her and she didn't know me. She never *would* know me. She'd be dead or gone in two days' time – having feelings of shame or remorse over what I'd done and was about to do was useless, ridiculous, and dangerous. So fucking dangerous.

"You almost took my breath away," I told her, giving her my most leering smile. "Such beauty in such pain."

"I am in no pain," she said. "If you've come to give me

another letter, shoot another video, then do it. Don't pretend you're here under the guise of giving me dinner."

I took a long, sweet look at her body and let the sight of her cause a spike in my cravings. "Perhaps I am here for other things."

I waited to see fear in her eyes but there was none. There was something else though, something I'd only seen once or twice in her face, hovering around the surface. It was curiosity. For good or for bad, it was as if she was interested in seeing just what else I could do to her. Or perhaps, for her.

She looked away, breaking our heated gaze, and hugged her knees tighter to her chest. "Well, if you are here for other things, then do them."

I clucked my tongue. "You are a strange one, Luisa. You should know better by now than to tempt the devil." I reached forward and traced an invisible E on her back with my finger. She flinched at my touch but still let me do it. I wondered now what else she would let me do. I wondered if I reached my hands into the bath and stroked her breasts, if she'd surrender like last time. Or would she fight back? Or would she welcome it, want it?

I could bet she'd never come before, never had an orgasm. I found myself savoring the thought of giving her both pain *and* pleasure.

I traced an invisible R, imagining the finished product, telling myself it would look beautiful. Then I trailed my fingers over to her shoulder and down her arm into the warm bathwater. I gently caressed her nipple, as if by accident, and watched her closely for her reaction. Her nipple reacted exquisitely.

She closed her eyes, and in turn I closed mine, taking in

the rich, sweet smell of her wet skin, listening to her breath catch and release.

"Did you like that?" I whispered.

I could hear her swallow hard. "I'm just waiting for the knife," she said softly.

My eyes snapped open and I stared at her. Of course she couldn't find anything pleasurable when there was blood to be drawn.

"And you shall get it," I said quickly. I retracted my hand and waved the bathwater away while I got to my feet. "Especially now since Salvador is working out a strategy to get you back."

She jolted, as if suddenly shocked, the water splashing around her. She stared up at me with horror, horror that wasn't meant for me. "You heard from Sal?"

"In a manner of speaking," I said slowly. I reached for the bath towel and held it out for her. "Come on out of the bath."

"I'd rather you do it here."

I frowned. "Your flesh is extra tender. It may hurt more."

"And I'd rather sit in a pool of my own blood." Though she said this with a hardened voice, her chest was rising and falling rapidly and she was nearly shaking. The night before I had seen how she reacted to going back to Salvador, but I hadn't quite realized it was that bad. I had to wonder what the fuck had been done to her.

And then I had to stop myself. It would only make this harder.

"Very well," I said. I folded the towel and placed it neatly on the sink, then whisked the knife out of my boot. "You sure you don't want to have your dinner first? I made it. Fresh produce from town and everything."

"I prefer the blade," she said. Then she leaned forward even further, gathering her hair tight to her side, making sure her back was completely clear. What I was doing had no effect on her, it was as if she wanted it. I was getting further and further away from breaking her and deeper and deeper into something else, something more troubling.

I leaned over her, and with one hand at her small, delicate neck to steady myself, I began to cut the E. I didn't do it nearly as deep as the I and it took much longer. I kept hesitating, something I knew she was recognizing, but it couldn't be helped. When it was finally over and the last cut was made, I watched the blood run down her back, like it was crying crimson tears, and the water around her waist became tinged with pink.

Before I knew what I was doing, I placed my lips on the wound, tasting the salt of her blood, the purity of her veins. I wanted to soothe the damage I had just created and feel the vitality of her existence pulse beneath my skin.

To her credit, she didn't flinch. She let me kiss her back and take my time doing so. She let me be a vampire, high on her blood and after her soul.

"I wanted to break you," I murmured against the blood. "I wanted to destroy you, ruin you. But you would not break. You will not break. Why won't you?" My last words were barely a whisper.

She pulled away from me and looked at me over her shoulder, her eyes expressionless even as they gazed at my red-stained lips.

"Give me back to Salvador," she said, looking deeply at me, "and I promise you, you'll never be able to piece me together again."

I could see that she was right. The truth felt like a tiny sliver in my heart.

I swallowed the feeling down and straightened up. I gestured to the towel. "Dry yourself off. Your dinner is getting cold. I'll be waiting out there to make sure it doesn't go to waste."

I left her in the bathroom and closed the door behind me. Once I was alone in the room, I put my hands over my face and breathed in deeply, trying to get a grip. Things were happening and unravelling at a breakneck pace and I had absolutely everything on the line. Whatever fucked up . . . *feelings* I was having for Luisa weren't real; they couldn't be. Feelings never got you anywhere, only instinct did. And my instinct was telling me to run, to distance myself, to get ready to pull the plug on her because either way, even with my name on her back, she wasn't mine. She was either Salvador's or she was dead, and in the end, they were the same thing.

It didn't take long for Luisa to emerge from the bathroom, wrapped in a towel, looking angelic and breathtaking. She stared at me curiously, and I wondered what she could see on my face, if anything. I couldn't let her see anymore.

She walked over to the bed and sat down on the edge of it, eyeing her cold food with little interest. I knew better than to try and make her eat it. In fact, the best course of action was just for me to go.

"I'll be seeing you tomorrow," I told her brusquely as I turned on my heel and headed for the door. I wondered what she'd think about my hasty departure, then I had to remind myself that I couldn't care.

"Why do you want to break me so badly?" she asked quietly, just as my hand went to the doorknob.

I paused and thought about the truth. Without looking back at her I said, "Because I want to destroy beautiful things before they can destroy me."

There was silence to that. But when I opened the door, she let out a low chuckle. I paused and turned around to look at her.

"Wow," she said dryly, her mouth quirked up in an amused smile. "She really did a number on you, Ellie," she added, as if I didn't know who she was talking about. As if there would ever be another *she*.

I slammed the door shut in front of me, wincing at the discomfort that radiated out from my chest. I turned to face her and managed to keep my expression still, my voice flat and cool. "Don't say her name."

Luisa frowned. It felt like a kick to my gut.

"Don't look at me like that either," I added.

"Like what?" she asked.

"Like you pity me." It shamed me to say it.

"But I do pity you, Javier Bernal," she said, her voice dripping with superiority. "I pity you a great deal. Such a cruel, tough man still licking his wounds."

I was across the room and at her bedside in one second. I grabbed her arm and yanked her close to me until my lips were grazing her earlobe. "The only wounds I've licked," I whispered harshly, "are yours."

Then I released her from my grip and got the fuck out of there before further damage could be done.

CHAPTER TWELVE

Luisa

I t's funny what time can do to a person. It's funny what a childhood, a few years, a couple of months, a week, can do to a person. My childhood made me believe in the people that loved me, that The Beatles were right and love was all we needed. My few years at the bar made me realize life wasn't fair and that the world was full of cruel people who preyed on the weak. A couple of months of marriage made me see how fucked my life was, how I was trapped in the famed golden prison put forth by the country's narcos, how there would be no escape. And a week as a hostage let me know just how damn fed up I was with every moment of time that had passed before it.

I had changed this past week, in ways I wasn't even able to understand. Without realizing it, I was starting to relate to Javier Bernal instead of fearing him. I saw his desire to make me break and I felt that same desire, to make others break, the ones that hurt me all this time. He was getting his revenge on the woman who had left him, whether it was by becoming more successful or by humiliating and overpowering me. I understood now the vengeance that rocked through him, because the need for it was starting to rock through me. That anger deep in my belly continued to uncoil, threatening to be let loose. I wasn't sure what would happen if I set it free – probably nothing helpful since I was but a woman in a man's game – but if I could have that rare chance to be part of the game, I felt like nothing would be able to stop me.

After he left me in the bedroom, my thoughts kept sweeping over our conversation. I saw he had the ability to hurt, and I saw his even greater ability to lie. While he acted callous and cruel, I could see deep into those golden eyes of his and know when he was hesitant, when he felt bad or ashamed. I could see his feelings, emotions, buried so far beneath his dirt that they almost didn't exist.

But they were there.

The truth was, however, as much as Javier may have felt something over his quest to ruin me, I also knew reality would trump emotion. When tomorrow came and Salvador got in touch with him, I knew that Javier would hand me over. And if he didn't, I knew that he would have to kill me. Oh, I figured he wouldn't do it himself – his emotions wouldn't let that happen. But Este would do it. Or The Doctor. Or Franco. I would be killed, possibly in the most horrific way, because that was the way things went. Whatever Javier might have felt for me, he was no idiot. He was cunning, manipulative, and he had his pride. A lot of pride. Cartel leaders did not let hostages go because of bleeding hearts.

He would have me killed because he had to. Then he would go on with his life, looking for another opportunity to get ahead, to bury the ghosts of his own past. I would be a memory in a week. Some other form of revenge would take my place.

In the other scenario, at least I could keep my parents safe. If Salvador bargained for me, that meant he really wanted me as his wife. To have and to hold and to rape and to abuse, but he'd still have me there, and in turn I would take it and have my parents stay alive. I would put up with whatever I could for as long as I could.

Then, maybe one day, I'd get them far away and safe, before I killed Salvador. I would definitely die in the process, but I would die with a smile on my face.

I fell asleep with those thoughts. When I woke up, I was surprised to see Javier bringing me my breakfast. I thought he would have avoided me again like he did before, but there he was at my door, bringing me a tray of food, like a butler with a taste for blood.

My blood. I remembered the shivery sensation of his lips as they kissed my wounded back, both soothed and revved up by the strange feeling. Now he was standing before me, and I couldn't help but feel my skin thrum like an electric fence.

Javier usually looked elegant but today he was dressed down, as down as one can go. He was wearing black lounge pants that were tight at his hips and loose in the leg, and a damp white tank top that clung to his upper body through sweat. His longish shaggy hair curled at the ends from being wet, his charismatic face covered in a light sheen.

I'd never seen Javier look this worn and raw, though his confidence still shined through, just as that watch never left his wrist. Oh, to be that woman who destroyed him so thoroughly. I found myself envying this Ellie woman and wondering what kind of a man he was with her. Their relationship obviously never began with a knife. He had broken her heart just as she had broken his, which meant at some point there was love to give and love to take. It was nearly impossible to think of this man being capable of love.

But not completely impossible.

He came over to the table and put the tray of food – fruit, this time – down on it. I found myself studying his body, starting to understand how Ellie must have become enraptured with him. If I had met him under other circumstances, perhaps I could have felt the same. It could have just as easily been Javier who waltzed into the bar, looking for a wife, for a conquest.

Then again, that didn't seem like something Javier would do. He would have seen that as too . . . desperate. He had intelligence, good looks, and charm, whereas Salvador did not.

"What have you been doing?" I asked him after he gave me a dry "good morning."

"Boxing," he said, looking down at himself, as if he had just remembered he was half-dressed.

Was that the truth, or had he wanted me to see him like this? There was something so lithe yet masculine about his body. He was the complete opposite of Salvador in every way, and I couldn't help but admire it, the sharp V of his hip bones as they disappeared into his pants, the taut flatness of his stomach, the firmness of his chest, shoulders, and arms. He looked every bit the boxer, someone who worked hard for his body, who possessed skill that begged to be tested. Since he always moved like a panther or a snake, easy and controlled, I'm not sure why his athleticism surprised me, but it did.

When I looked up at him, his lips were stretched into a wry smile and his eyes sparked with amusement.

"Do you have an interest in boxing?" he asked. "Or just in me?"

I quickly looked away, ashamed that he caught me ogling him so blatantly. He must have thought I was quite the fool. Still, my eyes went back to him, this time focused on the tattoos he had on the inside of his biceps. One said Maria. The other said Beatriz and Violetta.

"Who are those women?" I asked cautiously.

His eyes became vindictive slits. "No business of yours."

I ignored him. "People you killed? People you know? Ex-wives?"

He sucked in a deep breath before he sat on the edge of the bed, hands clasped between his thighs, and stared down at the floor with a dreamy look in his eyes. "You know, once I went fishing with my father."

Okay. This was unexpected.

"We were in La Cruz, just north of Nuevo Vallarta. Nice town, you know? Marlin fishing was really big there, still is, I'm sure. My father was a marine mechanic, so we had free use of his clients' boats whenever we wanted. Well, I'd always wanted to go fishing. Hell, I suppose I just wanted to spend time with him since we never ever saw him. Occasionally, he'd give me and my sisters money to get ice cream and candy, but other than that, he was never around. I always questioned that, you see. Even at a young age."

He cleared his throat. I didn't dare move or make a sound in case he stopped talking. I needed to know more.

With a shake of his head, he went on. "I was an idiot when I was a boy. Ignorant. Anyway, we went out. It was a stunning day, calm seas. We didn't go quite far enough to get the big fish – my father said he wanted to be close to shore in case he was needed for something. But it didn't matter, I enjoyed being out there more than anything on earth. He was even kinder to me than normal. I remember he wiped sunscreen on my nose, tousled my hair, you know, like a real father would do. It was the best day that I could ever remember, better than when my neighbor, Simone, showed me her tits. Better than that. And then I ruined everything."

"How?" I found myself asking.

"I asked too many questions," he said, giving me a poignant look. "I asked why my father worked so hard for being a marine mechanic. I asked why he was never home, what he was really doing, if this was really his job. I got a whack across the face. He had never hit me before and he never hit me again, but I'll always remember that feeling. The shock. Then he turned the boat around and we went back home, empty-handed. He didn't say a single word to me for days. Whatever closeness, love, I had felt for that brief time on the water, that was gone forever." He sighed and stared up at the ceiling. "Years later, when I was sixteen, he was shot. See, I had always suspected on some level that my father worked for a cartel. I just never had the proof until he was killed. I figured perhaps he asked too many questions, too."

I felt my heart throb with compassion. He probably didn't deserve it, but my heart knew no different. "What about the rest of your family? You said you had sisters? How many?"

He gave me a sad smile. "I had four sisters, Alana, Marguerite, Violetta and Beatriz. Now I have two. I also had a mother, Maria. Now I have none."

"All related to the cartels?"

"To live and die in Mexico," he said, getting to his feet. "That is the way."

"Violetta, Beatriz, and Maria . . ." I stated.

"They are the reasons why family gets you killed," he

finished, his voice hard. "As does love. And as does asking too many questions. Do you understand?"

I swallowed thickly but nodded.

"Good," he said, flashing me an insincere grin. "Now, since this is your last day in our beautiful safe house, I figured I'd ask you what you wanted to do today."

"Do today?" I repeated incredulously. "Are my choices eat food, get Tasered, or become a human carving board?"

"I was thinking maybe you wanted to do something else for a change."

As strange as it was to think it, the idea of change scared me. Things were bad for me, but I always knew they could be worse. In fact, tomorrow they would most definitely be worse and I was in no hurry to experience that already.

The look in his eyes softened as he held out his hand for mine. "Come with me," he said. "You have nothing to be afraid of."

"Only you," I pointed out.

"Only me."

I wasn't sure why that made me smile, but it did. I was starting to fear I was becoming as sick and twisted as he was. Then I realized that perhaps that was nothing to fear.

I put my hand out and he grasped it, his palm warm and soft, his fingers strong. He pulled me up to my feet, and I realized I was only wearing a long t-shirt and no underwear. I don't know why I was suddenly self-conscious, considering the way I was yesterday, considering I'd had my ass in his face a few days ago, but I was.

"I need to get changed," I said, looking away. He had brought me close to him and I could feel those eyes of his tracing my skin, from my toes to my lips.

"Do you want me to give you a minute?" he asked. "Because I'm afraid I've already seen everything. In every way possible."

I ignored that and pulled away from him, reaching for a pair of shorts, the shorts I had been captured in. I slipped them on, revelling in their familiarity, then knotted the t-shirt above my waist. Like hell I was going to bother with a bra.

"Low maintenance," Javier commented.

"It's easy when you're held hostage. I'm surprised I'm still brushing my teeth."

"Well, you don't want to turn into a savage."

I gave him a funny look. It was times like this that I could almost pretend I wasn't his captive at all, like my fate didn't hang in the balance of tomorrow.

I put on a hard face. "So, where are you taking me? Aren't you going to, well, look more appropriate?"

He shrugged. "We're just going for a ride. Tomorrow is a day for suits. Today is a day to . . . relax." I tapped my foot and he went on. "I've heard there's a beautiful waterfall here at the end of the road. Apparently you can see the Pacific from the heights. I thought we could go there."

I couldn't figure out just how sincere he was. "You're just going to take me on a car ride?"

"Don't look so concerned," he said. "You won't be able to escape."

I figured that much. He opened the door and we stepped out into the hall. Immediately, the repulsive pig that was Franco was at our side. Javier seemed on edge around him, his eyes burning into him like a warning, while Franco handed over a pair of handcuffs.

Franco then went down the stairs, and Javier slipped one cuff over my wrist and held on to the other one before taking me outside into the sunshine. There was a black SUV – the narcos' car of choice – running in the driveway. Franco climbed into the driver's seat and Javier put us both in the back, making sure the other end of the handcuff was fastened to the handle above the door. There would be no escaping from this vehicle, not unless I wanted to be dragged to my death.

We rode in silence for the first bit, the only sounds the crunch of rock beneath the wheels and my heart pounding loudly in my chest. It was jarring being out in the real world, so much so that I had a hard time taking it all in. It wasn't until Javier put down my window and the fresh mountain air came pouring into my lungs, that I remembered I was alive, even if only a short time. Lush, tropical foliage covered the road on both sides, and birds squawked happily from the trees. It was beautiful outside, and I realized that this was indeed a gift for me.

Yet, I had to wonder who all of this was for. Me? Or for the tiny speck of a conscience I knew he had.

I shifted in my seat and studied him for a moment, sitting there still dressed down in his top and lounge pants, looking more like an ordinary – albeit handsome – man.

"Why are you doing this?" I asked.

He stared out the window for a moment, as if he didn't hear me. "Because it is your last day here, your last day in my presence. I wanted to make it memorable."

"My last day on earth," I said grimly.

He gave me a lopsided smile. "Well, tomorrow you will either be gone . . ."

"Or I will be dead. It's pretty much the same thing."

He frowned. "I feel like Salvador knows how very precious you are. If I were him, I wouldn't let you go."

"But you're not him."

"No," he said with finality. "I'm not."

"So how are you going to kill me?"

His dark brows shot straight up. "Excuse me?" he asked incredulously.

"I said, how are you going to kill me? I know how most *sicarios* kill women. Through strangulation. Are you going to choke me?"

He rubbed at his chin, his eyes still bewildered. "Choking belongs in the bedroom, Luisa, and if you stayed around me long enough, you'd find that out for yourself."

I shrugged and looked at the trees rushing past, the way the road climbed and climbed. The air was turning cooler by the moment, the land smelling sweet and earthy. I felt like every sense was turned on, heightened, perhaps because this really was the last day.

"Choking is a horrible way to kill someone," Javier went on, his voice heavy. He placed his hand on mine, and I looked to him in surprise at the gesture. His expression was grave, his lips set in a hard line. "To feel someone's life slip out of your hands is not enjoyable."

"Is any killing enjoyable?" I asked coldly.

He raised his chin. "Yes. Some are."

"So how are you going to kill me?"

His grip tightened on my hand. "Why are you talking about such things?"

"Because it is the truth. Is it Franco here?" I asked, jerking my chin to the monkey driving the SUV. "Will he do it? Lower me into boiling water until the little parts of me burn, until you cut those bits off, until I pass out and you revive me and you do it all over? Will you sprinkle me with acid?

Gouge my eyes out, rape me with a burning hot tire iron and leave me in a room to die? Don't think I haven't learned a thing or two about being a narco-wife. I know how your business is conducted." My voice had become higher at the end and I realized how heated I was getting. I needed to calm down.

I took a deep breath and looked away from his face, his face that was still searching mine, seemingly in disbelief.

After a few thick moments passed, the tension in the car mounting, he removed his hand from mine and said, "You will be shot in the head."

A stone dropped into my stomach. The truth.

"I see," I managed to say.

"It is fast and painless. You won't feel a thing. Just hear a loud noise, perhaps some pressure. And then it will all be over."

"Are you going to do it?"

"No," Javier said. "That is not my job."

"I would like you to," I said, looking back at him. "I would like you to pull the trigger."

He frowned, shaking his head slightly. "Why?"

"Because I am your responsibility. And you are the boss. Don't become like Salvador, letting the people below you do your dirty work. Own up to the problems you created. Handle them yourself, like a man." I leaned in closer, close enough that I could see my reflection in his eyes. "I am yours. Act like it."

A faint wash of panic came across his face. "I am not finished with my name."

"Then take me back home and finish me."

Now he was really taken aback. He gestured to Franco and

the world outside. "But we haven't reached the waterfall. The view is breathtaking, I—"

"You wanted to make my last day memorable." I cut him off. "Then you should do what I want. I want to go back to the safe house. I want you to finish your job. I want to be done with all of this. I want to be done with you."

I could see Franco eying him in the rearview mirror, unimpressed that I was ordering around his boss. But I didn't care.

Javier watched me for a few beats, a darkness swirling in his eyes. Finally he said to Franco, "Turn around, we've seen enough."

"Yes, boss," he said, now glaring at me. I turned and stared out the window, taking in the sights that I would possibly never see again.

It didn't take long before we were back at the safe house and Javier was taking me up to my room. He practically shoved me in there and quickly locked the door, acting almost like he was mad at me.

I was alone again. But I knew not for long. He wouldn't stand me up, not after what I said to him. He had too much pride.

So I sat down on the bed and waited.

Javier came just after nightfall. Perhaps he was a vampire. His shining knife, caught in the moonlight, acted as his dutiful fangs.

He came in the room and flicked on the bedside light, which gave off a dull glow. He was wielding the blade in one hand, still dressed down, but in jeans and a tight white t-shirt. He didn't say anything to me, just stared down at my body.

There was a strange emptiness in his eyes, and I had to wonder if he was really here or somewhere else in that peculiar head of his.

We both knew what he was here to do; there was no point discussing it anymore. I no longer feared his knife; I'd grown accustomed to it, just as I'd grown somewhat accustomed to him. I unknotted my shirt and pulled it right over my head, not caring that I was bare-breasted in front of him.

He bit his lip and I could see his chest rise and fall, as if he was trying to catch his breath. But he still motioned for me to turn over. I did as he asked, feeling as if we were doing a well-choreographed dance and this was our final performance.

Javier climbed on the bed, straddling my thighs, his groin pressed against my ass, and I felt that familiar yet still foreign hardness. I wondered why he never tried to have sex with me, particularly since I seemed to turn him on so much. Pleasuring himself onto my back was one thing, but there was a distance to it. I wondered why he had never forced himself on me, why he never tried to get inside me.

I wondered what would happen if he suddenly did. A growing part of me realized that I kind of wanted him to try. I wouldn't fight him off. I wanted to participate, to be involved for once. I wanted to know if it was possible for sex to be different than the cruel, painful game I'd always had to play.

These were dirty thoughts. And yet I couldn't push them away.

I heard him breathing heavily and felt a finger trace the previous letters in his name. He traced them over and over again, as if in a trance, and the knife never once pressed into my back.

"Why are you hesitating?" I asked him softly.

His finger paused. I heard him swallow. Finally he said, his voice sounding rough in the dark, "Because I don't think I can."

My breath caught in my throat. "Why?"

"Because I think your last night should bring you no pain."

"There is no pain, Javier," I assured him. "Not anymore. I want you to finish your name. I am more yours than I am Salvador's."

Silence thickened the room. His erection grew harder, and finally he shifted against me.

"What did you say?" he asked.

"I said I am more yours than I am Salvador's," I repeated, as truthful and sad as it was. "So finish branding me. I want the knife. I want your name."

I think I might want you. You, the man who might pull the trigger.

I felt him lean over me, and the tip of the blade pressed in slightly, not enough to break skin. "Tell me again," he said, "that you want my name on you."

"I want your name. I want it to say Javier. I will wear those scars proudly." *And I will show the world that I survived it all, to the end.*

"Tell me you want me," he said huskily.

I stiffened, wondering if he had somehow learned my thoughts.

"Tell me you want me," he said again, "and I'll do it."

I decided to shed my self-consciousness. "I want you," I whispered. Then I said it again, until it sounded right, until I knew it was true.

Javier dug the blade in one sharp motion. I sucked in my breath, feeling a mix of pleasure with the tingle of pain. He finished the final sections of the R with gusto, his work quick and seamless. I felt the blood begin to pour from the wound. In seconds, he was kissing it, soothing it with his lips and tongue, absorbing the blood. He was so unbelievably tender, even after such an act of cruelty.

I closed my eyes, not wanting him to stop.

He slowly moved his lips away from the wound and began kissing down my spine, his tongue zig-zagging over it. I arched my back toward his mouth, an involuntary reaction from my body, wanting more contact, the wet heat of his lips.

"Do you like that?" he whispered as he paused at the small of my back.

I decided to be honest this time. "Yes," I murmured.

"Tell me you want me again," he said.

"I want you."

His hands slipped around my waist and under my pelvis and began undoing my shorts. "Tell me you're mine."

"I'm yours," I told him, suddenly feeling both turned on and afraid of what was to come, afraid of the unknown, of the change between us. But I didn't want to fear anymore, not tonight.

"Good girl," he said throatily. "Such a good girl." He grabbed the hem of my shorts and quickly yanked them off so my bare ass was exposed. I heard him groan at the sight of me. "A very, *very* good girl," he whispered. "And I'm about to do very, very bad things to you."

He ran his hands up my calves, my thighs, my ass, up the sides of my back all the way to my shoulders where he kissed the wound one more time. Then he reached under me and flipped me over until I was on my back. I winced from the pressure of the bed on my cuts, but he took no notice and pinned my hands above my head with one hand.

He placed his other hand on my neck, squeezing delicately. My eyes widened in surprise.

"The thing about choking," he said slowly, his voice dripping with lust, his eyes glazed with passion, "is both parties have to be ready for it. You, my beauty queen, are not. But I do know what you are ready for. Something to erase all your pain. Something . . . memorable."

He lifted his hand off my neck and leaned in so close, I was sure he was going to kiss me. My lips parted, wanting it. But instead he went for my ear, licking the lobe, and said gently, "I want you to relax and lie there. When it feels good, you grab my hair and pull hard until you're sure you're hurting me. I look forward to it."

Then he let go of my wrists and started making his way down, kissing my chest, my breasts, his tongue doing smooth circles over my nipples. He bit them and I cried out, from the shock and pain and the warmth that came afterward, a warmth that spread down my core and between my legs, making them spread open.

He kissed and sucked down my stomach, at my belly button, and then headed lower. I tensed up, afraid, but I felt him pause. I lifted my head to see those sharp lustful eyes staring at me with such want, I wasn't sure if he was going to kill me or fuck me.

"Just relax," he murmured, and his eyes never broke away from mine as he passed over my pubic bone and placed himself between my legs, his arms hooking on to each thigh. "I will do all the work." He looked down between my legs, bare and vulnerable. "You have a beautiful pussy, did you know that?"

My cheeks flamed and I chastised myself for feeling so bashful.

His face lowered even further and my body stiffened in response.

"I want to feel your clit throb between my lips," he whispered, his breath sending electricity through my thighs. When I didn't say anything – I couldn't, I was frozen in shock – he lifted his head from between my legs and gave me a curious glance. "You've never had an orgasm before, have you?"

I shook my head.

He grinned with easy carnality. "Do not worry. I'm very good at giving girls an orgasm for the first time. And for every time after that."

Then he placed his mouth on me, and a million volts of electricity ran through me, making me flinch. The feeling slowly melted away though as the wet warmth of his mouth spread all over, and I found myself relaxing into the most foreign sensation that had ever touched my body. His tongue slowly lapped up and down my slit before concentrating on my clit in slow, easy circles. I knew how my body worked, I just never touched myself before, never realized the pleasure that could be had.

I started thinking I was an idiot for not doing so all this time, but soon all thought was being sucked out of me and into his mouth. I was only sensation, this beautiful feeling that his lips were bringing me. I felt my whole body both relax and tense, and I began to raise my hips into his face, craving deeper contact when his tongue became whisper light.

"That's my queen," he said into me, and the vibrations caused me to squirm. "Your pussy tastes seductive, more delicious than milk and honey. I should drink you with my tea in the mornings."

I moaned, not even blushing this time. I just wanted him, needed him, to continue. I found myself reaching for his hair, burying my fingers into his smooth strands and gripping them. I pulled his face further into me and his tongue started to fuck me, entering in and out.

Now I was bucking my hips, craving him, wanting more.

"You're so wet, I'm drowning in you." He groaned. One of his hands left my thighs and he pulled back slightly. Suddenly he put one of his fingers inside me and I found myself trying to clench around it. "You want so much, it's beautiful."

"Just keep going," I said breathlessly, my back arching, my fingers wrapping tighter into his thick hair.

"I'll keep going until you are coming."

"How will I know?"

"Well," he said slowly, and though my head was rolled to the side and I couldn't see him, I knew he was grinning. "It will feel like this."

His tongue started flicking my clit harder just as his finger began to thrust and curl inside of me, pressing against my wall repeatedly. The pressure in my core began to build rapidly, my limbs stiffening, my breath escaping me. I held on to his hair as tight as I could while I felt like my whole body was on pause, that moment before falling when you're in mid-air, when all time stands still, when breath and heartbeat and bloodflow all stops.

It was the most beautifully exquisite torture.

Then everything broke loose. My body became a wave of

fire, of pulsating light, of air and heat and explosions that all went off at the same time. I was completely unaware of any sounds I was making – I think I was screaming – and I hadn't realized I was yanking on Javier's hair so hard that I lifted his head right off me.

I lay there, writhing, moaning. It was like being Tasered but only with pleasure. Then, as my eyes stopped rolling back into my head, as I began to catch my breath, I was hit with a second wave.

Only this one was pure emotion. I felt like my heart was light and fluttery, and there was pain and sadness and joy and regret and anger, and every single buried feeling being unearthed. I was beside myself, unsure of how to process what had just happened to my body and what happened to my soul.

And Javier, this horrible man, this narco, my captor, he was right there on the bed beside me, wiping his mouth and gazing at me before tucking my hair behind my ear. I could only stare at him in pure bewilderment, my eyes wide, my mouth open, trying to breathe, to remember who I was and what I was to him.

But I could barely remember any of that. I was feeling a pull to him stronger than anything before. This man was capable of such cruelty and violence, yet he had pleasured me, giving me something I'd never had. Well, the sated look in his hooded eyes told me that he found it nearly as pleasurable himself.

He rested his hand on my cheek, soothingly. "You better get some rest," he said. "Big day tomorrow."

And then more of the real world, of my life, came back, pecking away at the golden wave I was still riding, making my heart slow.

The thing, the crazy thing, was that as much as I didn't want tomorrow to come, I also didn't want him to leave. I wanted him to stay with me. At least until I fell asleep. I needed him, the little comfort he could give me on my last night.

He was staring at me expectantly, like he wanted me to ask him. Or he wanted to ask himself. Maybe we could do something else to pass the time. Maybe I could do something for him. Maybe it wasn't time to say goodnight.

But then he sat up, perched on the end of the bed, and smoothed down his hair. There was another moment where he licked his lips, his eyes flickering, his mind caught in some internal dialogue.

I almost said something. I opened my mouth and almost asked him to stay, as foolish as it was.

He got up and picked up the blade from the other side of the bed, sliding it into his boot.

"Goodnight Luisa," he said, and I knew the moment was over.

I couldn't find the words to say goodnight to him. He gave me a quick, almost grave smile, then left the room, the lock turning loudly behind him.

It was the loneliest sound.

I lay there naked, remembering the feeling I just had moments ago, a feeling I would never get back.

I let a tear fall, my emotions still running rampant in me, and then gratefully drifted off to sleep before the thoughts of his touch could turn into thoughts of his bullets.

CHAPTER THIRTEEN

Javier

I had woken up with the taste of her pussy on my lips. Proof that it hadn't been a dream.

Men who think they have to rape and violate in order to assert their power and control have no idea what they're missing. Real power comes in giving a woman pleasure. Real control is knowing you've taken that woman to another place, another plane of existence, and you're the only one who holds the key. I gave Luisa what she wanted, what she needed, and she would never be the same again.

In some ways, the same went for me.

But today of all days was not the time to dwell on such accomplishments. Today I had to separate my impulses toward Luisa and focus on the big picture, the task at hand.

My empire had so much to gain, so much to lose, and it all rested on one man's feelings toward a beautiful little woman, lying in bed in the room above me. I knew now that Salvador didn't love her – he wouldn't have abused her like he did, she wouldn't have hated him so much, and he wouldn't have let this charade go on for so long. But pride was easily confused with love and I knew how much of that he had. Too much self-love could be utterly destructive. I needed to play that card.

"Javier?" The Doctor asked.

I looked over at him, remembering what was going on. I was sitting down in the shitty little office, The Doctor in the seat across from me, Este and Juanito who had just returned from their travels, standing by the door. Franco was outside in the hall. By Luisa's room I had more guards than normal, just in case she panicked during these final hours.

On the desk was the old-fashioned flip cell phone Salvador would be calling. It couldn't be traced, but we would still destroy it after anyway.

"Yes?" I asked, tapping my cigarette and watching the stem of ash flake into the ashtray.

"How would you like for us to dispose of her?"

It was the way The Doctor said this, so callously, as if we were talking about garbage, that bothered me most of all. Naturally, I couldn't show it.

"I think a bullet to the head would suffice," I said quickly, before puffing back on the smoke. I'd already gone through half a pack that morning.

He cocked a brow at me, the lines in his forehead deepening. "Is that so? Don't you think we have to send a better message than that?"

I narrowed my eyes at his questioning. "What message is there? This isn't a secret killing, we don't have to bury her facedown. We have her, he doesn't obey, we kill her."

"But you know how sweet torture can be," he said with a wistful look on his face. "And it has been too long."

I stared at him, at the white Panama hat on his head that gave him this air of sophistication that hid all his depravity. "And you know I don't like women to be tortured."

"Right," he said slowly. "You think it's ugly."

"It *is* ugly."

"Are you sure it's all women," Este spoke up, "or just Luisa?"

What a fucking shit disturber. I gave him a dull look as I blew a cloud of smoke toward him. "*All* women."

He grinned and crossed his arms. "Interesting. You know, I could have sworn I heard you torturing her last night. There were screams . . ."

"Would you like another knife in your shin?" I asked. "No? Then shut the fuck up. For now, that is your job. Shutting the fuck up."

"No need to get violent again," The Doctor said, leaning back in his chair. "Not today. It's fine, Javier, if you don't want to torture Luisa. A bullet to the head will work, as long as we can remove her head afterward. And other parts of her. We'll mail it out to Cabo San Lucas, have Juanito here display her just so on the steps of city hall. It's her city, and that city has avoided the violence of the cartels for far too long, don't you think?" He ran a finger over his mustache, smiling at the thought. "Yes, that would send the right message. It will show the world, the whole world, that we don't fuck around."

"Um," Juanito said, speaking for the first time that morning, "wouldn't it also show that Salvador doesn't fuck around? I mean, if I saw a cartel boss's wife's body, I would assume that it was because he didn't negotiate. That his own wife wasn't worth it. That says some seriously fucked up shit right there."

Before I had a chance to run that terrible scenario through my head, the phone rang, causing us all to jump.

I snatched it up before anyone else could. It was a horrid ringtone to boot.

I flipped it open. "Hello."

"I take it this is Javier Bernal." The man's voice was raspy, heavy, like talking was an effort.

"I take it this is Salvador Reyes," I said.

"You're correct. I'm sorry I haven't gotten back to you earlier. You see, it took me some time to figure out who you were." He snorted in through his nose and I heard him spit on the ground. I grimaced. "I'd never heard of Javier Bernal. But one of my friends pointed out that you were the one arrested in California. Rumor has it that you were turned in by a woman, is that right? And now you appear to have my woman."

She's not your woman, I thought, but the thought didn't stick around for long.

"That I do. I have your wife, Luisa. Pretty little thing. You really shouldn't have let her out of your sight."

He grunted. "Have you ever tried to tell a woman what to do? It's not always easy to lay down the law."

His jovial tone was making me troubled.

"You've heard our demands, then," I prompted him. I looked over at The Doctor, Este, and Juanito who were all watching me, on edge.

"I did, I did," he said. He cleared his throat and spat again. "I did. And you must know that I love my wife very much. So very much. But you're asking a great deal from me. The Ephedra lane is a lot of money, a lot of work went in to that. Surely, as one master to another, you can appreciate that. I'll have no problems securing another one, but you get so attached to these kind of *things*." I could practically hear him smiling over the phone. The happier he sounded, the worse the knot in my gut.

He sighed. "How about this. Give me another week. I'll see what I can work out."

Every instinct told me to tell him there was no deal. That I was negotiating here, not him. That I was the one in control. I wanted to tell him that it was over, and I would personally fuck and kill his wife, and then I would hang up the phone. My instincts told me that because that's what they had been trained to do.

But my instincts were pushed to the side. "Fine," I told him. "You have another week exactly. If you don't deliver, we will. Her raped, mutilated body will be on the front page of every newspaper. And perhaps a few toes in your morning cereal. Goodbye."

I quickly snapped the phone shut and pushed it away from me. I hadn't realized I was breathing hard, my chest racing. Everyone was staring at me, seemingly in shock.

"What?" I snapped.

"You negotiated?" The Doctor asked in disapproval. "Javier . . ."

I pulled a cigarette out from behind my ear. "So what? It's another week. What's another week when we can get what we want instead of nothing at all?"

"You're giving him the upper hand."

"How? How the fuck am I doing that? I have his wife. If he didn't want her back, he wouldn't have asked for an extension." I lit the cigarette angrily then leaned forward in my chair, my eyes blazing into his. "You've done this a million times. Sometimes people can't come up with the money right away. So we work with them. We all know that is how this is done."

"For civilians," he said slowly. "That is how it is done with them. Salvador doesn't need to come up with anything, he has everything. He is playing us."

I shook my head. "No, you are wrong."

"This woman is clouding your brain," he said, getting to his feet. "I should just do us all a favor and kill her right now."

I shot up, leaning across the desk, fury rocketing through me. "You do that and I will kill you." I jabbed my finger at him. "You know I will. I will torture you the same way you torture everyone, and I will smile the whole fucking time."

He stared at me in surprise before his face crumpled into laughter. "You are serious. I like that about you, Javier. I like your edge. So, a word of advice then from your elder – don't lose it."

With that he turned and walked out the door. I looked over at Juanito, wondering if he had any more interesting anecdotes, but he quickly followed in The Doctor's footsteps. Only Este stayed behind. He closed the door behind him and then sat down across from me, putting his hands behind his head.

"Well, that was a doozy," he remarked.

"What did I tell you about shutting the fuck up?"

He nodded, looking away. "Yes, yes, I should do it more often. I'm just curious, Javi."

"About what?" I asked in annoyance. My heart was still racing along, my pulse beating wildly against my watch.

"About what you hope to gain from all of this."

"That's fairly apparent."

"Is it?" he asked as he picked up the cell phone and began to dismantle it. "You know at the end of next week, you'll still have to either kill her or send her on her way. You're delaying the inevitable."

"I'm delaying what I can to get what I want."

He shot me a look. "Look, I want to fuck Luisa just as much as you do. Or perhaps, just as much as you have. Her screams last night were not from being tortured. I'm not that much of an idiot."

I wasn't sure if I should own up to what I did; after all, I was the "master" as Salvador had called me, and that was our right as the master, the boss, to take what we wanted. Or I wasn't sure if I should gloss over the whole thing and pretend nothing happened. I didn't know what would be better for Este to hear. So I said nothing.

He continued, "I also know that another week with her is a mistake."

"How so?"

"It will be harder for you to . . . say goodbye."

"Then you don't know me very well."

He shrugged and displayed the phone on the desk, now in tiny little pieces. "That's true. I don't really. I should, but I don't. But that doesn't mean I'm not concerned for you."

"And why would you be concerned about my well-being?"

"I dunno. Being a good friend, I guess."

I laughed. "Friend. That's a good one."

His expression grew serious. "This organization means a lot to me, almost as much as it does to you. I just don't want us to be in over our heads. I don't like that Salvador has control back and I don't like that this might leave us looking like assholes." He bit his lip, thinking something over. "Are you still in contact with that chick from the DEA?"

"Lillian Berrellez," I told him. "And I haven't been in contact with her for a while."

"Do you think if things go south with Salvador, we could

give her Juanito? He can give her all the intel. They could pinpoint one of his safe houses, one of his mansions. I'm sure with some extra inside info, they could make an arrest, make it happen."

I shook my head. "I am not a snitch, Este. There is still honor among cartels. We don't rat each other out to the Americans."

He snorted, shaking his head like I'd just said the most ridiculous thing. "Oh, come on, Javier. You and your stupid moral code that doesn't exist. There is no honor. How do you think Chapo was caught before Salvador took over? Huh? The cartels put up those wanted posters around the continents, not the Mexican government, and not the American one. This is a new Mexico. There is no code among men because there are no men anymore. Only monsters who sit behind their desks and give orders." At that, he looked at me with a touch of exaggerated disgust.

"You think I'm a monster?" I asked. Funny how Luisa said I wasn't.

"I think you'll get there one day," he said carefully. "If you don't mess up."

He was talking around me and I hated it. I waved my hand at him. "You're starting to bore me, Este. Go and pack everything up."

"Where are we going?"

"Back to my place."

"What about a safe house?"

"I miss nice things."

"You can't bring Luisa there."

"I can do whatever I fucking want," I said, and instinctively reached under the desk for the gun I had put there. Este picked up on it and nodded, quickly leaving the room. He was right. He wasn't that much of an idiot after all.

Once he was gone, I was alone with my thoughts. Then my thoughts became too convoluted for me to wade through. So I got up and went to tell Luisa the news.

As usual, there was no answer to my knock. I opened the door and poked my head in. She was up, staring out the window, wearing that hot pink dress again, her hands behind her back. She didn't look over at me when I came in the room. I was glad. It gave me a few private seconds to appreciate the marvelous things her ass did to my dick. I had another week of this luxury.

"I have news," I said, clearing my throat.

Her shoulders tensed up but she didn't turn around. "Oh? Good or bad?"

"I'm not sure. What would be good news to you?"

"That you'll just let me go free."

I pursed my lips. "Well, that means I have bad news, I'm afraid. Because I can't let that happen."

She didn't say anything to that. I walked over to her and paused at her back. I lifted up her thick, soft hair and placed it gently over her shoulder, and peered at my name underneath. It looked less ugly now that it was done. I began to swirl around in the memory of the night before, the way she begged for me to finish it, to brand her, the way she told me she wanted me. I closed my eyes briefly and took in a deep breath through my nose.

"My name looks good," I said softly.

Her shoulders slumped. "Am I going back to Salvador?" Pure desperation tore through her voice.

"No," I said.

"Are you going to kill me?"

"No."

Finally she turned around and looked at me, puzzlement on her beautiful face. "Did you even hear from him?"

I nodded.

"What did he say then?"

I ran my tongue over my teeth. "Well, we've made a new bargain." Her eyes widened. "He said he needs time to give me what I want. I gave him one more week."

A cynical smile flashed across her lips. "You see. He doesn't want me."

"You sound happy."

"You have no idea what happy sounds like," she sneered, her eyes flashing with bright fire. "I am only relieved, but I am still here and I still face the same fate in a week. You've bought me more time to face my own death. How can I be happy about that?"

I'd be lying to myself if I didn't feel the way my heart pinched from her words.

I stepped closer to her and brushed her hair back over her shoulder. "I think I showed you last night just how easy it can be to pass the time," I said, lowering my voice. "I think you can find happiness in the time I've bought you. Don't you?"

She rubbed her lips together and looked away.

Where was that sexually curious girl from last night? I leaned down and grazed her satiny earlobe with my lips. "You're mine for another week, Luisa. Why not make it count? The tip of my tongue was only the tip of the iceberg. Trust me, you'll want to see – and feel – the rest."

I slipped my hand around the small of her waist, relishing

in how large it felt around her, and started kissing down her neck. Her nape was so soft, so seductively fragrant with just her own scent that it took a lot of effort to stay the course, to not throw her down on the bed, rip her dress off, and fuck her brains out.

She relaxed into my touch, into my lips and tongue, but it wasn't long until she pushed me back, her hand on my chest.

"No," she said, her voice uneven as she stared up at me.

I raised my brow. "No?" I removed my hand from her waist and used it to straighten my tie. "All right then."

I turned around and strolled to the middle of the room. I gestured to the clothes scattered everywhere. "I suppose there are more pressing things to deal with. You'll need to pack up everything."

"Why?" she asked, her hand at her heart.

I smiled. "It's no longer wise to stay here. I'm taking you home." She froze and I quickly went on. "Home to my place. No more safe houses, no rented mansions. You're coming to stay with me."

"Is that . . . safe?"

"My darling, you can't get any safer. I spend what I earn. I have informants at checkpoints outside of my local town who report all new people moving in, people who may be part of rival cartels. I have *sicarios* patrolling the town, searching for new vehicles, new people that may have gotten past the checkpoints. It's just as controlled as any federal agency. In matters of safety, I spare no expense. The same goes for shoes and liquor."

At that she glanced down at my shoes, perhaps noticing their quality craftsmanship for the first time. And they say women were always first to notice fine clothing.

Then again, Luisa was born poor. Her knowledge of wealth and style was only thrust upon her in the last few months, lost in the mess of abuse and brutality. I could smell that depravity waft in over the phone that morning, the sickness that was Salvador. I kept trying not to think of them together, of the things he must have done to her, but hearing his voice made it all the more real. I started to wonder how the hell I would be able to give her back to him in a week.

"Are you okay?" she asked me.

I blinked, bringing myself back to the scene.

"Yes, fine," I said quickly. "I'll come back in a few. Then we'll be gone."

CHAPTER FOURTEEN

Luisa

It took me a few moments to wrap my head around the new situation. When Javier came into my room, I was certain my world was about to change forever. Either Salvador was making the trade and wanted me back, or Javier would have to shoot me in the head – or at least get someone else to do it. I hadn't been kidding when I said I wanted him to pull the trigger. It only seemed fair, and if I was going to die because of him, he was going to suffer.

To have a week of your life extended was an odd thing. I wasn't sure if I was grateful or not. It was another week of uncertainty, but it was still another week of being alive. A week held chances, surprises, and possibilities – if one was in an optimistic mood. I wasn't, of course. No one in my shoes would be. Though I had to say I felt my knees threaten to give out when Javier started kissing my neck.

That man's lips did things to my skin – shocked me, gently, with warm electricity – and I found myself wanting him to raise his head and bring his lips to mine. I wanted to know what *that* felt like. But I wasn't about to give him the upper hand. As much as I didn't want to say no to him, as much as I fantasized about a repeat of last night, I did say no.

And to his credit, he immediately backed off. Didn't even

try to make me feel bad for it. Javier definitely followed his own set of morals and honors, and it was strangely fascinating trying to uncover each one. A whole week of discovery lay before me. I suppose that was the only bright side to everything. That, and the fact that I was still alive.

The only thing that really worried me – other than my outcome in seven days – was the fact that we were leaving the safe house for his compound. I had no doubt that the place was well protected but it couldn't have been a good thing that *I* was going there. I was still considered the enemy, hostage or not. I was Salvador's wife and could return to him, report back to him, spy for him, all to re-enact revenge on my cruel captor, Javier Bernal.

It was almost as if Javier was trusting me, though he had no reason to.

And for some reason, that scared me.

It wasn't long until I was "packed." I just shoved all my clothes back into the bag that they came from. I no longer thought of them belonging to someone else, except when I had to hike up the long skirts so they wouldn't drag. They were a part of me, part of this disturbing transition from one life to another. Some of the articles had bloodstains on them that wouldn't come out with soap and water, but I didn't care. I liked the stains, what they meant, what I'd survived.

Esteban came up to my room to get me, limping slightly. I asked him the other day what happened. He wouldn't say, which made me think he was getting too cocky with Javier for his own good. I was glad he had been put in his place.

Unfortunately, he wasn't alone. I could see Franco and a guard leering around outside the door. In Esteban's hands he had a blindfold and handcuffs.

"What's going on?" I asked, trying not to panic.

"You don't like kinky games?" Esteban asked with a smirk, coming toward me.

I instinctively took a step back.

He stopped and gave me a wry look. "Oh, come on, hey. I'm just getting you ready for your journey. You don't think we'd actually let you see where we are taking you."

I suppose he was right. So I was just trading one golden prison for another.

"Now be a good girl," he said. "And we won't have to hurt you."

At that, the old doctor stepped into the room holding out a syringe. Like hell I was going to let them drug me.

"I think I've grown tired of being the good girl," I snarled.

Este frowned, and I took that moment to pick up the lamp beside me and bash it into his head. I got him right on the bruise from where I'd smashed the rock into him. He swore as the glass shattered all around him, but I was already jumping across the bed and going for the other lamp, ready to fight off the doctor.

But when I turned around, Franco was coming into the room and shoving the doctor aside. The dull, mean glint in Franco's eyes and his veiny muscles meant that there was no way I could fight him off, even if I managed to grab a piece of glass and gouge it in his eye. Nothing would stop him.

He lunged for me, his hands hard on my chest, and he pushed me. I flew back against the wall, my head striking it, producing a shower of stars in my vision. Suddenly I felt rough hands grabbing my arms, squeezing them until I thought they would break like twigs, and through the throbbing in my ears I heard people shouting.

The next thing I knew there was a loud bang, a shot, and the blurred vision of Franco began to slip away. His grip on me loosened and now he was swearing his head off in between screams of pain.

I squinted, trying to see past the waves of dizziness and stay upright, and I saw Javier standing in the doorway, a gun in his hand, pointing it right at Franco who had turned around and was yelling at him. I looked down and saw him trying to clutch his foot, blood seeping out of his shoe and onto the floor.

"The next time you touch her," Javier said, his eyes crazed with burning rage, "I will remove the foot I just shot. And your other one. Then your hands," he stepped closer, the gun still trained on him, "and your shriveled cock." He aimed the gun down at Franco's crotch. "And then I'll piss on every single wound. I'll take your head last, so you can see each piece of you disappear, and then I'll piss in your skull. Do you understand?"

Franco didn't. He told him to fuck off.

The room seemed to freeze.

But Javier marched right up to him and pistol whipped Franco across the face, a man twice his size. He whipped him so hard that blood spurted out of his mouth and sprayed onto my arms and chest. I held my breath, so certain that Franco wasn't going to take that. But he did. Power was everything, and Javier had power. He just proved it.

Javier shoved him out of the way and gave me a quick glance of concern before he turned and faced everyone else in the room, a guard at the door, the old doctor with the syringe, Esteban who was holding his head and cursing.

"All I asked of you fucking delinquents was to bring Luisa

to me." He glared at the doctor. "I did not ask for her to be drugged. I did not ask for Franco. This should have been an easy process. Now I have another reason why I have to do everything my fucking self if it's going to be done properly." He jerked his chin at Esteban. "Leave the blindfold and the cuffs and everyone get the fuck out of here before I lose my temper again."

The men obeyed with no hesitation and left Javier alone with me.

He sighed and rubbed his hand down his face before he turned to look at me again.

"Did he hurt you?" he asked wearily.

"No worse than you have," I answered.

He nodded. "Good. Because I meant what I said."

"About?"

"About him touching you. I don't want anyone touching you. I won't let it happen. You won't have to worry about that."

"I don't know, you seem like a very touchy feely bunch here," I said humorlessly.

"I'm serious," he said, taking a step closer to me. He ran his hand down the back of my head where it hit the wall, gently cupping it. His eyes bore into mine and I couldn't look away. "I will protect you. I promise, and I keep my promises." He paused, licking his lips. "The only person I won't be able to protect you from is me."

I believed it. And in some messed up way, I was okay with that. I could survive him, his touch, his anger, his passion, because I was starting to understand him. I just couldn't survive anyone else.

"All right," I said slowly, still locked in his gaze. I wondered what they were seeing in me, deep down. There was no way he could look at me like he was, his stare so absolutely penetrating that I felt it in my heart, and not see something. I wanted to know what it was, who I was in his eyes.

But he looked away suddenly, breaking the spell, and pressed his hand to the back of his neck. "I'm afraid I'm still going to have to blindfold you and put you in cuffs. But I promise, you will not leave my side."

I nodded and bit my lip while he picked up the cuffs and the black satin sash from the bed.

I dutifully held out my hands for him. "Do you prefer in front or behind?"

He smiled openly at me, and it was the most shockingly beautiful sight. He looked so damn young, almost angelic. "Oh, my beauty queen, you should know I like it every way possible."

"I meant the handcuffs," I said, though it came out in an uneven whisper. I was still a bit shaken.

He cocked his head at me. "Well, just in case," he said. "The more informed you are, the better off you'll be. Let's take it from behind for today." He quickly walked around me and pulled my arms back, snapping the cuffs over my wrists, which now felt heavy and weighted with the cold metal.

I swallowed the tiny prick of fear that was forming in my throat as he reached around me and placed the blindfold over my eyes. The world went dark, save for a tiny sliver of grey light at the bottom, and he tied it securely behind my head. Now I was one hundred percent powerless and completely in his trust.

I could only pray that he really did keep his promises.

He gently grabbed my upper arm and put his mouth to

my ear. "Now I'm going to pick up your bag and take you down the stairs to the car. I'll put you in first, then I will come in right after, and we'll be on our way. If you need us to stop to use the washroom, well, there are plenty of trees. I'll try not to watch you too closely."

I raised my brow, the fabric barely budging from the movement. "How courteous."

I could sense him smiling. "I've been called worse."

True to Javier's word, he literally did not leave my side during the excruciatingly long journey to his compound. And, as he had said, he was even there when I had to pee. I was trying to avoid it, but wherever he lived was an eight hour journey, and even I couldn't hold it that long. There's nothing quite like trying to pee in the jungle with a blindfold and handcuffs. I suppose he could have taken the blindfold off for just those moments, but from the sound of his laughter ringing through the trees, I could tell it was funnier this way. To him, that is.

It was near the end of the ride that I found myself falling asleep. I must have dozed off for quite some time, because the car jolting to a stop woke me, and when I raised my head, I realized I had fallen asleep on Javier's shoulder. The feel and smell of him must have been strangely comforting. I felt embarrassed for some reason but said nothing, wondering why he had let me sleep that way.

"We're here," he said in a quiet voice. In the darkness, it washed over me like silk.

I heard the doors open and felt his grasp on my arms as he gently pulled me out of the vehicle. I gulped in the air, still smelling fresh and sweet. Mountainous. It was cool, making my skin erupt in goosebumps. It figured he would have a fortress somewhere up high. I started to miss the dry, hot desert air and sea breezes of Los Cabos. I started to miss a lot of things.

I was brought down a smooth path that felt like cobblestones beneath my shoes, and unfamiliar voices greeted Javier from all sides. I was ushered inside, across a tile floor, then up a long, curving flight of stairs. He took me down a lushly carpeted hall and finally into a room.

The door clicked shut behind me. Locked.

"Where am I?" I asked as he led me across the room. The floor here was tiled but I nearly tripped over a rug. His grip on my arm kept me upright. I expected him to remove the blindfold by now, but he didn't.

"We're in my room," he said. His hands went around my waist, and he picked me up and placed me back down so I was sitting on something lavishly soft, like a fluffy cloud.

His room.

His *bed*.

My pulse began to quicken.

"Don't look so scared," he said. "My room is a very good place to be." He leaned over me and I felt his hands go to the blindfold. I thought he was about to untie it, but his hand slipped down to the back of my neck and he gripped me there.

"I have been dreaming about you in my room," he murmured, his grip massaging my neck. "About what I would do to you if I ever got you here. And here you are."

I had expected to be brought to my own quarters, to be left alone or brought some food. I hadn't expected this. This was taking me completely off-guard, and the handcuffs and blindfold weren't helping at all.

"And what is that?" I somehow managed to get out, though the words felt lodged in my throat.

"Do you want me to tell you," he said, pulling down the front of my dress so my breasts were exposed, my nipples tightening from the air, "or would you rather I show you?"

"I'd rather you tell me," I said warily, even as his lips so softly grazed the tips of my nipples, causing a flood of need to spread through me. Now I knew for sure what cards were on the table.

"And I'd rather I show you," he said. Suddenly he was pushing me down on the bed and flipping me over so that I was on my stomach. In one quick motion he pulled my ass up in the air and flipped my dress over my hips. "This has to come off." He pulled my underwear over my cheeks and down my legs, taking his time.

This position felt awfully familiar. "You're going to come all over me," I said.

"No," was his response. I tensed as I felt a hand skim between my legs, sliding up toward where I was becoming increasingly wet and hot. "I'm going to fuck your cunt with my fingers and your ass with my tongue."

It took me a full moment for what he said to register. Then it hit me like a brick.

"What?" I gasped, utterly shocked.

He put one hand on my ass cheek and began to knead it with his fingers. "I've been staring at your perky, firm, heart-shaped ass for too long. I want you to clench around me as you come, I want to experience you from the inside out." He paused long enough to kiss me, slowly, on both cheeks, while one of his fingers slipped inside my opening, his thumb on my clit.

"And what if I say no?" I asked. I swallowed, trying to gather up the desire to say it. But it wasn't there.

"Don't you trust me?"

"Not exactly," I admitted breathlessly. He hit a sweet spot that made my back arch, my eyes clench shut, my body want more of it, so much more. I was surprised at how fast it was betraying me, like an addict after a fix.

"Let me rephrase that," he said. He plunged his finger in further, causing me to release a moan. "Don't you trust that I can make you feel better than I did last night?" He rubbed at me harder, increasing the pressure, making me swell. "Don't you trust that I can make you come so hard, you won't be able to stop yourself from screaming my name?" His tongue teased the top of my crack. "Don't you trust that I can give you things you've only dreamed of?"

I did trust that.

"Well?" he asked.

I nodded my response.

He stopped what he was doing. "I need to hear you say it."

"Yes," I said quickly, eager for him to continue. "I trust you."

"Good," he said soothingly, kneading my skin again.

"Isn't it . . ." I started, then decided it was too embarrassing to say.

"What?" he asked, his voice rough and low now, like sandpaper.

I bit my lip as the pressure continued to build inside me. *How do I say this?*

"You're a very dirty man."

"Filthy," he corrected me. He smacked my ass lightly, causing me to jump. "Oh, that's just fucking beautiful."

He did it again and again, not enough to hurt but enough to sting. Each time, he licked the place where his handprint would have been. Then, with one hand he gently pried my ass cheeks open. I couldn't help but cringe.

"You need to relax," he whispered. "This won't hurt. And I'm sure you took a bath this morning, didn't you?" I murmured yes in response. "Then you're clean and you have nothing to worry about. As for me, I'd take you anyway I can. It's all exquisite to me."

He was right. He was filthy.

"Relax, Luisa," he said again. "Relax."

And so I tried.

The first contact from his tongue made me shudder. The sensation was so entirely new to me, but what wasn't at this point? Yet his mouth, lips, tongue, were all warm and wet and gentle, and I found my body immediately relaxing into the steady motion. I pushed aside all thoughts about how unpure this was. Purity had done nothing for me anyway. It was better to be dirty. It was better to take what you could. It was better to embrace your lustful, needful, animalistic side because that was the side that *lived*.

I let those languid thoughts roll through me until they were replaced with deep-seated desire. His tongue became more forceful, entering me with an in-and-out motion that matched up with the same rhythm as his thrusting fingers. He was completely fucking me in every way and I was letting him more and more, my body opening up, craving him.

"Oh, god," he said, pulling away slightly. I could feel a

trickle of saliva roll down my crack. "You feel like velvet. You taste like sweet cream."

Then his tongue returned again, making my body shiver and rock from the sensations that were blurring my mind and shocking my senses.

At the sound of his fly unzipping and him moaning into my ass, I knew he had started to pleasure himself while pleasuring me. Suddenly I wanted nothing more than to do it for him. I was surprised at my desire – after what I'd been put through, I'd never wanted a cock near me or my mouth. But now I wanted him. I wanted to see him naked, see his cock, see what he looked like, wrap my fingers, lips, tongue around him and give him the same kind of ecstasy he was giving me.

But there was no time for that because he was just as skilled as he was relentless. His mouth and fingers brought me to the edge of a frenzy, the pressure building inside me from so many different sources that it had to give. My arousal splintered, rocketing through my body in hard, violent waves. I cried out, yelling Javier's name, my hands curling into fists behind my back, pulling against the cuffs.

He came too, loud, angry sounding grunts, but I was so far gone I barely heard him. I was swept away on that ship of emotions again, keeping pace with my body that was still spasming into his mouth and hand. I was so overwhelmed by everything rushing to the surface that I found myself sobbing quietly into the bed as the world ebbed and flowed around me.

There was a long pause, then his zipper went back up.

He placed his hand gently on the small of my back. "Luisa,"

he said, his voice throaty but touched with concern, "are you all right? Did I hurt you?"

I shook my head. "No," I mumbled into the soft bedspread. "I'm fine."

The truth was, I didn't know if I was fine or not. I didn't know anything except I had experienced something so achingly familiar it brought my head back to a moment in my life. What I felt just then was the same thing I used to feel when I drove to work in Cabo San Lucas, when the sea air flew in through my open window and I felt I was more than my reality, as if I were an element like the sun and water. Something simple and whole and everlasting.

I just never imagined that something like sex – or whatever just happened – could make me feel that way. It made me feel like a fucking queen. A rush of anger went through me as I cursed Salvador for nearly ruining me, for tricking me into thinking pleasure was one-sided, that sex was such a horrid, disgusting, cruel act. I could have died with that in my heart, never knowing the truth.

Javier's hands were at my wrists now and I heard him undo the cuffs, carefully taking them off. My arms burned in pain as I tried to bring them forward, and he gently eased me over onto my back, running his hands down my arms calmingly before removing the blindfold from my eyes.

I blinked rapidly at the intrusion of light, my eyelashes wet from the weak tears. I looked up at Javier's face as he leaned over me, his cheeks flushed, his hair messy, his eyes glazed. He smiled shyly and put his hand on my cheek. "My darling. You're going to be my undoing."

Javier

She looked so soft and delicate beneath me that I had meant what I said. Her beauty, her very essence, the way she cried out my name as she came around me, they were starting to fray my ends. It was only in that very moment that it didn't frighten me because my own completion was still rippling through my body. If only my cartel could figure out how to export this kind of high.

Granted, I'd much rather have made her come first then thrust myself inside her. My hand was getting a bit tiresome, and I knew how velvety soft and slick she'd feel around my dick. I wanted to shoot my semen high inside her and then watch it all run out between her legs and onto the sheets. She needed to be stained on the inside.

But that wasn't an option. If I fucked her, if I even kissed her, I would lose control of everything I kept chained together. It had happened years and years ago – with Ellie – and I wouldn't, couldn't, let it happen again. I had paid too dearly a price.

Still, the wetness around her eyes, the pretty way her mouth parted as she stared at me, was making it hard, in more ways than one. Even earlier, when she fell asleep with her head on my shoulder, the smell of her hair intoxicating me, I didn't have the courage to make her move. I enjoyed every second of the ride home.

And now, she was here. In my home. Everyone said it was a mistake to bring her here, but I didn't care in the slightest. Their opinions had become so tiresome and predictable. The fact was, she would be safest here. This was my throne. This was where I held all the power and all the control.

It would be nice to have a queen, even if just for a week.

"I'm sorry," she said.

I stared down at her in confusion, tucking a few strands of sex-mussed hair behind her ear. "Why?"

"For doubting you."

I smiled. "Most women do doubt . . . *that*. But if they're brave enough to be open-minded and own their sexual curiosities, they are greatly rewarded."

Her forehead furrowed slightly and I realized that alluding to other women probably wasn't something she wanted to hear. Oh well, I wasn't going to pretend I hadn't fucked a million women.

I cleared my throat. "Do you want to take a bath or something? I have a large Jacuzzi. I have a lot of things here you may enjoy."

She shook her head. "Am I sleeping here?"

I slowly sat up, distancing myself from her a bit. "No. You have your own room. Down the hall. I can assure you it is much nicer than the shithole you were in before."

She smiled weakly and I helped her into a sitting position. She tugged on her dress, covering up her perfect breasts. "The other place wasn't so bad . . ."

"Perhaps not to you," I said. "You've only known luxury a short while."

She tilted her head and looked me closer in the eye.

"What?" I asked, alluding to her intrusive gaze.

"Tell me about your sisters," she said. "The ones who are alive."

My face must have fallen because she looked ashamed and quickly said, "I'm sorry. That sounded callous. I meant, tell me about Alana and Marguerite."

I bristled. It wasn't exactly a favorite subject. I wondered why she was digging around. Was she trying to get information to use against me down the line, to hurt the rest of my family? My paranoia still fit me like a glove.

It was a glove that had kept me alive.

"I'm just curious," she said softly, looking away. "Never mind."

"It's fine," I said, smoothing on my mask. The last thing I wanted was for her to know what affected me. "What do you want to know?"

She shrugged. "Where do they live, what do they do, what are they like?"

"Well, they are both very pretty. Twins, you see. Which also makes them major pains in the ass. In the past, we weren't so close, but after Violetta . . . we became closer. I try and talk to them every month or so. I offer to send them money but they rarely accept it." I shrugged. "It's a good thing, I guess. Alana is a flight attendant in Puerto Vallarta. Marguerite is in New York City."

"Wow."

"I suppose," I said, absently running my hand over the bedding. "It seems so clichéd to me, to go live in that city. She fell in love with some filmmaker and I guess he treats her well. I don't know. She comes to visit Alana once in a while, but I am not sure if they are even close anymore."

"Do you love them?"

I shot her a sharp look. "Of course I do. Why would you ask that?"

She didn't say anything. I took the opportunity to turn the tables on her.

"Tell me about your parents."

She gave me a wry smile. "Oh, I see how this works."

"Give and take," I said matter-of-factly. "You should know this by now."

She nodded and her face crumpled a bit as she opened up. "My parents are lovely, loving people. Even though we grew up with nothing, they gave me everything they could. I wasn't an unhappy child. You're not unhappy when you have unconditional love. They made sure I had every opportunity that was available to me, and even though I knew how the other half lived, I didn't want for much. Then," she closed her eyes, "then my father started acting differently. My mother, she's blind, you see, and my father was always able to work enough to support us all, even though I helped out when I could. But now he was forgetting things, slipping into trances. One day I forced him to a doctor and they told us he was developing Alzheimer's." She took a deep breath and turned slightly away from me. "It set in pretty fast. He is – or he was – getting worse by the day. I had plans for university, you know. I was hoping that the money from the pageant I had won and maybe a scholarship would get me to school. But I couldn't do that. I couldn't be that selfish."

I shook my head vigorously, hating her selflessness. "Oh, but you should be, my darling."

"But I'm not," she said sharply. "So I forgot about that and decided to get a full-time job. I was lucky enough to work at Cabo Cocktails for three years. I was able to keep my job with a bit of . . . luck." A flash of disgust came across her face then vanished. "I took care of my family. I paid for everything. I did everything I could for them, just so they could be happy. I think I made them happy. I pray I made them proud."

I could feel the sadness leaking out from her heart. I couldn't help but be tainted by it.

"And how was your job?" I asked.

She shrugged. "It was a job."

"Was your boss nice?" I asked because I knew the types of men who ran those kinds of places, who hired women who looked as gorgeous as she did.

She pressed her lips together. "Bruno taught me that men were wicked and unkind."

I swallowed a pit of hate. "Did he rape you?"

She shook her head. "No. He didn't. But . . . he did other things. Not just to me, most of the other girls were . . . subjected to his advances. But he did seem to have a special fondness for me. I don't know why. Perhaps because he figured I was a virgin."

My blood started pumping hot, my face prickling with heat. "I'm going to bring you his head one day," I told her with one hundred percent conviction.

She gave me a wry look. "It's in the past. It doesn't matter anymore."

I rubbed the back of my neck, feeling the strain build up. "It matters. It all matters. Jesus. Luisa, your life has not been fair. Doesn't that anger you?"

"No," she said earnestly. "What's the point of yelling at the sky, it's not fair, it's not fair? It doesn't change anything."

She didn't seem to understand the power her rage could give her. "But if you get angry enough, it could change everything." Our eyes held each other. "I think I'd like you if you were angry. Very angry."

"Would you like me to start with you?"

I bit my lip, wanting her to unleash on me. It would be gorgeous. "Yes."

She smiled stiffly. "Maybe some other time." She got off

the bed, rubbing her arms up and down. I couldn't tell if she was cold or she was bringing life into her tired muscles.

"It's been a long day," I said, feeling strangely awkward. I got up too and adjusted my suit before gesturing to the door. "I'll take you to your room."

She complied and we didn't say a word to each other as I took her by the arm and down the hall. Her eyes took in the photography of world landscapes that I had adorning the walls in gilded frames, noted the various closed doors that all led to guest and employee rooms.

Finally we came to her room, and I led her inside, flicking on the lights. It wasn't exceedingly large, but it had a lovely en suite bathroom with a claw-foot tub and brass fixtures, walls with moldings, and a large four-poster bed, much like mine. An antique desk and chair were placed in front of the bay windows that overlooked the pool and hot tub in the gardens of the backyard. She'd be more impressed when the morning came and she saw the beauty around her more clearly.

I let her go and nodded to her clothes that were already hanging in her closet. I had called ahead and gotten the gardener, Carlos, to go out and fetch her some brand new ones as well, items that were properly fitted to her body. The man sure sounded embarrassed when I gave him his orders – I'd made him buy undergarments as well.

"If you need anything," I said, walking toward the door, "the phone by your bed is a direct line to my room."

She looked at me blankly, perhaps just overwhelmed. That couldn't be helped. I put my hand on the knob, ready to turn it.

"Wait," she said in a small voice.

I turned to look at her. "Yes?"

She glanced at the bed. "Do you think . . . do you think maybe you could sleep with me?" I frowned. "Or, or just stay until I fell asleep."

I straightened my shoulders, not allowing myself weakness. "I would if I could."

"But you can," she said, taking a step toward me. "You can do anything. You're the boss."

And a boss still has to answer to himself.

"Goodnight, Luisa," I told her, locking her in her new cell.

CHAPTER FIFTEEN

Javier

I was having a nightmare. I was on the fishing boat with my father, only I wasn't a boy anymore. I was the way I was now, thirty-two and wearing a suit. My father looked old, far too old to be alive, and had a Panama hat on his head. Every fish he reeled in he injected with a syringe, some kind of red poison, and threw them back. Soon, the whole ocean was filled with floating, bloated, dead fish everywhere you could see.

He ended up catching something really big on his line, enough that the whole boat started to tip over. When he finally managed to reel it in, we saw it wasn't a fish at all.

Luisa was hanging on the end of the line, her neck broken. The giant hook was through her throat and blood poured down from the wound, staining her body red. Her eyes were lifeless, like the dead fish that were slowly turning as red as she was.

"What part of her do you want to eat first?" my father asked me with a bloody smile.

I thought I woke up screaming. But it wasn't my screams at all that I was hearing.

They were Luisa's.

In a second I was in my pajama pants, a .38 Super in one

hand, and I was running down the dim hallway toward the room I had put her in earlier. I kicked down the door, not even bothering to open it, and to my utter horror, I only saw Luisa's legs on the floor, sticking out from alongside the other side of the bed. Franco's beefy form was over her, his face grinning. I couldn't see what he was doing, but I could guess.

Guesses were good enough for me.

I aimed the gun and shot him in the stomach, wanting the fucker alive. He howled, and before I knew what I was doing, I was running across the room and shoving him off of Luisa and tackling him to the ground. He tried to get up, but I head-butted him, breaking his nose. I pistol-whipped the same spot I did earlier, then quickly frisked the weapons off of him. I tossed them away and rolled his heavy, writhing body to the side. The rage, the living anger I had inside of me, was threatening to completely take over, something I rarely let it do, but I had to take care of Luisa first.

Then there would be no helping me.

I looked to her, my eyes wild, mouth open. She was grabbing her throat and coughing, trying to sit up, both cheeks red and swollen from where he had hit her. Her shirt was up around her breasts, and her underwear was crooked, halfway down her thighs.

Jesus Christ. If I hadn't gotten here in time . . .

"Luisa," I whispered, reaching for her. She looked at me with fear, total and utter fear, and tried to scoot backward and away from me. The bed and nightstand was blocking her exit.

I raised my palms as I went toward her on my knees. "Luisa, it's okay," I said as calmly as I could. It wasn't easy. "I'm not going to hurt you."

She shook her head, panicking, her hands clawing at the sheets as if she were trying to climb up on the bed. I gently grabbed her arm, but she pulled it away and started shaking uncontrollably, tears streaming down her face.

I was frozen in my own form of panic. I was watching her destruct. I was watching her break. And it hadn't been me who broke her.

"You promised," she gasped between her heaving sobs, crying into the side of the bed. "You promised."

Her words sliced through me like the slickest blade. I had promised. I promised I wouldn't let anyone hurt her. I promised to protect her.

I broke my promise. And by doing so, I ended up breaking her after all.

Suddenly Este was beside me, trying to make a grab for her. I could hear The Doctor behind me, peering over Franco, remarking on my shot, how long it would take for him to die. But I remained there on my knees, stuck in that moment where I finally ruined Luisa. The coldest, blackest rage had a hold on me, and after a while, it was all I could feel.

Fury became my captor. My hands were bound in shame.

Eventually, The Doctor pulled me up to my feet and poured a vial of bitter liquid in my mouth, moving my jaw so I would swallow it. I could barely stand and found myself pitching over but The Doctor held me up. He was saying things but I couldn't hear anything above the blood roaring in my ears. Fragments of my nightmare came rushing back.

"So what are your plans with him?" The Doctor asked. His words found their way into my ear, sinking in for the first time and penetrating the fog.

I looked to him in slow surprise. I was sitting in my chair

in my office, The Doctor across from me, smoking a cigar. "Oh, so you're finally here," he said with a nod. "Nice of you to join the real world, Javier."

"Where is Luisa?" I asked thickly, taking in my surroundings, wondering how catatonic I had been.

"Don't worry about her," he said with a flick of his wrist. "She's with Este and Juanito in the kitchen. She's drinking tea. She's a little bruised but she's fine otherwise."

Fine? He hadn't seen her destruction the way I had. That strong, beautiful woman folded over from too many years of fear.

I couldn't stop seeing her eyes.

"Franco didn't get a chance to rape her," The Doctor went on, smiling slyly. "But I still think we should let him suffer, don't you?"

"As much as humanly possible," I said, my jaw clenching. My hands kept opening and closing, making fists. "I want to do everything that I told him I would do."

"Either he wanted to test you or he had a death wish. Regardless, the man is a dumb fool and we don't need dumb fools in our family, now do we?"

I shook my head absently, not really listening. I was already fantasizing about my revenge. I looked over at him. "You can revive him, right, if he dies or passes out?"

He chuckled. "Well, I can't revive him if you remove his head, so save that for last."

"That is the plan."

He got up, a gleeful tone to his voice. "Tell me what tools you need and I'll set things up in my office."

The Doctor's office was in the small guest cottage on the property. It's actually where the Doctor lived. I wanted his torture house to be as far away from me as possible. Screams were so disturbing when you were trying to eat dinner, though now I wished his office wasn't soundproof. I decided I would leave the doors and windows open and let everyone hear exactly what we were doing to Franco.

"I want a saw," I said. "A very rough, strong saw. The kind that really rips flesh and gristle and bone. I want a jar of acid, something to dip toes and fingers and tongues in. I want a cattle prod. I want a red hot poker. My Taser gun."

"I see. Would you also like a rat and a bucket? Medieval torture never goes out of style." He went over to the door. "Franco is unconscious upstairs, but I'll get him down. I stopped the bleeding because I wasn't sure what you wanted to be done with him. He'll be awake and ready for you by the time you come by."

I swallowed hard, the anger continuing its course up and down my body, firing off in electric flames. I was going to make Franco pay. I was going to make him regret he ever looked in her direction. Then I was going to make Luisa see what I do to those who hurt her. I was going to make her look at him. And then she'd know exactly what I'd do for her.

This was all for her.

Luisa

The screaming started at four in the morning, about two hours after Franco had attacked me, and continued on well into the afternoon. At first it rattled me, bringing back memories of being at Salvador's and the torture I had to hear, and it kept me from sleeping.

Not that I could sleep at first anyway. I knew Este and Juanito were always around, watching me. I suppose their job now was to protect me since Javier was out exacting torture, but that didn't mean I trusted them. Who would protect me from them? Still, Juanito seemed safe enough, maybe because he was young and reminded me of a boy I grew up with. And to his credit, Este didn't appear to hold any grudges over me attacking him again.

After a while though, I was able to rest, my head on the island in the middle of the chef's kitchen. When I woke up around ten a.m., light streaming in the kitchen, Juanito was serving me tea and toast, the latter of which I refused. I had no appetite. It was then that I noticed the screams were still coming from the cottage – the doctor's office – though they were weak now and sporadic. They no longer had an effect on me. I was able to ignore them, and perhaps, if I was honest with myself, I was starting to enjoy them.

Just a little bit.

I had been lying awake in bed, daydreaming about a life I never had, when Franco came and knocked on my door. At first I thought it was Javier, coming to stay the night with me. It was so embarrassing when he turned me down, and I hated myself for being so needy and vulnerable in front of him. I just didn't want to be alone. I had my reasons and my reasons all came true.

Once I saw it was Franco, I screamed. I could see it in his eyes, that vile tar, that blackness, what he had come for. I expected him to lumber toward me with his injured foot, but he was fast. He threw me out of bed and onto the floor, and after he punched me a few times, my cheekbones taking most of the hits, he started strangling me with one hand. With his other hand he squeezed my breasts painfully and started to yank down my underwear.

With Salvador, I had learned to stop fighting back. I learned to stop struggling. He had always told me it was his right as my husband to do whatever he wanted to me and that I had to do whatever he wanted to him. Even if I had been one of his whores, he would probably say the same thing. It was his right simply because he was Salvador Reyes.

But I wasn't going to let Franco rape me, not without a fight. So I struggled. It was all in vain. His grip on my throat was so strong that I felt all the life drain out of me. The edges of my vision grew black as I gasped for breaths that I couldn't take in. I thought I was going to die on that floor, completely helpless while he had his way with me.

The thought of dying like that did something to me. It made me so afraid that I couldn't even function.

When Javier came in and shot Franco and I was free, my first instinct was to get away, to escape. All the formalities and politeness, and yes, lust that Javier seemed to show for me didn't seem to matter anymore. He was supposed to protect me, and I was a fool to believe a lion would ever shelter a lamb, especially from his own pride.

But, of course, there was nowhere for me to go. There was no escape from the golden prison. So Esteban and Juanito took me down into the elaborate, shiny-clean kitchen where they looked me over and took care of my bruises. And as they did so, as the screams of Franco began to ricochet throughout the surrounding jungle, a dark mass against the hazy blue of the pre-dawn sky, my fear began to melt away. It began to change inside me, as if all the chemicals were taking new forms and shapes.

My fear turned into anger. And when I woke up to Franco's waning screams of agony, I let the anger wrap around me like a cloak.

Javier had asked why I wasn't angry enough.

It was because I didn't let myself be.

But now, it was a part of me. The coil had unraveled. And I wasn't letting it go anywhere. Not anymore.

I was halfway through the cup of tropical green tea – judging by the excess amount of boxes in the cupboards, I gathered it was Javier's favorite – when the Devil himself showed up, standing in the hallway.

Javier had never looked worse. His white dress shirt was stained with blood, as were his jeans. He had circles under his eyes, his hair was messy and damp, and his gaze was blank, as if he were sleepwalking, even though he was looking right at me.

"Luisa," he said in a rough, strained voice. "Would you like to see what I've done to him?"

I stared right back at him.

"Yes," I said without hesitation.

He looked taken aback for a moment – perhaps he wasn't expecting me to want this. But I did. I wanted to see what justice looked like. I wanted to see what his anger was capable of.

He glanced briefly at Esteban and Juanito, perhaps delivering wordless orders. I got out of my chair and joined him at his side. We walked down the tiled hallway, past large rooms that held many secrets, until Javier opened the French doors out into the blinding brilliance of the backyard.

The gardens around the lawn and the pool area were absolutely beautiful and impeccably landscaped with the most exotic and colorful flowers you could imagine. There were bushes of red bougainvillea and white gardenia, pink plumeria, blue and purple orchids, magenta and yellow hibiscus, and birds of paradise, all of them expertly blending into the lush green grass and flowerbeds. Hummingbirds and butterflies filled the air, and dragonflies darted above a pond filled with koi fish and floating white lotus.

For a moment I was so stunned by their beauty and elegance, how tenderly cultivated and cared for they were, how seamlessly they seemed to thrive, that I forgot why we were outside. But beyond the dazzling blooms and shining heat of the morning sun, there were cries of pain and a man being tortured, and I was yanked back into reality.

I wanted to say something to Javier, ask about the garden, tell him how gorgeous it was, but now was not the time. As usual, I was caught between beauty and depravity.

I'd be lying if I said I wasn't a bit fearful as we approached the cottage, the door wide open, beckoning us into the darkest places. Javier put his hand at my elbow and gently pulled me to a stop just outside.

"Are you sure you can handle this?" he asked, his eyes focusing on my bruises.

I raised my chin. "Yes. Don't worry about me."

He squinted at that, studying me, perhaps worrying after all.

"Very well," he said. "Come on in."

The first thing I noticed when we stepped inside was the strong smell of ammonia that burned the inside of my nostrils.

The second thing was how spotlessly clean the room was, considering the messy state Javier was in.

The third thing was what made me fall ever so slightly into

Javier. His hands went to my shoulders, and he held me up, and I willed myself to stay conscious, to take it all in, even though it was all too horrible to take.

On a metal table in the middle of the doctor's office, lay Franco. He was completely naked – but he wasn't *complete*. His feet and hands were gone, bloody, cauterized stumps in their wake. His genitals had also been removed in a choppy, ragged manner. His torso was covered in hundreds of festering burn marks. Remarkably, he was alive. His head was propped up in a vise-like clamp that pressed down on his head and up on his jaw, his eyes staring at me, dull and milky.

The doctor was standing over him with a syringe poised at his heart, ready to inject him with the drug that would prevent him from losing consciousness. Judging from the amount of needle marks on his chest, this had been done many, many times.

The closest thing I had seen of torture myself was when Salvador was about to perform the "double saw" on an informant. It was enough to see the man, hung naked from his feet, upside down, with the saw positioned between his legs. I knew that was one of the most gruesome torture techniques, and I thanked my lucky stars I had gotten out of there before I saw any blood spill.

What Javier did didn't seem that much better. And because Franco was still alive, I knew it wasn't over yet.

"Take a good look at him," Javier said in my ear. "Look at his face. Look at the monster that he is."

I did. And I didn't just see Franco. I saw Salvador too. I saw Salvador's men. I saw Bruno. I saw all the men who ever wronged me, all the faceless cartel men out there who were wronging women left and right.

And I tried to imagine seeing Javier there, too. After all, he had kidnapped me, tortured me, humiliated me, and in the end, broke his promise to protect me.

But I just couldn't. The man had a hold on me that I couldn't even begin to understand.

"Franco," the doctor said to him. "That over there is Luisa. Do you remember what you did to her? What you wanted to do to her? Javier warned you, did he not? You were a dumb fool for breaking the rules – all along you knew this was the price you'd have to pay." The doctor looked at me, his voice chillingly glib. "Luisa, if you can perhaps give him a smile. It will be the last thing he sees."

I wasn't sure how it was possible, but I managed to plaster a smile on my face. It might have even reached my eyes.

"How beautiful," the doctor commented. Then he reached over, and with two quick twists of a lever on top of the clamp, it tightened around his head. There was a crunch as all the teeth in Franco's jaw shattered, blood pooling out of his mouth and onto his throat, then a faint, wet pop as his eyeballs fell out of his sockets, dangling by their optic nerves.

That was all I needed to see. I turned around, glancing up at Javier who was watching me with an unreadable expression.

"I'm ready to go now," I said quietly.

Javier nodded and looked over me at the doctor. "Keep him alive for a bit longer. Then remove his head. With the knife, not the saw."

"Yes, Javier," the doctor said, a trace of awe in his voice.

I stepped out back into the sunshine and heat and the birds that called out their beautiful song from the nearby trees.

Had all that just happened? How did so much ugliness co-exist with this?

"You must be tired," Javier said to me, gently leading me back the way we came, down the groomed gravel path that took us past the pond and gardens and back to the house.

"I'm okay," I said. Truth was, I felt like a million tons of caffeine was moving through me. It must have been the adrenaline. I was amazed I wasn't throwing up.

As we passed by the pond, Javier nodded at the lotus blossoms.

"Those are my favorite, you know," he commented. It was as if everything in the cottage had been a dream.

"The lotus?" I asked. Despite everything, I couldn't help but admire them again. "They are beautiful."

"Yes, they are." He stopped and stared at the flowers for a few moments. "I love the lotus because while growing from mud, it is unstained," he said, as if he were reading something aloud. He glanced at me. "A Chinese scholar once said that. I agree. It represents everything that I am not."

We started walking again. We were almost at the house when I said, "You must feel your soul is dirty then."

He gave me a wry smile. "Oh, my darling. No," he said, opening the French doors for me. "I don't even have a soul."

CHAPTER SIXTEEN

Luisa

For the rest of the day, I was given free rein of the house. I wasn't sure why – maybe Javier was extra confident in his security, or perhaps with Franco gone, he believed I had nothing to fear. I didn't know, but I did take every moment to explore what I could.

Downstairs was a game room with leather couches and a bar. There was a dart board on the wall and a billiard table in the middle. It was styled to look like one of those gentlemen's clubs: lots of dark mahogany, green-glass lamps, and gold fixtures. I stayed in that room for a long time. It was quiet in there, and the heavy curtains blocked out all the light from the outside. I wondered how often Javier used the room, if he came here to escape, have a drink, pull a limited edition hardcover book from the shelves and immerse himself in it. I wondered what kind of a life he had day to day, when he didn't have a hostage in his house.

Hostage. The word was starting to sound foreign. I was still a hostage, his captive, and yet when the word ran through my head, it had no meaning. I wasn't anything anymore . . . I was just me and I was just here.

After some time, I went to investigate the other rooms on the main floor. There was a small but state-of-the-art gym, some guest bathrooms and bedrooms, a large, immaculate dining room that housed a table that could fit at least twenty people, an open living room with a flatscreen TV built into the wall, and the kitchen.

Upstairs there were more bedrooms, as well as a few doors that didn't open, and one door that I didn't even try.

From that door I could hear Javier's voice on the other side, talking to Esteban. I couldn't make out what they were saying – the door was thick and their voices were muddled – but I knew it must have been Javier's office.

I kept walking past it, not caring what they were saying. They were probably discussing me, about what was to be done with me when the week was over. I wondered if Javier was at all having a dilemma over Salvador's upcoming deal, if he was still planning to shoot me in the head, or if torturing Franco had awakened some kind of appetite.

I wondered if it was scaring him. When I asked him to stay with me last night, I wasn't the only one who had been afraid. For one quick moment, like a burst of lightning, I saw fear in his eyes.

I made sure not to forget it.

Later, I ended up falling asleep on my bed, a science magazine I had snatched from downstairs open on my lap. It was dark out and my stomach was growling. I vaguely remembered Esteban coming into my room and telling me there was dinner for me, but I was so out of it he must have let me keep sleeping. I suppose I had been more exhausted by everything than I thought.

I glanced at my bedside clock. It was eleven p.m. I'd crashed for hours.

I groaned, trying to shake the grogginess out of my head.

For a moment I thought about my parents, wondering where they were, if they were still being taken care of. The caretaker made them go to sleep at ten every night, but I knew sometimes my mom stayed up later, listening to her audiobooks.

My heart clenched at the thoughts and I had to willfully force them away, otherwise, I would weaken. There was no time for weakness anymore.

I got up slowly and changed out of my rumpled clothes, and into a camisole and boy shorts that had magically appeared in my dresser drawers. They were lilac and made of the finest silk, fitting my body like they were made for me. I used the washroom, splashed water onto my face and combed back my hair, then opened the door to the hall. To my surprise it opened, which meant I was still allowed to be free. I smiled to myself and quietly padded down the hall. The house was still, and I wondered if I could raid the kitchen for something to eat without waking anybody. Obviously there was a security system set up and cameras everywhere which relayed to a guard somewhere, but I didn't care if they saw me getting a late night snack.

When I passed by Javier's office, I saw his door was open a crack. The light inside was on, spilling faintly into the hall. I thought this odd since everything Javier did seemed to happen behind closed doors.

I paused, listening, and heard the clink of glass. Taking a deep breath, I gently pushed the door open.

There was a click and I saw Javier sitting behind his desk, a gun pointed straight at me.

I froze.

"Oh," he said, his voice sounding odd, "it's just you."

He quickly put the gun away and picked up the glass beside

him. Ice cubes rattled in smooth, brown liquid. An antique bar globe was open, a half-empty bottle of scotch taking prominence.

"Sorry," I said breathlessly. My heart was still going a mile a minute from the image of the gun aimed at my head.

He nodded, not looking at me, and waved his glass at the room, scotch spilling over the rim. "Come in then, come into my office. Close the door."

I did so and took two steps into the middle of the room. I pretended to admire how tastefully it was all decorated, but instead I was studying him. Was Javier . . . drunk?

"I see you've found your new clothes," he said, his eyes feasting on my body, drinking me in like the booze at his lips. "You're gorgeous." He tossed the rest of his swill back and then wiped his hand across his mouth.

Yes. He was drunk.

I swallowed, feeling slightly nervous. I wasn't sure what Javier was like when he was drunk. Bruno became bold and disgusting when he had too much, while all of Salvador's vile actions were magnified. Javier was always so cool, calm and collected. To see him slightly unhinged threw me off.

That said, it was also intriguing. When one was drunk and the other sober, the sober one held all the cards and all the power.

"Are you okay?" I asked.

He tore his eyes from my body and poured himself another glass, nearly getting scotch on his elegant desk. "I'm fine. Why wouldn't I be?"

"You're drunk."

"I'm not," he said as his brows furrowed. "I'm just having scotch."

"Half a bottle of it."

He looked back at the bottle absently. "Oh. I already went through a full one earlier. Men like me must know how to control their liquor."

"Men like you," I mused. I walked over to the desk, completely conscious of the fragile garments I was wearing. I placed my hands on the desk and leaned down, staring at him. "Tell me more about men like you."

He must have caught the cynical tone of my voice because he looked at me sharply. "What do you mean?"

"I mean," I said carefully, wanting to push his buttons but needing to be cautious at the same time, "tell me why a man like you is sitting alone in his office, getting drunk. Don't you have body parts to clean up in your torture chamber? Or is that the hired help's job? You seem to get them to do all your dirty work."

His mouth set firmly, and a muscle ticked along his jaw. "I don't enjoy telling a lady to shut up. But I'm not above it."

"And how do you do that?" I asked, unfazed and unwilling to break away from his simmering stare. "How would you shut me up?"

He ignored that. "Why are you here?" he asked in a measured voice.

"I was just curious as to how my captor was doing. You had such a busy morning, chopping off limbs and such."

Suddenly he was out of his chair and leaning across the desk, his glass of scotch sloshing over. His face was inches from mine. I could see the flecks of brown in his amber irises. If I looked hard enough, I wondered if I could find that soul that he pretended he didn't have.

"Do you think I enjoyed that?" he growled, grinding his teeth. The smell of alcohol and tobacco wafted toward me.

I didn't move. "Yes. I think you did."

"I did it for you."

A smile tugged at my lips. "I think you also did it for you. I think you enjoyed giving Franco what he deserved."

He frowned but didn't back off. "So what if I did? He deserved everything he got. I told him that, I warned him what would happen if he ever touched you again. I never make empty threats."

"Why did you care so much if he touched me?"

He blinked, swallowing hard. "Because you're mine," he said, as if this was common knowledge.

"Because you carved your name in my back?"

He looked at a loss for words. He shook his head briefly. "No."

"Then why?"

He broke away and flopped down in his chair, staring off at a painting on the wall. "You should go back to bed."

"I'm not going anywhere," I told him. I walked around the desk so I was blocking his view. "If you think I'm yours, then you have to deal with me."

"You're becoming a pain in the ass."

"But you like my ass so much."

He glared at me. "What are you doing? What do you want from me?"

I went right up to him and hunched over so I was at eye level. He wasn't going to escape me that easily. He was drunk and he was close to breaking.

"I want to know why you're drunk." I cocked my head. "Is it because of me?"

He looked away from my gaze and didn't say anything.

"Is it?" I prodded, my voice rising. "Is it because of me?" I shoved at his shoulders. "Answer me, dammit!"

His eyes widened and I saw that fear in them again as he looked at me. "Yes," he said, barely audible.

"What?"

"I said yes!" he bellowed, grabbing me roughly by my arms as he shot up out of his chair. "Yes, fucking yes, it's all because of you!"

Even though his eyes were enraged, there was a vein pulsing along his throat, and his hold on my arms was tight, I wasn't afraid.

But he was.

"Why?" I asked.

His brows knit together in confusion. "Because I broke a promise. I never break those. That's not *me*."

I stepped closer into him so my chest was nearly against his. His perplexed look deepened. "I don't think you know yourself quite as well as you think you do."

His voice lowered. "Is that right? Well, then you tell me who I am, since you know me so well," he said tauntingly.

I rubbed my lips together, and I saw the way he focused on them hungrily. His breathing was heavy now, like he was fighting to keep himself together. I didn't want him together. I wanted to undo him.

"You're afraid," I whispered.

"Afraid of what?" he asked incredulously.

"Afraid of me."

He snorted in open disbelief. "Ridiculous. You?"

I looked at him more closely, until he was all I could see, and I was all he could see. "Yes. Me. You were afraid to stay with me last night, you're afraid of what you'll have to do at the end of the week, you're afraid to see me as a human fucking being. Afraid, afraid, afraid!" I angrily jabbed my finger into his chest. "You're nothing but a coward!"

His nostrils flared, and for one small breath I worried I made a mistake, that the beast would be unleashed and he would hurt me.

But a different beast was unleashed altogether.

He grabbed my face, his fingers pressing into my jaw, and kissed me so hard that it stole my breath. It was quick and violent and his lips were soft only for a second before he pulled away, breathing hard. He stared at me in thinly veiled shock, as if he couldn't believe he had done that.

My lips tingled from his absence and I tried to regain my footing in our battle.

But I couldn't think and there was no time.

His eyes sharpened with intensity, and suddenly he grabbed me again, this time one hand behind the back of my head and the other around my waist, jerking me toward him. My chest pressed up against his so tightly I could feel the rapid beating of his heart through his shirt and tie.

His lips engulfed mine, hungry, eager and wild. He kissed me deeply, thoroughly. Luxuriously wet. I felt like my feelings were sediment at the bottom of the sea, and he was shaking me loose, stirring me free, until it was swirling around both of us, clouding everything. I kissed him back, my pace easily matching his frenzied one, an appetite unleashed. Our tongues and lips melded like satin and sparks, and the more I got, the more I wanted.

My hands found their way into his hair, and I gripped his thick, silky strands, tugging on them until he whimpered softly into my mouth. He spun me around so I was leaning back against the desk, and I found myself writhing against him, trying to alleviate some of the pressure that was building between my legs.

He pulled away briefly, his eyes heavy-lidded, his mouth wet and parted, and quickly lifted me up in the air, placing me on the edge of the desk. He pulled down my camisole so my breasts were free and tended to them while he started ripping off his tie.

I grabbed the back of his head and yanked him closer to me as his lips encircled my nipple, sucking deeply at one then the other. I felt like I wasn't even myself, or maybe I was myself and I was just waking up. But I wanted things more dearly than I'd ever wanted them before. I didn't even ask for them, I made them happen. Javier was awakening me.

He worked my nipples into hard peaks, flicking them until I was gasping with need. Then he stopped and looked up at me, that wonderful mouth of his grinning at me while he ripped off his shirt. "Is this what you want?" he asked hoarsely before continuing.

"It's what I need," I said, my words punctuated by my own groan.

"Then I'll give you everything," he said. He yanked the camisole over my head and kissed me passionately again, his mouth snaking down my neck, washing me with his tongue as he pushed me back on the desk. My head was resting uncomfortably on a stack of papers but I didn't care.

When his lips got to my stomach, I expected him to pull down the thin, lacy shorts I had on. Only he stepped back. I looked up to see him swiping a letter opener off the desk. My eyes widened, and before I could say anything, he reached between my legs with the blade and made a quick slash down the center of my shorts. The edge of the metal didn't even come close to grazing my skin.

"I told you it was a hard-earned skill," he said slyly, stabbing the letter opener into the desk so it was sticking straight up. My god, even during foreplay there had to be knives around.

While I marveled over that with a mix of trepidation and excitement, he undid his pants, which only made those emotions double. He brought his cock out into his hands, hard, long, and judging by the look in Javier's eyes, somewhat dangerous. I breathed out slowly as I took in the sight of him. I thought by seeing him naked, he would be vulnerable in my eyes, but he was the complete opposite. His body was a fine-tuned machine and he owned it one hundred percent.

"You do realize," he said huskily, removing his pants, shoes, and socks until he was totally bare, "that once I go down this path with you, this is all I'm going to want, all the time."

"So I better like it then."

He grinned and it did funny things to my heart, just as the sight of his cock was doing funny things to my body. "My beauty queen, you know you'll like it. What you don't know is how much you'll *love* it."

Then his smile vanished and his expression was replaced by greedy lust again. He came forward, spreading my legs wider and climbing on the desk between them. "I'm going to fuck you and fuck you hard. I'll make sure you come, but I've been wanting to do this for a fucking long time and it's going to be rough. Do you understand?"

I nodded. "Yes."

"Yes, Javier."

"Yes, Javier," I said, though I couldn't help but smile.

"That's my good girl," he murmured as he started nibbling on my neck, sending shivers over my skin. His fingers entered the slit he created in my shorts. He slid his thumb over the swell, swirling it around until I let out a guttural moan. "But," he went on, biting my earlobe now, his breath hot, "what I really want is for the bad girl to come out." He paused and moved his face so it was right above mine, our lips inches from each other. "So, if you're feeling particularly . . . passionate . . . I invite you to hurt me the best that you can."

Before I could say anything to that, he reached down and wrapped his hand around his cock, positioning himself at my entrance. Instinctively I clenched up, afraid.

He put his hand to my face, his fingers trailing lightly over the bruises. "I'll go in slow," he said, assuring me with his confidence. "If I went in fast, this would be over in a minute."

With my heart in my throat, I nodded, and he slowly pushed himself in. Because I was tense, there was pain, but his movements were steady and controlled, and I soon found myself expanding, letting him inside. I ended up wrapping my legs around his waist.

"Good," he whispered, his eyes shutting in concentration. "Keep your legs and hips up, it will make it easier for you." He exhaled loudly and groaned. "Oh, Jesus, you feel so tight, it's like fucking an angel."

"I'm no angel," I said breathily, letting his width fill me.

"No. You're a queen." At that he thrust himself in, all the way to the hilt. My eyes flew open and I stared up at him while the realization that he was deep inside me hit. I didn't know what I was doing. But it felt so damn good, and so strangely right, that I didn't care.

I had let this man inside me.

It was going to be hard to get rid of him.

"Do I feel good?" he asked me, his impassioned eyes searching mine as he slowly pushed in and out, taking his sweet, torturous time, getting in deeper and deeper.

"Yes," I said, gasping, finding the need to both stare into him and look away. It was so intimate being able to gaze into his hypnotic eyes while he made me feel so alive and electric. "You feel good."

I didn't feel like I was very good at talking during sex but he didn't seem to care. His nostrils flared at that and he grunted. His breath was becoming shorter as were his thrusts into me. "I can make you feel more than good," he said.

He reached down between my legs and started stroking me. Now the pleasure was doubling throughout my body, from the wet swirls of his fingers to the thick fullness of him inside me. I loved watching his shaft drive in and out as he fucked me, loved the way his arms and shoulders rippled from the strain. I couldn't take the bliss anymore. It wasn't long before I was coming, crying out and digging my nails into his back.

"That's it," he grunted, "fucking scar me, mark me, make me bleed."

I dug my nails in further and rode out the wave just as he started picking up the pace. He was an animal. He started fucking me and fucking me hard, as he promised. I held on, even as the desk started to move from his strong, sharp thrusts and my head began to thump against the surface. It was turbulent and rough and half-crazed, and yet I was loving it. I loved watching Javier lose all control because of me.

The power felt incredible.

It wasn't long before he was coming and I made sure to take in every single detail. The way his brows scrunched up, his hair stuck to his sweaty face, and how he closed his eyes, his back arching. His jaw went rigid – every part of him went stiff – right before the violent release that had him groaning loudly and gasping for breath.

He collapsed on top of me, careful not to put his full weight on my body. His cock was still inside and I could feel the wetness start to trickle out of my legs. While he slowly regained his breathing, he propped himself on his elbows on either side of my shoulders and coaxed my hair behind my ears.

Javier was beautiful when he'd just come, when he was still inside me, softening. There was a gentleness to his eyes, an easiness to his smile. This was what I'd wanted to see all this time, just a glimpse of the boy behind the man, and the man behind the monster. He stared at me so tenderly and openly that I knew he had a soul. It didn't mean it wasn't stained and filthy, but it was there.

"So?" he asked, running his thumb over my lips. I could smell myself on his fingers. It was the smell of us together, good and bad, captive and captor.

I cleared my throat. "So," I repeated, finding my voice. My world was still a million spinning colors because of that orgasm.

"So I'm going to pick you up and bring you to my bed," he said simply. "And we're going to do that all over again."

I blinked. "Already?"

His mouth quirked up. "I warned you."

That was true. Still, I thought I'd be heading back to my room to be alone again. Even though that's not what I wanted last night, it was something I needed now. I needed time to separate myself from my hormones and reflect on what had happened with some distance and space. I needed to think about the power I earned and all the ways I needed to keep it, especially now that I knew my sex was his weakness.

But as I let him scoop me up into his arms and carry me, while he was naked, down the hall and into his bedroom, I realized he was my weakness as well.

I had the feeling that we weren't through with ruining each other.

CHAPTER SEVENTEEN

Javier

I woke up with a dry mouth and a pounding headache. I was hung over, something that didn't plague me very often. I rarely got drunk – you couldn't in this business, not when you were at the top.

But yesterday I had been a different man. I had become a man enslaved to shame. Not for what I did to Franco. I felt zero revulsion or regret over torturing that man. Even when he begged me to stop and I took out my dick and pissed on his gaping wounds, I didn't feel bad about that in the slightest.

No, my shame was because of Luisa, because I had failed to protect her and because I had broken my promise. I never made them in vain. I had meant what I said. As strong as she was, I knew there was a fragile casing underneath that could crack under the worst circumstances. All this time I wanted to break her, and the only way that I could have was by doing something I would have never made myself do.

I guess that said something about me, that I had a limit to my ruthlessness. But if I didn't have my own morals and my own code, who would? Someone out there had to lead by example.

I rolled my head over and took in the sight of Luisa sleeping beside me, pretty much hanging off the edge of the bed, her back to me. She was wearing one of my dress shirts, oversized on her petite frame, but I couldn't recall why. Perhaps because it looked fucking hot.

She seemed to be in a deep sleep, her sides rising and falling, her hair spilled around her on the pillowcase. Part of me yearned to reach out and feel it between my fingers, to wake her up by kissing her shoulder. But I had to keep those urges to myself. I was surprised I even let her sleep in my bed and hadn't sent her back to her room.

Memories of fucking her on the desk were followed by several rounds in the bed. That's why I didn't send her away.

In all reality, I made a mistake. A big one. I shouldn't have succumbed to her. I shouldn't have kissed her, shouldn't have fucked her. I knew it was a dangerous road to go on for me, to allow myself to be intimate with her, to be inside her. Watching her come while I was buried deep in her pussy was like a religious experience and it flamed my devotion. It spurred an addiction and made me insatiable for the next hit. It was in my nature to crave sex like I craved water, and I knew too well how cravings could derail even the most solid plans.

I exhaled through my nose, trying to focus on said plan instead of her. There was nothing wrong with a man having sex with a woman at his disposal, provided he would still be able to get rid of her at the end. It was expected of me, in fact, to be using Luisa every way I could. Most captives were treated far worse. The complication came at the end of the week, when she would be gone, one way or another.

But I just couldn't make myself think about that, about the hard choices that lay ahead. I had to believe I would do the best thing for me and my cartel. I would make the right choice, as ruthless as it would be. I had to trust that about myself and then let it go. The dilemma would be dealt with then and only then. Until her days were up and Salvador made his call, I was going to pretend that Luisa was here under different circumstances.

I was going to make the best of her.

Carefully, I eased myself out of bed, not wanting to wake her, and made my way to the bathroom. I flicked on the lights and briefly admired my naked reflection in the mirror. Though I boxed in order to beat any opponent – I'd lost a fight once and never intended that to happen again – I also did it to have my body look as good as possible. Judging from the hungry look in Luisa's eyes last night, it hadn't gone unnoticed.

I brushed my teeth, gargled mouthwash, and decided to run a bath and put on the Jacuzzi jets. My limbs were quite sore, not just from the sex but from the things I did to Franco. Rubbing a clit to completion and sawing off someone's foot seemed to use all the same muscles.

It wasn't long before there was a knock at the bathroom door.

"Yes?" I called out, craning my head to see.

The door opened and Luisa poked her head in. Once she spotted me in the bath, she looked flushed but she didn't leave. "Sorry," she said.

I smiled at her bashfulness. "Don't be sorry." I patted the rim of the tub. "Come over here."

She scurried across the tiles, my linen shirt billowing around her, and planted her perky bum beside me. She looked down into the tub and quickly looked away, a small smile on her lips. For obvious reasons – mainly the sight of her – I was already erect, the tip of my dick poking out of the moving water.

"How did you sleep?" I asked, my wet hand caressing her bare legs. I watched the goosebumps erupt on her flesh.

"Surprisingly well," she said.

"That shouldn't be surprising. I wore you out."

Her eyes went soft and held mine for what felt like an infinite amount of time. "Yes. You did."

I nodded at the water – well, at my erection – and skimmed my hand along the surface. "Come, join me."

She pursed her lips, seeming to think about it, before shaking her head.

I grinned at her. "That was a command, not a suggestion."

Before she could protest, I reached forward, put my arm around her waist, and pulled her down into the water. She cried out, half-laughing, as she plunged in on top of me, water splashing over the side of the tub. My shirt was immediately soaked, but I didn't give a fuck.

"Come here," I whispered, bringing her down on my chest, one hand gripped firmly behind her neck. I loved holding her here, so delicate, so powerless. I stared up at her face, the wet ends of her hair tickling my skin. Bringing her closer, I kissed her softly on the lips, teasing the rim of them with my tongue until she let me in. Even in the morning she tasted delicious.

I cupped her ass and gave it a firm squeeze, grunting a little. I needed to control myself – I was already so turned on, stiff and swollen, that the littlest thing could set me off. I had a reputation to keep.

"Ride me," I told her before I held her lower lip between my teeth and tugged. "Ride my cock. Impale yourself on it."

She raised her brows. It probably didn't sound hot to her but it sounded oh so fucking perfect to me. Sex needed to be a little rough and crude to balance out the elegance. A touch of tasteful violence goes a long way.

I reached down, moving my floating shirttails out of the way, and found her bare pussy. I pressed my fingers against her clit, applying just the right amount of pressure to get her started. Her lids drooped and a lazy smile graced her lips.

"You like that, don't you, my beauty?" I said, keeping my pace consistent as I slid my fingers down through her folds and teased the opening of her cunt. It was so tight, begging me to penetrate it, that I sucked in my breath in anticipation.

She nodded and I thrust a finger inside her, her body stiffening around it before relaxing. "Tell me you like it," I coaxed her.

"I like it," she said throatily, shutting her eyes and embracing the pleasure.

"Do you want my cock inside you?" I whispered, licking the shell of her ear.

She moaned, nodding quickly. "Yes."

"Then ride me like a queen." I put my hands around her hips and scooted her back. She grabbed onto the edge of the tub for support while I held her with one hand and kept my dick rigid with the other. She slowly, carefully, lowered herself onto me. It was excruciatingly deliberate, my balls tightening as my body already begged for release. Such a fickle beast it was.

She let out a breathy moan, her fuckable lips parting, and her head went back, exposing her throat. She felt like a velvet glove around me.

The sight of her riding me, my wet shirt clinging to her breasts, my cock going into her tight pussy, was almost too much to take. I kept a firm grip on her hips, holding her tight, so I was in charge. That was the thing about having a woman on top. They think they're in control, that they've got all the power, but that was never the truth. I was controlling this ride. Every thrust, movement, swivel – it was all mine.

I kept the pace slow, the rhythm easy, as the warm water splashed around us, the jets blasting against our skin. The sounds of our moans and heavy breathing echoed throughout the room, bouncing off the shiny glass and tiles. Just when I knew I couldn't take much more, I sat up slightly while keeping her on me. I put my thumb against her clit and reached around and teased her ass with my index finger.

She inhaled sharply but I merely grinned at her. "Keep the pace," I commanded as my finger pushed in between her cheeks. "I'll bring us both home."

She did, moving her hips continuously while I fingered her rosebud, her muscles contracting around me. From the way she sank deeper into my finger, I knew she was enjoying the stimulation, wanting more. I exhaled carefully, controlling my breathing as best as I could. When I was ready to come, I raised my knees so my hips slanted under her and simultaneously flicked her swollen clit back and forth.

She gasped, her eyes rolling back in her head and began crying out, loud as hell. God, I loved how vocal she was. Her body shuddered, and she clenched hard around my dick until I couldn't hold back. I grabbed her hips and kept her moving as she came until I was letting loose inside of her, coming in torrents.

Nothing in this world ever felt so fucking good.

I kept her rocking back and forth, slowing her gradually as her body grew limp from the exertion. Finally she fell on top of me, her breasts pressed against my chest, and she buried her face just below my ear. I heard her breath even out, felt the warmth of it soothe me. It was quiet and satisfied. It brought me a strange bit of peace, something I hadn't felt for a very long time.

We lay there for a long time, her breathing in my arms, until the jets shut off and we were surrounded by silence.

Silence that was quickly shattered by a knock at my bedroom door.

I covered Luisa's ears with my hands and yelled, "What do you want? I'm busy!"

I heard Este say something muffled and then my bedroom door opened. "I need to speak with you," he said.

"Well stay right the fuck where you are. I'm in the bathroom."

"Doing what?"

Luisa raised her head to give me a look and I let go of her ears. I gave her a sympathetic smile then hollered, "None of your fucking business! Give me a minute."

"I'll be in your office."

I heard my door click shut.

I groaned, straightening up in the tub. "Sorry," I said to her. "Business."

"Right," she said as she leaned back on her heels. "Business."

We exchanged a loaded look. We both knew what the business was.

I could see how our fucking was about to make things a lot more fucking complicated.

I quickly got out of the bath and dried off, wrapping the

towel around me. "I'll come right back," I told her as she hoisted herself out so she was sitting on the edge of the tub, staring down at her feet in the water. "And you better be naked, lying on my bed with your ass in the air, waiting for me."

At that, I left her in the bathroom and quickly got dressed. Black silk shirt, black jeans. I hurried out my door, shutting it behind me, and went down the hall to my office.

Este was already sitting in the chair, making it swivel back and forth while he sipped on a Tecate.

"It's still early," I said, nodding at the beer as I came around the desk and sat down.

He took a swig and shrugged. "I've had a hell of a time the last few days."

I cleared my throat and folded my hands neatly on the desk. "Well, I suppose that makes two of us then."

He cocked a brow. "Oh yeah? I suppose all the sex is helping."

My eyes narrowed. He needed to be careful. Out of my peripheral I could see the letter opener sticking straight out of the desk. Then the memories of slamming Luisa on the desk last night began to seep into my brain.

"Oh, you've got it bad," he commented snidely after a moment.

I snapped to attention. "Why did you call me here, Este?"

"For obvious reasons. We need to talk about the girl."

"And why is that? Is she bothering you?" My hackles were going up. I couldn't help it.

"No, not me," he said, finishing the beer and putting it on the desk. I watched as the cold drops of condensation ran down the side, heading straight for the fine finish. I reached over and quickly slid a thin coaster under it before it was too late. My desk had been abused with too much scotch and cum last night as it was.

"Then who?" I asked.

"Well," he said, "she's making you bother me."

"Who told you to speak in riddles, Este?"

He leaned forward and looked me dead in the eye. "I'm afraid you're putting yourself and the cartel in jeopardy."

I sighed and pinched the bridge of my nose. "We have already been over this."

"But now you're fucking her."

"So? I know you fuck things too, on occasion. Whores and your hand."

"I'm worried you've been compromised."

I shook my head in disbelief. "I think you worry about all the wrong things, and I think you forget who you're talking to. Since when does fucking someone compromise anything? It's my damn right to use the hostage any way I please. Don't get all jealous just because I'm not sharing her."

"I'm not jealous," he said. "Not much, anyway." He eyed my half-empty bottle of scotch. "But you were drunk last night, which meant something had gotten under your skin. It wasn't what you did to Franco. It was what he did to her. And if that affected you, a little abuse and attempted rape, how the hell are you going to kill her when this is all over? Or deliver her to Salvador, if that ends up being the case? You won't."

My gaze grew flinty. "Don't tell me what I will or won't do. Remember what you used to say about assuming, how it makes an ass out of you and me. Don't be a fucking ass, even though you're so good at it."

"Funny," he said, slowly getting to his feet. "Anyway, I thought

I'd bring it up again. I'd hate for the others to start thinking the same thing."

I got up too, pushing my chair back. "How about you let me worry about that?"

He gave me a self-assured look. "Just don't grow a mangina."

I snarled at him and unzipped my fly, swiftly bringing my dick out into my hands. "Does this look like a mangina to you?"

He blinked and looked away, shielding his face with his hand. "Jesus, Javier. Put that thing away."

I kept my cock out for a moment, stroking it once, before putting it back.

Este peeked through his fingers and lowered his hand when he saw it was safe. What a homophobe.

"Is it always hard," he asked, "or just when you're looking at me?"

"Just when I have a wet cunt in my bedroom, waiting for me to stop talking to you so I can go back and fuck it. What do you have?" I waved at him dismissively. "Why don't you go and enjoy your hand?"

He made a sound of displeasure and started to leave. "One more thing," he said, pausing before he opened the door.

"Yes, what now?" I asked curtly, resisting the urge to roll my eyes.

"Where is Luisa right now?"

I frowned. "I told you. In my room. Waiting to get fucked."

"Alone?" he asked, drawing out the word.

"Yes, *alone*," I said, mimicking him.

"How many guns do you keep in your room, Javi? A nine millimeter under your pillow. Your thirty-eight super in your drawer. An AR-fifteen under your bed. Am I right?"

I didn't say anything although my pulse quickened curiously.

"I'm just saying," Este said gravely. "Be careful when you open your door." He left the room with a morbid look on his face.

Shit.

But Luisa wouldn't shoot me. Would she?

Of course she fucking would, I told myself quickly. *She's still your fucking hostage and she'll do anything to escape.*

I exhaled sharply and picked up my pistol from underneath my desk, quickly checking the chamber. I really fucking hoped I wouldn't have to use this.

I left the office, seeing Este head down the stairs in the opposite direction. Some backup he would be anyway. I gripped the gun in my palm and eased myself down the hall toward my bedroom. I paused outside the door and put my ear to it, listening. I couldn't hear a thing.

Taking in a deep, steadying breath and hoping for the best, I quickly turned the knob, my gun down by my side, and pushed the door open with my shoulder.

Luisa was on her knees on the bed, naked, my 9mm in her hands and aimed right at me.

I automatically had my gun pointed back at her.

The sexiest Mexican standoff I'd ever been involved in.

"What are you doing?" I asked, taking a cautious step toward her, not lowering my gun for a second.

"Leaving," she answered, her eyes hard. She was distracting as all hell, her tits and pussy and that gun. I don't think I'd ever been so turned on so quick and in such an untimely situation.

"It doesn't look like it."

"I'm going to ask you nicely to let me leave, and if you don't, I'll shoot you."

A grin broke out across my face. My god, she couldn't be more perfect.

"If you shot me, you'd kill me," I said, taking another step. "Then who would make you come all the time?"

"My fingers," she said, her double grip on the gun tightening. "And I'd shoot you in the knees. I don't want to kill you. I'm not that bad."

I cocked my head. "No, you're not. But you could be."

Her face remained serious. "Please, Javier. Don't make me do this."

"Don't make *me* do this. You know the minute you shoot me, I'm going to have to shoot you. And I hate to brag, but I'm a terribly good shot, no matter the range. The odds of you hitting me, even from this close, are very low. Have you ever even fired one of those before?"

I could see she was taking aim at a spot right beside my head, perhaps to scare me, perhaps to kill me. "Easy!" I yelled at her quickly. "If you let that gun off, everyone in the house will be up here and I won't be able to protect you from them."

A venomous expression came across her dark eyes. "You didn't protect me before."

"And I have been paying dearly for it," I told her sincerely, taking one more step so I was almost at the foot of the bed. "Luisa, please, put the gun down and let me get back to fucking you."

She shook her head. "I can't. I need to go. I need to make sure my parents are safe and then I'm going to disappear."

"How are you going to do that?"

Her lips pinched together for a moment. "I have a friend, Camila, she's in Cabo. I could call her and—"

"No," I stated, imploring her with my eyes. "You can't. You won't get to her in time, and she won't get to them in time."

"Please just let me go," she said. Her tone was weaker now, as was the look in her eyes. They seemed nearly lost and hopeless.

There was a peculiar hollow feeling in my chest.

"I can't do that," I told her gently. "You know I can't. I must keep you here until I hear from Salvador. If I let you go, it would ruin everything for me." I gave her a pacifying smile. "Besides, don't you know I've grown kind of fond of you?"

She swallowed. "You just want to use my body," she said, her voice dropping slightly as well as the barrel of her gun.

"And I've grown very fond of doing so."

As soon as I said that, I moved quickly. I lunged forward, hitting the gun out of her hands and it went clattering to the floor, then I tackled her into the bed, pinning her arms above her. Her eyes were filled with a mix of anger and desperation as she writhed under me.

I held her arms tighter, my face bearing down on hers. "I can't blame you for trying, Luisa. And I was the fucking fool who was thinking so hard with his dick that I didn't realize I left you alone when I shouldn't have." I lowered my head so my lips lightly grazed hers. "But you know what," I said huskily, "I don't regret any of it. Because that was the hottest fucking thing I've ever seen. And you, my darling, you're really starting to be a queen."

I bit her lip and tugged on it for a moment. "Now, if your adrenaline is pumping like mine is and you're done with gunplay for the day, I say I flip you over and fuck your brains out."

"You can be so heartless," she sneered against my lips, but she didn't turn her face from me.

I sucked her lower lip into my mouth and felt her body respond underneath me. "My dear, you don't need a heart to fuck. Just a big dick." I thrust my erection against her stomach for emphasis and grinned.

Her eyes widened appreciatively.

She was a goner.

CHAPTER EIGHTEEN

Luisa

I thought the days leading up to Salvador's negotiations would take forever. The not knowing, the fear, the anxious anticipation – they all had ways of making the time drag.

Instead, the three days passed by me in a blur of sex and ecstasy. It was naked flesh and intimate fluids, languid limbs and earth-shattering orgasms. It was Javier's eyes in a million different ways: intense during sex and soft after coming, playful while we were in bed and glacial when we were with others. It was the way our bodies melded together that was absolutely captivating, addicting, and strangely freeing.

I started to feel like I knew his body inside and out as he did with mine. I learned what he liked, what he didn't like, what he craved. I knew the things to say that would make him fuck me breathless, and I knew what to say when I really wanted to piss him off.

And all this time, these days of mindless passion, I never had the urge to run again. Maybe fucking me was one way of keeping me under control. Maybe me fucking him was doing the same. I didn't know. But as much as I feared my future, I made myself live in the now. The now was all I had, and I made sure to enjoy every last drop.

I knew very well what Stockholm Syndrome was. I knew it was common. I just didn't think it applied to me. Because the women who fell for their captors that way, it was considered so strange and unusual that it needed a clinical name. It was an issue that could be diagnosed.

The longer I was with Javier, feeling myself stir, my wings stretch and flutter, I felt as if there was something so terribly right about it. When a woman is captured from her home, she is forced to contend with another man, one who wants to bring her harm. When I was captured from my home, I was forced to contend with a man who was better than the one I was taken from. Bad still, of course. Javier was terribly bad. But he wasn't the worst. And when I caught him staring at me sometimes, I could fool myself into thinking that he could possibly be the best.

But Javier himself still remained an enigma to me, despite the feelings I slowly found myself needing from him. For all his grace and tenderness that he sometimes bestowed upon me, there was this shield, this wall up around him that, for all my beauty and blow jobs and sweet conversation, I could not penetrate. He kept himself distanced from me and it made me frustrated and a little mad. Not necessarily because I needed to know what he was thinking, what he felt for me, but because I hadn't done that with myself. The both of us knew something horrible was coming up, and he was the only one who had the strength to protect himself from it.

Me, I knew I was done for. But at least I got to live a little in the process.

At least that's what I kept telling myself.

"What are you doing out here?"

I turned to see Javier strolling toward me, hands casually

jammed in his linen pants pockets. I'd only left his side a few hours ago and had come out to sit on the stone bench by the koi pond.

"Feeding the fish," I told him, lifting a few pieces of bread I nicked from the kitchen.

He stopped behind me and gazed out thoughtfully at the lotus. A breeze caught a few strands of his shaggy hair, the sun highlighting the gold in his eyes. Times like this I could pretend I lived here and that there wasn't a horrible world outside the beauty and blooms.

He eyed the bread and ran his hand along his strong jaw in amusement. "You do realize that koi fish need special food."

I shrugged. "I thought they were like your pigs and they'd eat anything." The other day he took me down a path that passed through a clump of trees at the edge of the yard and we ended up at a farm of sorts. He showed me his pigs. I'd learned how Franco's body had been disposed of.

He took a seat next to me. "Not quite."

Somewhere beyond the flowers, the gardener Carlos, a nice little fellow, started up his lawnmower. The sound was so mystifying. It reminded me of the traces of suburbia and normalness I used to see when driving into Cabo San Lucas.

I glanced over at Javier, wondering if he ever found it odd how normal and peaceful his life seemed to be on the outside when it was anything but. I wondered if he orchestrated it that way, to keep all this beauty and elegance around him in order to balance all the bad. I wondered if he had ever come close to making this place even more domestic than it was, if he ever dreamed about having a wife, having children.

"So what happened between you and Ellie?"

He went rigid for a moment before his gaze settled sharply on mine. "Where did that come from?"

"I don't know. I'm curious."

His eyes narrowed suspiciously and he shifted in his seat. "Why are you so focused on my past?"

"Because the past makes you who you are. I want to know why you're this way."

"This way?" he repeated with a wry smile. "Luisa, I hate to break it to you, but I've always been this way."

"Then what happened? Humor me."

He clasped his hands together, his watch jangling.

"In a nutshell," he said with an exasperated sigh, "I was trying to help her get revenge. I was also trying to show her who she really was, or who I still thought she was. In the end, my help did nothing. She'd changed. She played me. She threw me under a bus so she could be with another man, some dumb fuck, and laughed while I was taken away. I'm sure she knew I ended up in prison. I'm sure it only cemented her decision to be *good*. That was all the thanks I got for trying to help." He shook his head, anger simmering in his eyes. "People are so fucking ungrateful."

"So she broke your heart."

He gave me a sidelong glance. "Don't mistake broken pride for a broken heart. No man wants to look like a fool. Because of her, I lost almost everything, and it took years for me to get it all back. That isn't something you can forget overnight."

Now I understood the shield.

A few moments passed us by. One white and orange fish did several laps around the pond, eyeing me hopefully every time he came near. I thought about what Javier said, how he saw something in Ellie that he wanted to bring out of her. Her truth.

Finally I looked to Javier and shyly asked, "Will you help me?"

His brow furrowed delicately. "Help you what?"

"Help me see who *I* really am."

He smirked. "I think you're already finding that out. One day at a time."

"But there are no days after tomorrow," I said, trying to keep my voice as flat as possible.

Tension broke the surface of his face but he reined it in. "I guess you're right. So what are we to do?"

Something, I screamed in my head. *Anything!*

I gulped my thoughts down so they didn't dare escape from my lips. "I don't know."

He eyed Carlos who was now mowing behind a flowering bush then looked back at me. "You do," he said, his heady gaze trailing to my lips. "What we've always done."

He reached for my shoulder and slipped off the strap of my dress with his index finger. His eyes fastened to mine as he gently eased me back so I was lying flat on the bench. In moments, his pants were unzipped, my underwear was pushed to the side, and my leg was straight up against his shoulder. He pushed into me in broad daylight, while the lawnmower whirred in the background and the flowers perfumed the air with their delicate fragrance.

Even though I felt completely exposed to the living, breathing world that whirled around us, I was absolutely captive to the private one between us. When I came, my nails raking down his back and into the loose linen threads of his shirt, I was holding on to more than just him; I was holding on to the day, the moment, the second.

The time where I was queen.

And where I was free.

CHAPTER NINETEEN

Javier

I t was the middle of the night when Luisa woke me, just a few hours before dawn, before the day came and I would get Salvador's call.

As usual, she woke me up in the most exquisite way – her naked body pressed against mine, hands in my hair, lips on my chest.

"What time is it?" I groaned, both from lack of sleep and from the way she pushed herself against my dick.

"Does it matter?" she asked softly.

I opened my eyes and made out her features in the waning dark. "No, it doesn't. Not when you're like this."

Her pearly teeth flashed in a gorgeous smile. "Good," she said. She trailed her fingers down the side of my face and that smile slowly vanished. I didn't even have to ask why. I knew why. I knew what was coming. I was doing everything I could to steel my mind against the impossible choices I'd have to make in a few hours.

"Javier," she whispered, my name sounding like heaven. "What are you going to do to me?"

I ground my jaw, trying to keep it together. "Don't ask me this."

"But you must know."

"But I don't know," I whispered harshly. "I'll know when the time comes."

"Will you promise to be the one to shoot me? Like you said."

"I never said I would do that."

"Will you promise?" she repeated, running her hands into my hair again.

"No," I told her. And I was telling the truth. "I will not shoot you. I will not harm you. I will not kill you. Do you feel any better?"

She shook her head, and I could see how wet her eyes were. A tear drop fell on my chest and the hollowness beneath it grew. "I don't feel better, because I know the others will. Salvador will not want me."

I grabbed her shoulders and shook her. "We don't know that!" I hissed.

"And then so what if he does! Can you let me go? Can you watch me go back to him, to be his wife again?" She pressed her fingers into her tear stain and swirled it around my heart in angry circles. "Is that what you're still capable of?"

Yes. I had to be.

"Luisa," I said carefully, looking into her shining, desperate eyes. "You can't save me."

She smiled, letting out a caustic laugh. "I don't want to save you," she said, bringing her face closer to mine. "I want to *join* you."

I stared at her, completely dazzled by what she had said. Even with everything that I was, she didn't want to change me, she didn't want to save me. Perhaps it was because I was so beyond saving. Either way, she saw who I was and all my filth and she wanted to roll around in it with me.

She had become my equal.

And in the morning she would become nothing.

"Did he say when he was calling?" Este asked with a hint of annoyance.

I couldn't even answer him. My eyes were trained on the new flip phone lying on my desk in front of me. It was the exact same scene as the week before, except there was one difference. Este was right. Luisa had compromised me.

It didn't mean I wasn't going to do what I needed to do. But it meant that though I looked annoyed on the surface, I was being crushed underneath.

"Well, Javier told him exactly a week," The Doctor said mildly. He adjusted his hat on his head. "I suppose Salvador could take him literally or not."

"If it's literal then he's already late," Este said. I could feel his eyes on me. "Are you sure Juanito is a good enough guard, Javi?"

I jerked my chin into a nod. They wanted Luisa guarded during this so I sent Juanito to do the job. The man had his flaws, but I knew he wouldn't hurt her and would obey me. Someone like Este couldn't always be trusted. My mind started picking that apart, wondering if perhaps one day I could get rid of Este before he attempted to get rid of me. My mind wanted to think about everything except what was about to happen.

"So what is our course of action if he wants her back?" The Doctor asked. "We shouldn't give her over until everything is absolutely secure. We need proof of the shipping lane. We need physical evidence before we do anything. This might mean holding on to her for a few more days. But I'm sure Javier can handle that, can't you boy?"

I barely heard him. My eyes willed the phone to ring, to get this fucking over with.

And, like God himself was the operator, the phone started dancing, vibrating on the desk. We all watched with bated breath before I snatched it up.

I waited a moment, that one golden moment where everything stayed the same, before I flipped it open.

"Hello," I said into the receiver, relieved at how strong my voice was sounding. I could almost fool myself.

"Javier Bernal," said Salvador, his voice dripping with false formality. "I'm glad you were waiting on my phone call. I almost forgot about it, you see. Nice to know you hadn't."

I pressed my lips together, hard, waiting for him to go on. He didn't.

"No, I hadn't," I said with deliberation. "So what have you decided? Will you deal with me or not?"

There was a pause and the other end of the phone erupted with laughter. It was so loud that I knew The Doctor and Este could hear it. They exchanged a concerned glance with each other.

"Deal?" Salvador spat out when he calmed down. "What was the deal again? An Ephedra lane for my wife? Javier, Javier, Javier. Have you seen my wife? Have you tasted my wife?" His voice grew lower. "If you're anything like me, you have."

I'm not anything like you, I thought bitterly.

"But for her beauty and body," he went on, "do you really think she's worth a shipping lane? You just might be dumber than I thought." He snorted and my chest constricted painfully.

"The world is full of naïve, brainless, helpless women like her. I can pick up another one. In fact, I already have. Several. So no, Javier, I will not be making a deal with you." He paused. "Chop her fucking head off."

The line went dead.

Everything inside me went dead. I slowly removed the phone from my ear and stared at it in my hands.

I had been wrong. Luisa had been right. Salvador didn't want her. I kidnapped her in vain. I wasn't getting anything in return.

It seemed fitting for a man who loved to fuck so much that I had royally fucked myself over.

"Javier?" The Doctor asked carefully. "What happened?"

I glanced up, meeting Este's eyes by accident. He immediately grimaced, knowing the look of failure.

"Shit," he swore. "No fucking deal, hey."

The Doctor made a tsking sound, leaning forward on his knees. "That is a shame. A real shame. All the time we wasted. And now we look like fools. Well, the only way we can recover from this, Javier," he said my name sharply so that I would direct my attention to him, "is if we show we don't mess around. And I know you don't. Look what happened to Franco. No idle threats there." He got out of his seat and peered down at me with curiosity. "You know we have to kill her and do it publicly."

I raised one finger to silence him. It was oh so hard to think when you could barely even breathe. "Give me a minute," I managed to say. My brain was working on overdrive, trying to figure out a way to save my pride, save my cartel, and save Luisa at the same time. I barely noticed Este leaving the room.

But I certainly noticed when he came back.

I looked up to see Luisa in the doorway looking beyond frightened, Juanito and Este with tight holds on either side of her. Her eyes flew to mine, and in an instant she knew exactly what was happening.

I'm sorry, I mouthed to her. I didn't know what else to say.

"Ah," The Doctor said, clapping his hands together gleefully. "Just the woman we wanted to see. Luisa, Javier has something very important and troubling that he'd like to tell you. Don't you, Javier?"

I wanted nothing more than to chop *his* fucking head off. My eyes burned into his but he took no notice. He had that look on his face, that dreamy, wistful look that preceded his torturing someone.

I slid my gaze over to her. "Luisa," I said thickly. "I just spoke with your husband. He doesn't want to make a deal. You were right. He wants me to chop your head off instead."

I suppose I could have said that more eloquently.

Her eyes widened for a moment before something passed over them, something that made them grow cold. She was retreating inside herself. I didn't want that to happen. I wanted her to fight back. Her fight would give me courage to do the same.

"I see," she said blankly. "Sometimes it's horrible to be right."

I nodded and looked to the men. "Do you guys mind excusing us? I need a moment with her alone."

The Doctor narrowed his eyes. "Javier, you know you have to do what's right for all of us. As gruesome as it may be."

"Please go," I said, my voice growing harder. "Now."

Juanito, Este, and The Doctor all exchanged a worried

look before they reluctantly left the room. As soon as the door shut behind them, I went up to it and locked it before turning to look at Luisa.

We stared at each other for a long moment. There was so much to say and yet so little.

"So this is it," she said.

I shook my head and went over to her, grabbing her face in my hands. "No. This isn't it. I won't let this happen if you won't. Tell me you'll fight this. Promise me."

She stared up at me in the open need to believe. "How can I fight?"

I licked my lips and looked away. "I don't know. The cartel will suffer – I will suffer – if we don't deliver. We all follow through on what we say we're going to do. If we say we're going to kill you, then we have to do it."

"Then find someone else," she cried out, her eyes dancing feverishly. "Go into the village, go and find a woman, a hooker, someone, anyone, anyone that looks like me. Bring her back here and tie her up and film it. Cover up her face in a bag and take her fucking head right off!"

I jerked my chin into my neck. Where had this brutal Luisa come from?

She smiled and shook me. "It will work," she assured me. "Killing another woman instead."

"No," I said, watching her closely. "It won't. They might want proof of your actual head."

"Then let me stay here," she said. "You don't have to kill me. You can tell them no. You're their boss."

"I know I am. But that doesn't help with pride, with image."

"Fuck your pride!" she yelled, her face contorted. "What the fuck has that ever gotten you?"

She didn't understand. "It's gotten me everything," I told her.

She made a sweeping gesture to the room. "All these dear things you love so much," she said sarcastically. "All your fucking flowers and your clothes and your money and the shitheads who work for you."

I rubbed my face in my hands, trying to get a grip, trying to get control back. I felt like I'd lost it many days ago, somewhere deep inside of her. No matter what I chose, I was going to suffer in some way.

"Look," I said carefully, slowly meeting her wild eyes. "If you stay here, even if the cartel can't save face, what do you think happens to your parents? If you run off into the jungle, what do you think will happen to your parents? If we kill some other woman and pretend it's you – what do you think will happen to your parents?" Her face fell and I took a step toward her again. "You're not thinking straight. You're thinking out of survival and instinct, and that's *good* because that means you're finally being selfish. But you've got a pure heart, my darling. You wouldn't be able to be selfish for long. I don't want you living or dying with that kind of regret on your shoulders."

She seemed to think about that for some time, her eyes staring at a blank spot on my shirt. I could almost see the wheels turning inside, that fight to survive and the fight to protect the ones she loved.

I hoped I wasn't included on that list.

When she came to a conclusion it looked like she was wearing the weight of the world on her face. She looked me dead in the eye and said, "I have to go back to Salvador."

I frowned, a bolt of panic going through me. "What? No."

She nodded and raised her chin defiantly. "Yes. It's the only way. I have to go back to him. I have to be his wife again. It's the only way I can live and keep my parents alive at the same time."

I grabbed her by the hand and squeezed hard, hoping to press some sense into her. "But you won't be alive for long," I hissed at her. "You know what that man will do to you. Christ, what happens when he sees my name on your back!"

"You never cared about that before."

"But I do now! You can't do this, this is a death wish for fuck's sake."

"I will do this," she said, her voice growing calmer by the moment, as if she had made peace with the horrible fear. "You'll let me go. Even better, you'll have someone drop me off in Culiacán. I'll wander around until someone spots me. The whole city knows who I am, the whole city is still under my power. I'll tell them what happened – that I knew I was going to be executed. I'll tell them I escaped and that I've come to beg my husband to take me back, that he made the right choice by picking his business, that there are no hard feelings. I will grovel. And to save his own face, to save his own fucking pride, he will take me back into his house." She swallowed. "And I . . . I will be his wife again. Just as before."

I was angry. So angry that my breath wouldn't leave my lungs. It took all my concentration to calm down, to start breathing in and out of my nose. Why did she have to choose this of all things?

"Luisa, please," I told her, hoping she could see the truth. "You will die. He will take you in on pride but you are nothing to him. Do you hear me? Nothing! You will last a week or two, and then he will kill you. And before that, you know what he's going to do to you. He—" I broke off, unable to finish the sentence. I couldn't even let myself think about it, but it was there, poking around in my brain. The sound of Salvador's voice, the fear I'd seen in Luisa's eyes, the brutality he'd proven he was capable of.

"And I will handle him as I handled him before," she said, almost proud. "This is the only way. At least I can say I gave it a shot. One more shot at life, as pathetic as it may be. And you? You only have to lose your precious pride among your workers here. The rest of the world may laugh at your faulty security, but I'm sure it will be something they'll soon forget. To Mexico, your cartel is still one to be reckoned with and your pride will remain intact. And you, Javier Bernal, will continue on as you had before. In a week, you won't remember me."

But she had to know, had to realize, how hard this was for me, too. If she did though, perhaps she didn't quite care.

"All right," I said, nodding at her. "If this is what you want, I can tell the others the plan. They won't like it, but they won't be able to do anything about it."

"Thank you," she said. She smiled at me with the strength of a million breaking hearts. It was the saddest thing I'd ever seen, and I'd seen a lot of sad things in my lifetime, things that would chase me to the grave.

And that's when I knew, with nothing but a smile, my Luisa, my queen, had broken *me*.

CHAPTER TWENTY

Luisa

I slept alone that night. In fact, I spent most of the day alone as well. After I learned the news and after I had come up with my own horrid plan, Javier told his comrades about what we were to do. They didn't take it well, as I figured. Este was pissed off like a whiny boy and even Juanito gazed upon Javier with an air of disrespect. I had to say, much as I mocked him for his foolish pride, there was a moment where I felt almost sorry for him.

The Doctor seemed to take it worst of all. In that calm, cynical, monstrous way, he berated Javier in every way he could. He called him weak. Soft. Pussy-whipped. He talked about me as if I wasn't even in the room, but those lewd insults about how good of a fuck I must be, well they meant nothing. All I cared about was putting my plan into action.

And, eventually, that's what happened. Javier lost face among his men but they would protect the cartel as a whole. I would be let go. The next day, Juanito would take me to Culiacán. I would look like I had just escaped from somewhere. I would have a story to tell. And then I would hope for the best.

I knew Javier wasn't happy with my choice – I wasn't happy either. I was actually so scared that I'd grown numb. I didn't let myself think about what might happen to me, I just knew it had to be done. My chances for survival were extremely low. My chances for vile abuse, torment, and torture were extremely high. Either way, I was in for a lot of pain.

But like I had done all week, I put that on the back burner. I tried to appreciate the last day I had in that house that, in the dying sun, became only golden and not a prison at all. I wished I had Javier by my side, but he was ignoring me, avoiding me. I knew it was for the best. I knew that if I was with him, in his bed, that it would make leaving even worse.

It's not even that Javier and I were lovers. We weren't really anything you could explain. What relationship we did have was fucked up beyond reasoning. It made no sense for me to feel more than just attraction to a man like him, and yet I did. I shouldn't have let my emotions excuse the things he'd done, the person he was, but again, I did.

I should have been grateful that he didn't kill me, that it wasn't even an option to him. A week ago, I would have been certain he'd take my head off, and with glee. Now he was willing to take a hit to his ego, not just to resist killing me but to actually let me go. Not to mention actually let me go through with a plan that I, his hostage, had initiated.

And yet I still wished for more. I wanted him to ask me to stay again. I wanted him to protest just a little bit more. There could be other ways around all this. He could go and take my parents somewhere safe and then keep me here as his. I would gladly stay. There might have not been any love in this house, but it was better than a house of hate.

I couldn't find the words. I didn't see the point. It should have been enough that he did, finally, see me as a human being. It's just that being a human being meant I also wanted what I couldn't have.

Him.

The next morning, after a fitful sleep, I was awakened by a knock and Este bringing me my breakfast. He was one of the last people I wanted to see.

"Thought you deserved this in bed, since it's your last meal with us and all," he said, shutting the door behind him with his foot and bringing the tray to the bedside table. He shot me a sidelong glance. "It's only because you're leaving that I can trust you not to bash me over the head with the bowl of fruit or something."

I didn't smile, I merely stared at him.

"No jokes today, hey?" he asked with a shrug. He sat down on the end of the bed, and I instinctively drew my feet toward me. "You know, Luisa, I think we may have gotten off on the wrong foot here. But I just wanted you to know, I like you."

I grimaced. "Is that supposed to be a good thing?"

"It's not anything," Este said. "I can see how Javier is so obsessed with you."

"Obsessed?" This was news to me.

"Don't be too flattered," he said wryly. "Javier gets obsessed easily. Though it doesn't happen very often with women. Considering the way things have gone for him in the past and his devotion to building an empire, I'm actually surprised at the way things have turned out."

"But you're unhappy about it," I said.

"I am. I think he's letting his feelings for you cloud his judgment. But things could be worse."

Feelings for me? I wanted to ask him to elaborate, to tell me more. But I realized how damn inappropriate that was, considering my dire circumstances, and internally chastised my heart for even skipping a beat.

Este studied my face. "Just so you know," he said carefully, a knowing look in his eyes, "his *feelings* for you only mean that he's not killing you. That's all. You can't get much more than that out of him. It's like getting blood from a stone."

"I know," I said quickly. "I never figured otherwise."

He nodded and patted the bed. "Good. Well, I suppose I should be off. I hope all of this is worth it, you know. You could just as easily disappear and get a new identity, a new life, a new everything."

I shook my head. "I couldn't do that. I have a conscience."

"And that *will* be the death of you," he said. "Juanito will come up and get you in an hour. It's a long drive, as you know." He got up and paused, as if remembering something. "Oh, and sorry again about Tasering you."

I stared at him coldly. "Really? I'm still thinking about hitting you in the head with this tray, just because."

He grinned. "I figured as much."

He opened the door.

"Esteban," I called after him. "Could you please send Javier up here?"

His face twisted doubtfully. "I'll try."

The door shut and I waited. When the hour ticked closer, I put on my dress and my running shoes, the only things I would be pretending I escaped in. I would have nothing else. No money, no ID, nothing. I stared at my face in the mirror. I wondered if Salvador would see the horror in my eyes and mistake it for where I had been, not where I was going. I hoped so.

Eventually, five minutes before the sand in the hourglass

was up, Javier came to me. He wore a mask of elegance and indifference, his unusually handsome features taking on the appearance of a sculpture. But I had no idea what the artist was trying to say: Here's a man in denial? Here's a man without a soul? Here's a man who will build empires and legacies, whose pride shaped the land? Or here is a man who for once in his life, doesn't know who he is?

Whoever the man at my door was, it was apparent this was the last place he wanted to be.

"You wanted to see me?" he said so formally that it cut worse than his blade.

"You weren't going to come say goodbye?" I asked him. He remained at the door. I remained near the bathroom. Neither of us moved.

"I was," he said, an air of defiance to him. "At the door."

"Oh," I said caustically. "How very kind and proper of you."

"Luisa," he warned.

"So after all you've put me through," I said, folding my arms, "you're just wiping your hands clean and pushing me out the door."

Indignation flared in his eyes. His hands clenched and unclenched, but he managed to keep his voice hard and steady. "This was your choice. You chose this."

"Because it's the only choice I have," I said. "Isn't it?"

Our eyes fastened on each other. I wanted him to come closer. I wanted to see something that wasn't there.

"Can't we go back in time?" I asked, my voice softer now. "When I believed I meant something to you?"

He swallowed and looked away. "You were always my captive. I was always the man holding the knife."

And again that knife was buried straight in me. I took in

a sharp breath, willing the pain away. "I suppose I shouldn't be surprised. Esteban said getting feelings out of you was like getting blood from a stone."

"Esteban doesn't know shit," he snapped, glaring at me. "What the hell do you want me to say? Do you think anything I say will make any difference to you? To me? To this fucking situation? Huh?"

"You could tell me not to go."

"I did!" he cried out, marching across the room. He grabbed me by the shoulders, his reddening face in mine. "I told you not to go. I told you there could be another way. You could go free, away from certain fucking death. But you're like this . . ."

"This what?" I goaded, watching his eyes spark and flame. "What am I?"

"A martyr," he said, spitting out the word. "You wear your nobility like a goddamn crown. I am so sick and tired of it, especially when I know there is a strong, unapologetic woman in there just dying to come out. I've seen her. I've fucked her. I want *that* woman to win."

"That woman will have to live with regret."

"That woman," he said, giving me a shake, "will *live*." His eyes sought the ceiling, trying to compose himself, but when he looked back at me, the fire was still there. The mask had slipped. "I know you love your parents, Luisa. But is their safety – not even guaranteed – worth your own life? Do you really think your parents want you to do this? Do you think this will make them fucking proud? If they're anything like me, they'll be angry as hell. They will live their lives with regret instead. Is that what you want to give them? A dead daughter and a lifetime of fucking sorrow?"

I was stunned. He grabbed my face with both his hands and stared at me with crazed intensity. "Be fucking *selfish*! Save your own life." He let go of me suddenly, turning his back to me, his hand on the back of his neck. "Lord knows I can't save it for you."

I watched his back, the strength of it underneath his navy suit jacket, wondering if it ever got tired of shouldering this world. It seemed all so easy for him to give orders, tell people what to do, and never have to give an ounce of himself.

"You gave me a reason to run," I said to him. "Give me a reason to stay."

He paused and slowly turned to look at me. "Give you a reason to stay?"

"Yes," I said, walking up to him, refusing to break my gaze.

His eyes softened, just for a moment. "What can I say to make you stay?" he asked, his voice barely above a whisper.

"Tell me you love me."

My boldness shocked him more than it shocked me. He stared at me, unhinged and absolutely bewildered, like he didn't understand. "I can't do that," he managed to say.

I had nothing to lose. "You can't because you don't."

He opened his mouth then shut it. He gave a small shake of his head, and then said, almost chagrined, "No. Because I don't know what that is anymore."

I placed my hands on his jacket, running them down his silky lapels. "Well," I said sadly, "it's what you feel for your suits. And your money. And your mansions. And all your power." I looked up at him. "Except you feel it for me."

There was a knock at the door. I reluctantly broke his gaze, his lost and helpless gaze, and looked to see Juanito standing in the doorway.

"So sorry, boss," he said nervously, trying not to look at us. "But it's time to go."

Javier nodded, clearing his throat. "She'll be right there."

Juanito left, and it was just the two of us again, and for the last time.

"I'm sorry," Javier said sincerely, reaching for my face and gently brushing a strand of hair behind my ear. I wasn't sure what he was apologizing for – for not loving me, for Juanito interrupting, for having to say goodbye. Perhaps he was apologizing for that first moment when he decided my life would be worth a shipping lane. It didn't really matter in the end.

"I'm sorry, too," I told him. Then I walked away from his touch and to the door, down the hall, and down the stairs to where Juanito was waiting for me in the foyer.

Waiting to take me home.

I did not look behind me. I did not look back. I kept my head high and conviction straight, even when Juanito placed the bag over my head, so I would still not see the way in and out of this place.

With his help, I got into the SUV that was running outside and told myself, for the umpteenth time that day, that I was doing the right thing.

It began to really worry me then, when the right thing started to feel so very wrong.

The drive back to Culiacán was longer than the drive to Javier's. I wasn't sure if it was the mountainous roads or Juanito's driving, or the fact that every mile we passed, my veins filled with ice-cold fear. The fact that I couldn't see didn't help, but a few hours into it, Juanito leaned over and pulled the bag from my head.

I squinted in the afternoon light. We must have been far enough from Javier's that it didn't matter what I saw. I guess I couldn't blame them for thinking that I might have ratted on their whereabouts. That thought made me wonder if perhaps Salvador was going to think I was a rat myself.

But once I entered his doors – if I even got that far – I would never leave them again. Whether I had switched sides or not, it didn't really matter. I knew I would die in that gilded cage.

Night was just falling, the sky turning into a brilliant blend of periwinkle and tangerine that made my soul hurt, when Juanito pulled the car to the side of the highway. He cut the engine and eyed me expectantly. "Well," he said.

"Well," I said back.

"This is where you get off." He nodded to the dusty shoulder that was riddled with garbage.

"But we aren't even near the city," I protested. "The sign said we had another two hours or so."

"True," he said, "but my orders were to drop you off here. How you get into the city is your own doing. Soon, there will be checkpoints, all from your husband's cartel. They'll be looking at each car. I can't risk being seen with you."

"So then, what do I do?"

"Hitchhike," he said.

"But that's so unsafe," I said. "I could be attacked or raped."

He gave me a melancholy smile. "What do you think's going to happen to you anyway?"

I flinched. The truth stung. "You're turning heartless, just like them," I warned him.

"Occupational hazard, I guess," he said. "It may save your life if you were to turn the same."

At that he nodded at the door, eager for me to leave his charge. I sighed my acceptance and got out. Though I had told Javier I wanted to be bound at the wrists, he assured me it wasn't necessary to make it look like I escaped. I was grateful for that. I needed every ounce of power I could get, even if it was just an illusion.

The minute my feet hit the soil, Juanito pulled away. I watched his red lights until he did a U-turn a few meters away. Then he roared past me, heading back to Javier, back to safety.

I'd never been so envious in my life.

I stood there for a long time, just a black figure against the darkening sky, the passing cars anonymous with their blinding lights, my hair and dress billowing around me in their wake. It wasn't until I summoned the courage to stick my thumb out that one car eventually stopped.

To my utmost relief, it was a middle-aged woman driving. I got in and kept quiet while she scolded me for being out on the highway. I didn't give her much of an explanation as to why I was out there – I was saving that for later – and I kept my face turned away from her so she wouldn't see the faded yellow and blue bruises that still colored my skin from Franco's assault.

She made good company, talking about her newest grand-child and how scandalous it was that he wasn't baptized yet, and how all the neighbors were flapping their lips. I wondered what it must be like to live a totally normal life. To fall in love, get married, have children and grandchildren. To drive to the supermarket and drink instant coffee and watch daytime television and go to church and take every fucking day for granted.

Because of her normality, we sped past the one checkpoint we saw. The armed men didn't even slow us down. We just kept driving through, their eyes trained only for people like Juanito.

When we finally arrived in the city and I asked her to drop me off at one of the busy plazas, I told her she was lucky to have all that she did. She only stared at me in disbelief. Then I thanked her and got out of the car. She drove off, shaking her head and talking to herself, and I wondered if I was going to be news in the morning, and if she'd be flipping through her morning paper and realize just who she had given a ride to.

Now, it was time to play a part, a me from another timeline, a timeline where Javier was the brutal captor and that was it. I closed my eyes, inviting the other persona in: frightened, relieved, jubilant at their escape. I looked around the plaza for someone who would know who I was, who would hear the underground tittering from the Sinaloa Cartel, who would first have to hear my story.

I found a musician – a *narcocorrido* singer – sitting by the side of a fountain, playing murder ballads on his accordion. The man, with his slicked back hair and soulful voice, glanced up at me as I hugged myself in front of him, shivering for show, and he immediately knew who I was. I was sure he had sung many songs about narco wives. Perhaps even one just for me. Sing me a song about Luisa, the one who was taken, the one who wasn't wanted back. The one who found her freedom in another man's bed.

It didn't take long before I was wrapped in a blanket and

being escorted into a police vehicle, flashing lights illuminating the plaza in red and blue. A few onlookers were
watching, camera phones out, recording my apparent rescue
as they would the murders that littered the city.

Once in the vehicle, the officers extra courteous, I was
driven in a different direction than I thought we'd go. Then
I realized that after my kidnapping, Salvador must have aban-
doned his old mansion for another one, for security's sake.

It made no difference to me; they all held the same horrors.

Soon we were driving past checkpoints – some operated
by other police, some by men with black ski-masks and automatic rifles – and then through the heavily guarded gates of
my husband's newest palace.

Once we came to a stop, the police escorted me out of the
SUV and straight up the polished steps of Salvador's front
door. One officer went to knock but the door was already
opening, slowly, ominously, like a scary movie.

Salvador stood on the other side, backlit from the foyer,
his ugly face cast in sinister shadow. He stroked along his
mustache and gave me a smile that even a crocodile would
be ashamed to wear.

"Luisa, my princess," he said cunningly, opening up an
arm for me. "Welcome home."

I looked to the police officers, wondering if I had enough
strength to turn back, to run, to plead for their help. But they
were paid handsomely by my husband, and their job was
about indifference to anything but money. There would be
no help from them. There would be no help from anyone.

I was on my own.

I gave Salvador a stiff smile as I walked into the house.

He slowly closed the door behind him and shot me a sly

look over his shoulder. "This took me by surprise. I must say I never expected to see you again."

"I know," I said, putting on the face of the scared yet sympathetic wife. "And I understand. When I saw I had a chance to escape, I took it. You'd be shocked at how immature Javier's men are. They are nothing like yours."

He smiled briefly at my compliment. "I'm surprised you came back *here*."

"You are my husband," I told him, hoping he bought the sincerity. "Where else would I go?"

He studied me for a moment, his jaw ticking back and forth. "I guess you're right." He took a large step toward me, his cowboy boots echoing on the floor. "It's too bad that you'll soon wish you hadn't."

My face fell. His lit up. "Sometimes," he went on, "you don't know what you've got till it's gone." He chuckled to himself. "I realized what I had wasn't even worth bargaining for." He shrugged and pulled at his chin as he looked my body up and down. "But that doesn't mean you aren't worth something. Get on your knees."

I opened my mouth in protest and almost said something I'd regret. Talking back to Javier had become a bad habit, one he had encouraged.

"I said on your knees, cunt!" Salvador yelled at me. He grabbed me by my hair and thrust me down to the floor, my knees taking the brunt of the fall. I heard his zipper go down but I couldn't make myself look up.

He made me look. He made a fist at the top of my head and yanked my hair straight up, my nerves exploding in pain. I looked past his rancid cock and right at his face. It was evil incarnate. He shook his head, clucking his tongue. "You hesitated, Luisa, and a woman never hesitates. Looks like I'm going to have to retrain you all over again."

The next thing I knew, his knee came toward my face. There was pain and spots and all the world went black.

CHAPTER TWENTY-ONE

Javier

The saying goes, if you love something, let it go. I always thought it was better to just shoot the damn thing so it'd never go anywhere.

But now I understood. Now that I didn't have a choice.

I suppose I could have said something. I could have told Luisa what she wanted to hear. But that would have been a lie. I didn't love her. I couldn't. That was something that was no longer applicable to the person I'd become. There was no place for it in my life; it didn't fit, it didn't work. Love didn't build empires, it ruined them.

What I felt for Luisa wasn't love. But it was curious. It was something, at least. It was deep and spreading, like a cancer. Yet, instead of only bringing pain, it brought purpose in its sickness. Her lips soothed me, her heart challenged me, her eyes made me bleed. My bed was where we held our exorcisms. She brought me peace. I brought her fire. Now the flame was out – gone forever – and there was a war raging inside me.

I went a full week pretending that nothing had happened. Pretending that nothing was eating me from the inside out. I wore my mask every day. I worked with Este on our next targets, our next hand in this game. A trip to Veracruz was becoming more and more possible. But that city no longer stirred fear in my heart, no longer played on bad memories. Those memories meant nothing to me anymore. There was something so much scarier raging just below my surface.

One night I woke up from a nightmare. I think it was the same as I had before, with my father and I fishing, Luisa on the end of the hook. It was hard to remember; the dream shattered into fragments the moment I woke. But the feeling was there. The unimaginable fear. This was the sickness manifesting itself. This was the war coming. This was what happened to me when I no longer had her to placate me.

And then I realized with certainty that I had been a coward this whole time. I was in my bed, safe and comfortable in the life I had created for myself. I wanted for nothing. And yet she, she was with Salvador. She had been there a week already and I couldn't imagine her state, if she was even still alive. She wanted for *everything*.

I didn't go back to sleep. Even though it was the middle of the night, I slipped a robe around me and left the house. I went to sit by the koi pond, the lotus blossoms looking ghostly in the moonlight. I stared at their white purity until the sun came up. Then, in that glow of dawn, I saw more clearly. The flowers were magnificent, but they weren't as the Chinese scholar had said. There were imperfections on their surface. There were stains. Their beauty didn't come from the fact that they were untainted, their beauty came from their resilience. They were proud to have grown from mud.

Even if my beauty queen was already dead, I knew what I had to do. There would be dire consequences for my actions, but there already were. What was the difference if I stirred up a little more trouble? At this point, it was pretty much expected of me.

Later that day, I told the men I was going away on a business trip to Cabo San Lucas. Este, being my right-hand man and all, insisted he come along for the journey, but I told him I needed to do this alone. I would be safe and I wouldn't be long – two or three days, at most. And if I happened upon the wrong people at the wrong time, then that was that. I knew Este would slide right in and replace me anyway.

I was a nervous flier. It was a quick trip across the water, but it still took a lot of composure to not drink all the alcohol available in first class. There was a man in the row across from me who stared at me like he might have recognized me. I only smiled back. Though this was risky, I also knew that most people would never do or say anything to me. Besides, my face might have been out there once or twice but Salvador was right – I wasn't on anyone's radar.

Though the airport was closer to San Jose del Cabo than it was to San Lucas, that wasn't my first stop. I wasn't lying to Este when I said I had business that needed attending to. This time, I wasn't going to give an order and watch someone else do it. I was going to get my hands very, very dirty.

It was all for her.

And it seemed the more I did for her, the filthier I got.

Once in Cabo, I took a long stroll around the town. I hadn't been here in a long time and was shocked to see how much it had changed. What was once a small marina was jam-packed with million-dollar yachts. Cruise ships hovered offshore while drunk teenagers on jet skis did circles in the azure surf. The beaches were filled with dance music and DJs announcing hourly body shots. The popular bars spouted Top 40 hits and celebrity-owned statuses.

The town had no soul. Perhaps this was good for tourists – indeed it was excellent for Mexico's economy, as were my drugs. But I could never live in a place that catered to the other half. Sure, the town was safe and the drug wars hadn't littered the streets. But where was the real Mexico? Where was the grit beneath the glamour? Where were the proud flowers rising from the mud?

I spent most of the day walking around, taking in everything. Despite all my misgivings toward the resort town, I still enjoyed myself. I was a tourist, just looking at all the sights. I was a man just looking for a bar, a place to get a drink.

And then I found it. It was barely distinguishable from all the other tourist traps.

Cabo Cocktails.

I went in and sat at the bar. Even though it was a hot, sunny day and nearing three o' clock, the bar was fairly empty. There was an old man nursing a beer at the other end of the bar and a couple in a booth. That was it.

The bartender, a cute girl with blondish pixie hair, was quick to serve me.

"A gin and tonic," I told her. "Perfect for a day like today." I gave her the smile that I knew could remove panties.

She smiled back but I could tell I had no true effect on her. She was probably into women.

"No problem," she said, and got to work.

"What's your name?" I asked her while she fished out a can of tonic water.

"Camila," she said, an edge to her voice that told me not to bother asking for more than her name. But I wasn't here for her.

I waited until she served me my drink and told me the price, then I asked what I really wanted to know.

"Camila, I'm wondering if you can help me," I said, smiling again. "You see, there's a girl who used to work here."

Her eyes widened. I wasn't sure what tipped her off I was talking about Luisa; perhaps it was my sharp suit, or maybe she'd been on Camila's mind. "And I'm very worried about her," I went on. "Luisa is her name. Have you spoken to her recently?"

She shook her head, her eyes darting around the bar. "No."

"But she did work here . . ."

She nodded. She looked to the old man at the end of the bar. I waved at him dismissively. "Don't worry about him. I just have a few questions and I'll be out of your way."

"Who are you?" she asked.

"I'm a friend," I told her. "One of the few that she has these days. So you haven't seen her around here then? She hasn't called you?"

"No. No, I haven't seen or spoken to her since a few days before her wedding."

"To Salvador Reyes."

She swallowed. "Yes. Tell me, is she all right?"

"I really hope so," I said. *I really doubt it.*

I knocked the rest of the drink back, feeling immediately refreshed and energized, and slid the money toward her. "One more thing."

"What?" she asked, a bit of impatience mixed in with her apprehension. I could tell she was a tough girl. No wonder Luisa and she had been friends.

"Is your manager around? I'd like to ask him a few questions about her."

She nodded and jerked her head down the hall. "Bruno. He's in his office, I think. He comes and goes."

I grinned at her. "Perfect."

I waited until she left to go tend to the couple in the booth, then I reached over behind the bar and picked up the knife she used to cut up the lime for my drink.

I caught the man at the end of the bar watching me with mild interest that only tired old men have. I flashed the blade at him and smiled. He shrugged and went back to his beer.

Making sure the blade was hidden from sight, I walked down the hall and paused outside the door that said Bruno Corchado on it. I gripped the knife in my hand, slightly sticky from the lime juice. It would have been better if I had my own, but airplane security wouldn't have let me fly with it in my boot or in my carry-on. Bastards.

I decided not to knock. I opened the door a crack and poked my head in.

"Camila," the man grunted in annoyance until he looked up and saw me. His annoyance deepened. He obviously had no idea who I was. Good.

I shut the door behind me. "Bruno Corchado?"

"Who the fuck are you?"

I shrugged. "I could be a customer coming in with a complaint. Do you talk to all your customers that way?"

He glared at me. It was pitiful. "I can see you're not. What do you want?"

"I wanted to ask you a few questions about your past employee, Luisa Chavez."

He smirked and rolled his eyes. "Haven't you heard? She's Luisa Reyes now."

"Is that right?"

"The bitch married a drug lord," he said. "Salvador Reyes."

I sucked in my breath. "I see. Well, good for her."

He picked his nose and then wiped it under the desk. My lips wrinkled in distaste.

"She was money hungry," he informed me, as if I was suddenly his friend. "She'd always come in here asking for money. Said it was for her parents. I bet it never was. But I don't know what the hell she spent her money on, actually. Not men. Maybe she was into women, too." He gave me a knowing look. "She was always such a prude. Doesn't mean I didn't get to have my fun with her, if you know what I mean."

"I know what you mean," I said, trying hard to keep my voice steady.

Bruno picked up on something anyway. "Aw, shit," he said, straightening himself in his chair. "You're not like a relative of hers or something?"

I cocked my head. "No. Though she does carry my name."

He frowned. I could almost hear the rust in his head as the cogs turned.

"It's on her back," I told him. "Where I carved it."

Before any panic could fully register on Bruno's face, I swiftly flung the blade out. I aimed for his upper neck, but it went straight in the hollow of his throat.

Good enough.

He gasped, wheezing for air, but the air would not come. His hands went for his throat, trying to pull the blade out as the blood began to run down his chest, but he was already too weak to grab the handle. He started to pitch over, falling for the floor. I was at his side before he could.

I grabbed him by his greasy hair, holding him up by the roots.

"No, no, no," I said in a hush, making sure to stare him right in the eye. "This is not over."

I grabbed the knife and quickly yanked it out. Now the blood was gushing from the wound, drenching him in seconds. But as beautiful as the sight was, I had to be careful not to get any on my suit.

With my grip firm in his hair, I leaned over to whisper in his ear, the blade poised at his bloody throat. "You know all those things you tried to do to Luisa," I said. "Well, I did them. I did them again and again, and she loved it. Maybe because I'm one of the few men who has ever seen her for the queen that she is. All you see her for is her beauty. I see her for *her*, stained and everything." I pressed the blade in harder. "And I see you for everything you are – a sleazy sack of shit."

I slowly, deliberately began to work the blade into his throat. He squirmed and kicked and fought against me, but in his current state, I was stronger. His will to live was pathetic, just like he was.

Eventually he stopped kicking. I kept cutting. When I was finally done, I was covered in a sweat and only a few drops of blood on my shoes and pants. They'd come out with a good wash.

I put his head into the garbage and pulled the bag out, making a knot at the end. I hoped it wouldn't leak through. Then I looked around the office. It was a mess before I came in, piles of paper and empty beer bottles scattered around.

The addition of blood and a headless corpse was barely noticeable.

I pushed in the lock on the door and quickly exited, shutting the door behind me. I couldn't see Camila around, which was a shame. If she had asked me what happened, I would have told her Bruno had a headache and didn't want to be disturbed. It was such a good line.

Soon I was out of the bar and strolling down the street again toward my rental car, bag of garbage hoisted over my shoulder. My first order of business was complete. Now it was on to the second.

I had a feeling it was going to be a lot harder.

"Excuse me," I asked the aproned-woman who came to the door. "But do Raquel and Armand Chavez live here?"

The women stared at me for a moment, slowly wiping her hands on her apron. I had left Bruno's head in an ice cooler in the trunk, so there should have been nothing too unusual about a smartly-dressed man standing on the steps. "Yes, they live here. Who is asking?"

I breathed out a sigh of quiet relief. So Salvador hadn't killed them yet, which meant that Luisa was probably still alive.

"I'm a friend of their daughter," I told her, smiling as genuinely as possible. "Could you let Raquel know that I wish to speak with her? It's rather important, I'm afraid."

Again she studied me. I had a feeling that Luisa personally hired this woman. She was bold and suspicious, just the kind of person she'd want to protect her parents. If my instincts were right, she probably had a gun very close by and knew how to use it.

"What is your name?" she asked.

"Javier," I told her.

"No last name?"

"Garcia."

"All right, Javier Garcia," she said. "I'll go get Raquel. Please stay here."

The door shut in my face.

I shrugged and took a seat on the bench beside a well-tended rose garden. I admired the flowers while I waited to hear the door open again.

When it did, I swiveled in my seat to see a beautiful, elegant older woman standing there. Her focus was on me, even though I knew she was blind.

"You wish to speak to me about Luisa?" she asked. I could see the caretaker hovering right behind her.

I started to rise but Raquel quickly said, "You stay right where you are. Don't get up. A friend of my daughter's is a friend of mine."

I really hoped she hadn't said that about Sal.

"Your senses are outstanding, Mrs. Chavez," I told her as she came down the two steps and on the path toward me, moving with grace and confidence, not needing any help at all.

She smiled, and I saw Luisa in her face. It did funny things to my gut, rotting it with sadness.

"Thank you," she said, "but this is just life for me. It doesn't need to be so hard."

"No," I said, "I guess not with this. You have a lovely new home." My eyes slid over to the housekeeper who was now leaning against the doorway, openly watching us. "And very watchful help."

"Ah, that's just Penelope," she said, waving her away. "Go back inside, Penelope, I'll be fine. This man is not going to hurt me."

Penelope reluctantly did as she asked, but even so I saw the blinds move and knew she was spying through the window.

"She's very paranoid," I noted, turning back to Raquel. "Is there a reason for that?"

She gave me a small smile. "Yes." But she said no more.

I didn't want to make Raquel paranoid, but I had to ask, "How come you're so sure I'm not going to hurt you?"

She sat down beside me and folded her hands in her lap. "You can read people's faces, can't you? I can read people's souls."

I couldn't help but laugh, but her smile and confidence never wavered.

"Oh, you're serious," I said, feeling slightly ashamed. I covered it up. "Well, I'll have you know I have no soul to read."

Now it was her time to laugh. "Of course you do!" she exclaimed. "You're here right now, aren't you? Now, tell me why, and you'll see that I'm right."

"Why I'm here?"

She nodded gently.

"Mrs. Chavez . . ."

"Raquel."

"Raquel," I started, "have you heard from your daughter recently?"

She shook her head, her hands trembling just a bit. "No. Not for at least three weeks. Do you know if she's okay?"

I sucked on my lip for a moment. "Truthfully? I don't know anything. But I don't think she is. I think Luisa is in a lot of danger and so are you. Salvador Reyes makes bad men look good."

"I know that," she said in quiet anger.

"And I know that he's no longer interested in keeping her as his wife . . ." I breathed in and out loudly. "And when that happens, she's as good as dead to him."

She stared up at the sky blankly for a few moments before she said, "What do you need from us?"

"I need to make sure you're safe," I said. "It's all Luisa ever wanted. She cares more about you than she does her own life and her own happiness." It's actually infuriating, I wanted to add. But even I knew when to keep my mouth shut.

"I know," she said, barely audible. Her eyes were watering. I really hoped she didn't start crying in front of me because I would have no idea what to do.

"If you're safe," I told her, "both you and your husband, and away from here, away from where Salvador can find you, then I can go and get Luisa. I can bring her back."

"That's impossible," she said. "Salvador Reyes is the leader of the Sinaloa Cartel."

"He is. And it won't be easy. I'll most likely die in the process. But there is a way to do it. There's always a way."

She seemed to take that in. She wiped away a tear with the back of her hand and nodded her head, as if agreeing to an internal conversation.

"Why are you doing this?" she eventually asked. "What is Luisa to you?"

"She's a friend." It wasn't quite a lie.

"You're in love with her," she stated, a wide smile on her face.

I shot her a look she could not see. "I care about her very much," I corrected her.

"Well," she said, not put off, "if that's good enough for you, that's good enough for me."

"Then you'll let me help you," I said cautiously, feeling like this had gone over easier than expected. I thought there would be a lot of protesting, a lot of yelling, a lot of doors slammed in my face or guns held to my head.

"Of course I will," she said. "And Armand will too."

"And you're trusting me, just like that?"

"Yes. I am. I told you. My senses are sharp, and you, my boy, have a very good soul, even if you choose to believe otherwise."

"I may not be as good as you think."

She smiled and waved at me. "Oh, I don't doubt it. I can smell the blood on you, after all."

I looked down at my pants, at the few dark spots that stood out against the navy blue. "I had some business to take care of," I tried to explain.

"I'm sure you did." I wondered how much exactly this woman thought she knew about me. It was fascinating and troubling all at once. But as long as she was willing to help herself and her daughter, I couldn't care.

"Will Penelope be an issue?" I asked, eying the house again.

"You're not shooting her," Raquel told me, "if that's what you're thinking."

I frowned. She seemed to have a pretty good handle on me after all. "I wasn't," I lied. "But will you be needing her in the future, or will someone else do? I can hire you anyone you want on the other side, but it's too risky to bring Penelope along with us. She's on the cartel's payroll, after all."

"Anyone kind will do," she said. "What do you mean the other side?"

"I can get you and your husband on a private ship leaving from San Jose's marina in thirty minutes. You'll go straight to Puerto Vallarta. There, I'll have someone meet you and help you get settled. You can trust her."

"Who is she?"

"My sister, Alana. She owes me more than a few favors." At least, in my mind she did.

"All right," Raquel said. "I trust you."

I smiled. "Normally you shouldn't, but in this case, I'm glad you do."

I helped her up, even though she didn't need it. Just before I was about to lead her to the door, she reached out and touched my face. She touched my forehead, my nose, my lips, my jaw, feeling delicately at each one.

"You're a striking man, I bet," she finally mused, looking satisfied. "All these parts that shouldn't work together but do."

I raised my brows and she gently took her hand away. "You could just call me handsome. Everyone else does."

Once we were back in the house, I told her to go get Armand and pack up everything important. Penelope started asking questions, panicking. I knew she'd either shoot me or stop them, so I stopped her before she could. It was just a sleeper hold of sorts, something to knock her out long enough until Luisa's parents were safe and on their way to Puerto Vallarta.

I quickly slid the body into the kitchen, making sure she wasn't visible to anyone passing by, and left her a great wad of American hundred dollar bills, knowing that it was worth more than she'd get in a few months' pay. It might buy her silence – there was no way Penelope wanted to own up to being the one who let Luisa's parents escape. It also bought Raquel peace of mind.

Armand was a bit more cantankerous than I thought, and even though he drifted in and out of confusion, he was willing to go wherever Raquel was telling him. Soon I was driving them to the docks and helping them onto a fishing boat that one of my men operated. It paid to have my workers everywhere.

Once on board, Raquel looked up at me and smiled. I'd be lying if I said it didn't creep me out a little, the way she knew where you were, the way she seemed to see into you without seeing you at all.

"Good luck," she said. "I trust that you'll do everything you can."

I nodded. She was right about that.

After I watched them leave, and their ship faded on the horizon, I put in the call to Alana. If she wasn't willing to help out, I had a few people on that end that would. Still, I didn't trust them quite the way I trusted her.

"Hello?" she answered, sounding short of breath. "Javier?"

"Alana," I said. "Is this a bad time?"

"No, no, I was just doing my workout video, it's fine."

I'd forgotten that Alana was a bit of a health nut. I hoped happy endorphins were running amok.

"Yes, well, so here is the thing." I launched right into it, telling her only what she needed to know – mainly that she needed to take care of two ailing parents for a few days. She tried to get out of it, telling me she'd get fired from the airlines for taking time off. I told her I would ensure that not only would she not get fired, but that I'd pay her three times what she'd miss. She told me she wasn't equipped to act as a nurse, and I told her I'd give her money to hire a short-term nurse if needed. I had an answer for everything, and I was very persuasive. I was also an expert in the art of guilt-tripping.

After she reluctantly conceded, she asked, "Who are these people, Javier? Why are you doing this?"

"Their daughter is important to me," is all I said.

"In what way?" she asked suspiciously.

"In ways I don't even understand. Thank you, Alana. I'll be in touch." Then before I almost hung up, I quickly said, "Oh wait. They'll have a cooler with them. There's what looks like a head of lettuce in there. Can you put it in your freezer at home? I want it there for safe-keeping."

"*Is* it a head of lettuce?"

"It's something I promised to get." I cleared my throat. "A gift. But for fuck's sake, don't peek at it."

"I wouldn't dare," she said dryly, then hung up.

I sighed and put my phone back in my pocket. I walked away from the turquoise waves and the fishermen, back to the car, back to the airport, back to Mazatlán and back to The Devil's Backbone. When I left again, there'd be no guarantee I was coming back.

CHAPTER TWENTY-TWO

Javier

"You're fucking crazy," Este spat at me, grabbing the ends of his hair and pulling on them. It was surprising to see him acting like a teenage girl, even for him.

"We all know I'm crazy," I agreed. "This should not be new information. It takes crazy to run this business."

"No, Javi," he said, sitting down in his chair in a huff. "What you're talking about isn't running a business, it's *ruining* a business."

I gently pulled at the ends of my shirt, making sure they were even. "And it also has nothing to do with the business. I go in and get her. End of story."

He narrowed his eyes, taking me in for a moment. Then he shook his head. "If you come back dead, that will affect the business."

I gave him a hard look. "And then you'll take over. That is what you've always wanted, isn't it? Me out of the picture."

He scoffed at that. "If I wanted you out of the picture, Javi, I would have made that happen a long time ago."

"No," I said, smiling slowly. "You wouldn't have. You can't. And you know it. No one gives a flying fuck about you because you haven't had to do anything to get where you are except just show up. People respect me. I worked for everything I've got. You'd last a few hours if you were ever to usurp me and you know it."

He rolled his eyes. "Point taken. You don't have to be so mean about it."

"If I wasn't mean, I wouldn't be me." I leaned forward, hoping he saw how serious I was. "And if I wasn't crazy, I wouldn't be me either. I know what I'm doing, Este."

All right, well that was a complete lie. I had no idea what I was doing or if it would work. I was guessing the odds of getting Luisa out – if she was still alive – were fairly high, but the odds of me surviving, or not being hauled off to prison again, were very low. But for once in my life, the odds were worth the risk.

Two days after I returned from Cabo San Lucas, I finally heard from Lillian Berrellez. She had been my absolute last resort, but I was at the point where I could admit that not only did I need special help in getting Luisa back, but I needed to shed a few points from my moral compass.

In old Mexico, the Mexico I aspired to be a part of, the cartels all operated around each other with an air of respect. Bargains were made – I give you something, you give me something. There were no ruthless, pointless killings in the streets. There were no innocents being raped, murdered, tortured. There were no 16-year-old versions of myself being taught to fire AR-15s. There were no gangs of punks running amok and killing people over fifty dollars worth of stolen cocaine.

We did our business to better ourselves and to better the country. We were vicious and violent but elegant and discreet. There was a dance to all of this, one that kept all things flowing in the right direction, a circle that ensured the smartest and brightest would stay on top, not the man with the most guns and the smallest dick.

And in this dance, there was a code. We are born as Mexicans and we die as Mexicans. Our problems stayed our problems. We never get the States involved in our affairs. The DEA, the FBI, the CIA, they were our enemies, and as cartels, we needed to unite against an enemy that thought they knew what was best for us yet had no idea how our business worked. The USA had no right to tell us, citizens of another country, what we could and couldn't do. They didn't live here, they didn't know. They only knew their privileged, fat, wasteful society while they pointed their fleshy fingers at us and blamed Mexico for all their problems.

When I was let out of prison, it was because I struck a deal with the DEA, an agency that was sometimes more corrupt than we were. I had promised to provide intel when it was needed – something I never wanted to do, something that went against my morals. I also paid a shitload of money.

Lillian Berrellez was a young, attractive, saucy woman who was born in San Diego to Mexican parents. I used to have more than a few fantasies about her while we were striking our bargains. She was a tough nut to crack though, completely devoted to her job, though obviously not above a little bribery. Though I had promised her intel, aside from a few things here and there, stuff that was of no use to her, I had never really given her any since my return to Mexico.

And the funny thing was, she never asked. I suppose she knew I would protect my country before I ratted any of my countrymen out, whether they were enemies or not.

But now, I was asking her. I was providing her with everything she needed to know about Salvador Reyes. I was making a bargain with the enemy across the border, all so I had a chance of getting Luisa out of there alive.

Luisa was a woman who never needed saving. But this time, I was afraid she did. It was too bad that I was going to be the one to have to do it.

"I just don't understand," Este went on. "Why Luisa? Do you want to start a family? Have kids until you have a son to carry your name, carry your empire? You're not the only one, Javier. All the narcos want that, all the narcos have that – except for you. But why her? You can find a hot, pretty woman who's a good lay anywhere. You could snatch them up in a second. It would be far less complicated. You don't need to love them to have a family. You just need a willing pussy." He considered his own words. "Or a non-willing pussy, if you're anything like most men."

A few seconds ticked by in silence. I eyed the bottle of scotch I had been imbibing on for the last week, grateful I was putting my days of misery and inertia behind me.

"I just want her," I found myself admitting. "That is all. It's that simple."

He sighed, running his hands through his hair. "Fine. And I know you don't believe me, but I am just looking out for you. It would be a million times easier for all of us if you just forgot about her."

"I've tried. I can't."

"At least let me come with you," he said. "You know if you go alone the DEA will take you. You're playing right into their hands. They'll arrest you."

"Berrellez said I wouldn't be touched," I said. Unless I killed Salvador, I finished in my head. Then she said all bets were off. They wanted that fucker alive. That was going to be the hardest promise to keep.

"And you trust that woman?" Este laughed.

"Not really," I admitted. "They could very well take in Sal and me at the same time. Two major cartel leaders in one raid. Wouldn't that buy them a larger pension and a watch. Headlines all across the country chanting, 'USA, USA!'"

"You do realize I'll probably never see you again."

I smiled quietly. "Bury me by the koi pond. And wait at least a day until you crack open the Cristal."

He chuckled and I added, "Oh, and if I don't make it out and Luisa does and you happen upon her again, promise me two things."

He sighed and crossed his arms. "What?"

"One, that you don't dare lay a finger on her or I will rise from my grave and fuck you up the ass. And don't you think I won't enjoy it – I'll be dead and I'll take any hole I can get. Two, that you tell her to see my sister Alana in Puerto Vallarta."

"And then what? Even I don't know where your sister lives."

And I intend on keeping it that way. "My sister will also be looking for her. I just want her to be aware."

He looked uneasy. "Word about this will get out, you know," he said gravely. "Everyone will know what happened and why you did it. All your enemies will know your weakness – your weakness is women."

"Women?" I repeated, confused by the plural wording.

He nodded. "Yes. Luisa. And your sisters."

"I don't think many know Alana even exists, and Marguerite is safe in the US."

"Fair enough," he said. "I guess you can keep Luisa safe,

if you get out alive." He got out of his chair, ready to leave. "Any last requests? Any more noses you want cut to spite your own face?"

"Yes," I said, twirling my watch around my wrist. "If you do take over, don't fuck it up. I didn't build an empire to have you come in and destroy it in seconds flat."

"Then don't fuck it up yourself," he said imploringly. "Don't do this. Let Luisa go and save your face, save your empire. Save everything you say you worked so hard to build."

"I told you!" I snapped, frustrated with his inability to understand, though even I was having a hard time understanding myself. "I tried. I just can't let her go. I can't let her die." I composed myself and added softly, avoiding the pity in his face, "I know that makes me a fool . . ."

"It makes you weak," he corrected me.

I swept a shrewd eye over to him. "Or maybe it makes me strong."

After all, a kingdom was only as good as its ruler, and a king and queen could do more damage together than a king alone.

"It makes you aggravating as all hell," Este said sourly. He sighed. "But you wouldn't be Javier Bernal if you weren't." He left the room.

I poured myself a glass of scotch and wondered if it would be the last scotch I'd ever have. Was Luisa really worth that?

But I knew she was. And if I really wanted to pretend I was still completely selfish, saving Luisa would save me from my own torture, my own demons. Not having her around was hard enough. Her absence ate at me. My dick throbbed for her when my own hand wouldn't do. She had given me something during the short time she was with me, something

I never knew I needed. Now it was gone, she was gone, and I'd become captive to the foolish notion that I could get it back.

It wasn't that Luisa completed me – she couldn't be the other half of my so-called soul. But she was all I could ever want, all I could ever need. If I was going to be swallowed by my own dirt one day, I'd rather have her with me, smiling and free.

❥

The next day, armed with as much detailed information from Juanito as possible – information I had already forwarded to Berrellez – I headed out on my suicide mission. I made sure I looked good. The finest silk and linen suit I owned. Black leather boots – a 9mm in one and my knife in another. Two .38 Supers in my harness under my jacket. A bulletproof vest under everything else.

I couldn't do anything to protect my head, but at least my hair looked good.

I had Juanito drive me to Mazatlán and drop me off at one of the high-end resorts.

I took my seat at a flashy bar overlooking a glittering blue pool, aviator shades keeping my struggles internal and away from eyes.

"Looking good, Mr. Bernal," a husky voice said from behind me.

I grinned to myself before I turned and shared it with Lillian Berrellez.

I looked her up and down. "You're also looking good, Ms. Berrellez," I said smoothly, in English.

She was a fairly tall woman, nearly my height, with a very

tight, curvy build. Her tits were huge and fantastic, and her ass was larger than an aircraft carrier. Her eyes were hooded, her lips gratuitously full, her hair big and light auburn, which somehow worked with her darkly tanned skin. She was wearing a black suit that fit her perfectly.

She smiled, cheeky as always. It was her way of making you think she liked you. I knew the truth – she was tough as nails and didn't like anybody, especially me.

"English?" she asked.

I shrugged. "It's good for me to practice."

"I'm guessing you won't need any practice for what we're about to do."

I gave her a sly look. "I'm not sure who you think I am and what I do all day, but I can assure you that I don't take part in government-operated raids on a daily basis. I'll be more of a fish out of water than you."

"Hey," she said sharply, though her eyes were still playful. "I'll have you know I helped initiate a bust in Culiacán that resulted in thirteen million worth of drugs and cash being seized."

"That was you?" I asked. "Oh, your parents must be so proud."

She glared at me. "Your English needs some work. You're not very good at sarcasm."

I finished up my drink and followed her through the hotel lobby and out to a waiting white SUV with tinted windows. I felt a bit like a lamb being led to the slaughter. I hoped they knew there was a lion underneath all my wool.

I climbed in the back, beside her, and was quickly introduced to her team before the vehicle roared off. There was the driver, Diego, a traitor to my country, obviously, and

Greg, a gruff silver-haired dope in his early fifties who didn't say much but obviously had a problem with the fact that Berrellez was sharing the operation with him. He only spoke up when he needed to take control.

While we chugged along the highway heading north to Culiacán, I was filled in on their plan. Naturally, I wasn't given very much to go on. Though I was thanked and told that the intel that Juanito provided was the final puzzle piece that helped them pinpoint where they thought Salvador might be, they gave me no background into how closely they had been watching him, how much they already knew, and how they got all their previous information.

I suppose they could have been doing the exact same thing to me, although I was a smaller fish to fry. Technically I wasn't wanted in the states anymore for anything, but I had a giant rap sheet in Mexico. My government did nothing to enforce it, but I wouldn't be surprised if the DEA tried to take things into their own hands. They'd say capturing Javier Bernal would make America a safer place.

Fucking morons.

But Salvador, Salvador was wanted for a few things in the USA. Cocaine trafficking charges and the murders of several DEA officers and officials were just some things that the DEA wanted to hang him for. The rest of his charges would come via the Mexican Attorney General. I had no doubt that the DEA and the PGR were working together on this, using Mexican soldiers who had no ties to the cartels.

Of course, it was always so hard to tell what side people were on here.

"Did you know that the character of Sinaloa is that of an angel and a devil?" I said to Berrellez as we started getting closer to the city, our vehicle beginning to snare up with traffic. "It was lawless and violent, even before the poppies started growing."

"Thanks for the history lesson, Javier," she said, not taking her gaze from the window. "It's a wonder you aren't from here."

"I merely live nearby. Besides, I'm all devil, no angel."

She raised a brow and looked at me with that perpetual smirk. "Is that right? Tell me again about the woman you are doing this for . . ."

I pressed my lips together, not wanting to share more about Luisa than I had to. If they weren't going to be so forthcoming with me, I wouldn't with them.

"She's an innocent woman who got taken in against her will," I finally said.

"She looked happy in her wedding photos," she noted.

"She wasn't," I said, my tone flinty. "And you know that whatever Salvador wants, Salvador gets."

"Sounds a bit like Javier Bernal."

"Well, we shall see then, won't we?"

"It's just strange you've taken an interest in his wife. I have a hard time believing you're doing this out of the goodness of your heart."

"Then keep believing that. But once you see her and you look in her eyes, you'll know. And you'll know there was no point in even having this conversation."

"What if she's already dead?" Greg asked from the front seat.

I shot him my most violent look. "If she's already dead, there's no difference. Her eyes will look the same."

It was something I was trying my hardest not to think about.

As much as I thought about Luisa, as much as I pictured her beautiful face, her fiery spirit, her pure heart, the way she felt like home when I was inside her, I didn't think about the way she was now. I couldn't even let myself imagine the horrors she must have been going through with Salvador.

For the second time, I felt total shame for carving my name into her back. That would bring her so much pain, much more than the pain I had given her. I hoped she wouldn't be too broken, when and if I found her. I hoped she'd still find that fight inside of her, that courage. I also hoped she wouldn't let her selflessness kill her, especially not for someone like me, who didn't deserve an ounce of it.

I wished I'd had the guts to realize what she had meant to me, back when I could have changed things. Now it was probably too late.

After a while, we came across our first checkpoint. Considering our vehicle and the fact that Greg, a white man, was in the passenger seat, I was certain we were going to be busted by Salvador's men.

But the masked gunman only waved us through.

"That was easy," I commented, twisting in my seat to watch them stop the car behind us.

"They're on our side," Berrellez said smugly.

"And what side is that?"

"Mexico's. They're your army."

"And Salvador's checkpoints?" I asked, waving at the distance in front of us. I knew there would be a few more and they wouldn't be on "our" side.

"Just trust us," she said.

Yeah fucking right.

But I had no choice. Soon we were pulling off the highway

and down a dusty road that seemed to head into nothing but
farm fields, rows of eggplant and tomatoes as far as the eye
could see. Finally the fields tapered off and we ascended up
into a forest, the road starting to wind.

"Where the hell are we going?" I asked. There was a
niggling feeling in my gut that perhaps they were planning
to off me.

They didn't answer. That didn't help.

Eventually, however, we came to a stop in a wide, mowed
field beside a rather large barn. The field was occupied by
at least seven black helicopters. Dozens of armed officers with
the words DEA emblazoned on their backs were milling
around. All of them were wearing goggles and helmets,
covered head to toe in protective gear and holding matte
black automatic rifles.

"Wow," I commented. "Very professional looking bunch."

"It's the DEA, what did you expect?" she asked, opening
her door.

I shrugged. "I thought it stood for Drink Every Afternoon."

She eyed me with impatience. "Come on, get out."

I did so, stepping on to the grass with ease and felt every
single pair of goggles turn in my direction. Here I was, Public
Enemy Number Two, and completely surrounded. I was
tempted to give them all a little wave but figured some
hotshot would probably mistake it as a threat and blow my
hand off.

"Now I'm going to go change," she said. "Want a gun?
They're brand new carbine AR-15s."

I pursed my lips. "Nah. Seems a bit impersonal, don't you
agree?"

She stared at me for a few beats. "How about protection?"

I grinned at her. "I don't use protection. Dulls the senses."

"For your body," she said in annoyance.

"I've got a vest underneath and a few pistols. I'll be fine."

"Your funeral," she said before she turned and headed toward the barn.

It wasn't long before she came back looking like a man. Every part of her was covered up in the DEA's armor, the long AR-15 held proudly in her hands. She smiled at me. "Well, I just spoke to the PGR. They have another five helicopters at their location, and they're about to set off. Are you ready?"

"To be thrown out of a helicopter? Not particularly."

She jerked her head toward a helicopter that was just starting up, its blades slowly whirring around. "Let's go."

Just like that, everyone around us started clamoring toward the waiting choppers. I climbed in with Berrellez, Greg, and four other men whose names I didn't know, nor could I tell them apart, and soon we were lifting off into the air. Though I denied an AR-15 and protection, I was still given a headpiece which I could talk to them through, something that was already useful, considering how loud the helicopter was.

"You look nervous," Berrellez said to me.

"I'm not the best flier," I admitted.

"Nothing to do with you being dropped off at the heavily-armed compound of the world's most wanted drug trafficker?"

"No," I lied. It wasn't that I was freaking out. It wasn't even that I was afraid. But there was a thread of apprehension that ran through me, tickling me from time to time. It wasn't often that I was out of my element, and beyond that, beyond the idea of dying fruitlessly, I was worried that I still wouldn't be able to save Luisa in the end.

"Good," she grinned. "I'm not nervous either."

To my surprise, the choppers didn't head toward the city of Culiacán, the hazy mass of roofs and rivers. They headed further inland, into the mountains. It seemed that Salvador had changed it up after we captured Luisa and had moved to another mansion. I had no doubt that the remoteness meant security was even tighter.

"Based on satellite images," she said, pulling out a mobile device and flipping through it, "there's a plot of land both behind the house and down the road by a few meters. We'll go as close to the house as possible. If the PGR aren't already there, we'll be the first on the scene. We'll all head out first, then you follow."

I nodded, understanding but not agreeing.

Suddenly the choppers swooped up, nearly missing a row of trees that protruded from a rapidly rising cliff.

And on the other side of them, settled in the middle of a plateau, was Salvador's house. It was a mansion not too dissimilar to mine, albeit with none of the class or beauty, with a few guards milling about and some stationed at the gates. Naturally, as soon as we started bearing down on the house, they started panicking and shooting at us.

The gunman in the chopper began firing back, taking out as many as he could before the pilot began a quick descent toward the green grass of the backyard.

Not going to lie – my heart was in my throat.

And I had to take every opportunity I could. As soon as Greg slid the doors open and the chopper was making its way past one wing of the house right over a small balcony, I made the sign of the cross, leaped past Berrellez, and jumped out.

Someone tried to grab me at the last minute, maybe it was Berrellez, but gravity had taken hold and I plunged about fifteen feet, landing straight on a glass table. It shattered beneath me and I lay there for a few moments on my back, the wind knocked out of me, staring blankly up at the black chopper blades as it continued on its way. The sound was incredible, hypnotic, until I heard Berrellez squawking in my ear.

"What the hell was that?" she yelled at me through the scratchy earpiece. I quickly rolled over in time to see someone coming to the balcony door. I whipped out my pistol and shot right through it, getting the figure before they could get me.

"You do things your way," I said to her, "I'll do things my way."

"Don't forget the deal. All bets are off if you end up killing him. We need Salvador alive!"

"Yeah, yeah," I said, and switched my earpiece off.

I scrambled to my feet, shrugging the broken glass off of me. Rapid gunfire erupted on the lawn though I couldn't tell who was firing the most and who was already winning.

It didn't matter though. I was after only one thing.

I gripped my gun and stepped through the broken glass door and into a cool, carpeted bedroom of Salvador's house.

Time to find my queen.

CHAPTER TWENTY-THREE

Luisa

At first I thought it was the end of the world. I heard the deep rumble slice through the air, felt it quaking in my bones, shaking the floor of the bathroom I was lying on.

I welcomed the end of the world with open arms. In fact, I think I smiled knowing that death was finally on its way. It had ignored my pleas for far too long.

But then, when I didn't die and the world didn't burn and crash around me, I realized that the sound I was hearing was helicopters. I tried to raise my heavy head to look through the narrow window above the shower. It was glassless now, as was the mirror. Salvador had taken them out after I had stabbed him in the forearm one day with a slice I broke off. It cut my hands up pretty bad and I received a round of electric shock torture for my disobedience, but damn had it felt good.

Through the window I saw a black helicopter fly past, heading right over the house and the sound built up, growing deeper. Then I saw another helicopter and another.

Something was going on. I should have been happy, just having a disruption to the daily monotony. I wasn't sure how long I'd been kept in the bathroom, perhaps ten days, perhaps two weeks? It was hard to remember. My brain wasn't functioning anymore since he stopped feeding me several days ago. I still had water coming out of the bath and the taps and the toilet, just to ensure I wouldn't totally die. If I was dead, how on earth could he torture me? How would he hear me scream?

Salvador hadn't even raped me aside from the first day or two that I had arrived back. I felt like that was purely to assert his dominance, especially after he saw Javier's brand on my back. He wanted to make sure that I belonged to him again. But to my surprise, the sexual attacks stopped soon after.

It was nothing to be relieved about. Salvador's big thing now was to torture me in other ways. I was no longer his wife that he could have every which way he wanted. He no longer *wanted* me. So I was treated like an informant, like a spy, like a hostage. I was locked up in the bathroom somewhere in his house and he would visit me . . . sometimes once a day, sometimes twice, sometimes once every couple of days, all his ways of keeping me in suspense.

Too bad I had become too numb inside to even care anymore.

The first week, he removed the nails from my pinky toes. While one of his men held me down, he slowly ripped the toenails straight out. I prided myself on not passing out, but boy did I scream. It was just what he wanted. After that, I did my best not to make a sound. I was able to make it through the Tasers, being the old pro that I was already, but when it came to the hot irons he applied against my stomach, well that I could never keep inside.

And while I was able to take the beatings quite well, the other day he took a hammer to my finger. He seemed extra angry, muttering something about my choice in hired help, and I was punished accordingly. I screamed more after he left, when I attempted to bandage my broken index finger to my middle one using a toilet paper roll and strips of the shower curtain I had painstakingly ripped off.

Now I was lying on the cold tiles of the floor, wondering if the end was coming or if the helicopters were only going to bring me more pain. I didn't even have the strength to crawl over to the door and see if I could hear anything.

Not that I needed to. Soon the air was filled with the sound of gunfire coming in all directions. People were no doubt dying. I wanted to smile at that. I wanted the whole world to burn.

I closed my eyes again and lay down my head, envisioning the madness that was going on outside, pretending that the good guys had come – whoever they were – and that Salvador would be caught in the crossfire. I hoped he'd die feeling like a fool.

Minutes passed and more helicopters sounded. More gunfire followed. I wondered what would happen if someone found me. Would they mistake me for being part of the cartel and shoot me on sight? Would they show me mercy? Or did the world hold worse things for me? It didn't seem possible.

Eventually I heard quiet footsteps on the floor outside, and when I opened my eyes, I could see a pair of boots underneath the doorframe, waiting on the other side.

I started smiling before I even knew why.

The door was suddenly kicked open, narrowly missing my face, and I followed the boots up to see a pair of golden eyes staring down at me. Waves of pain and relief swirled in them with startling clarity.

"Luisa," Javier whispered, immediately dropping down to his knees. He looked completely beside himself as his eyes searched my body up and down. He touched my face and I closed my eyes, leaning into the warmth of his palm. He was here. He had come. My beautiful, ruthless king.

"Luisa," he said, gently running his other hand down my side, feeling carefully for anything broken. "Stay with me, darling. I'm getting you out of here. Can you walk?"

I nodded. "I think so," I said, my voice so painfully raw.

He looked at my broken finger, at my toes, at the wounds in my arms and legs from the Taser, at the bruises on my face. The more he searched me over, the more broken he looked. I couldn't let him lose it if I hadn't yet. Now was not the time.

"I'll be fine," I said, trying to get to my feet.

He gripped me by my arms and carefully pulled me up. I wobbled a bit on my feet, dizzy from the lack of food, and fell into his chest. He immediately wrapped his arms around me and held me tight. It took everything I had not to break down crying.

He kissed the top of my head. "I should have never let you leave."

"I never should have left," I said softly. I had regretted it the moment I stepped into the house, the moment I realized that Salvador would probably have my parents killed anyway. For once, I hated how selfless I had been.

"I'm going to kill him," he growled, and I could feel the anger and tension starting to roll through him. "I want to kill him more than I've ever wanted to kill anyone. I want to do everything he did to you to him, but worse. I want him gone." He sighed in frustration. "But I made a promise not to."

That surprised me. "To whom?"

"The DEA," he said. "They're the ones who got me in."

"You made another deal with the Americans?"

He pulled away and stared at me intensely. I had missed his eyes so much, the power inside them, the passion and strength. "I would do anything to get you back. And I did."

"But your cartel," I started.

He shook his head. "It doesn't matter. None of that matters. Only you matter, Luisa, only you." In the distance, the gunfire reigned. He paused. "But it will all be in vain if I don't get you out of here. I'd tell you I need you to be strong, but I can tell you already are."

I managed a smile, refusing to let fear enter my veins anymore. I wouldn't fear with him by my side. We would make the world pay.

"Give me one of your guns," I said, holding out my good hand, which was thankfully my right one.

He grinned at me and reached into his boot, pulling out a handgun and placing it in my hand. "Try not to shoot the guys with DEA on their backs. We might get in trouble."

"Save that for another time?" I said, not really joking either.

He planted a hard kiss on my forehead. "Goddamn it, you're perfect."

He led me out of the bathroom and into the adjoining guest bedroom. We were almost out in the hall when one of Salvador's guards appeared.

Javier pulled me down and shot the man just as another guard appeared. From my position on the ground, I somehow managed to aim the barrel and pull the trigger.

I hit the second man right in the chest, and he stumbled backward against the wall before toppling over on his fallen comrade.

My heart galloped wildly, loudly, and it felt hard to breathe. I had just killed a man.

Me.

Just like that.

Javier looked down at me in awe before helping me to my feet.

"How did that feel?" he asked in amazement, peering at me closely.

My breathing had returned to normal and the adrenaline was starting to coax through my veins. My flesh tingled all over. I swallowed as I looked at him, sharing his wonder.

"It felt good," I told him honestly and not feeling the tiniest bit ashamed. "Almost like sex."

He shook his head, his nostrils flaring. "Stop that," he said gruffly. "I almost came just from seeing you pull the trigger."

He brought me to the hall, and after checking both ends, we ran down it, heading away from the gunfire that now sounded like it was coming from the foyer. He darted into the room of David, Salvador's asshole assistant, and I could see where he'd already come in. The French door and the table on the balcony were already smashed, David's dead body lying amidst the damage.

I spit on his body as we stepped over the corpse and onto the balcony. In the distance a helicopter was flying and I could see a few of them on the lawn. The grass was littered with bodies, most of them Salvador's men. Bullets still ripped through the air, though I couldn't see the combat.

"We'll go on the roof," Javier told me, staring up at it. "That way one of the helicopters can pick us up and we'll be safer. We can see anyone coming from below and we'll pick them off."

If we stood on the edge of the balcony's railing, there was a small overhang that would be easy to climb up on, at least for him. Escape was so near.

"I don't know if I can pull myself up," I told him, starting to panic a little. "I don't have much strength."

"I'll pull you up," he said confidently. He quickly eased himself onto the railing, balanced himself, and then jumped up onto the ledge, needing to pull himself up a few feet.

And while he was doing that, his back to me, I felt a gun press against my temple and an arm hook around my neck. I dropped my gun in surprise and it went skittering over the balcony edge.

Heavy breathing seeped into my ear.

Fear gripped my heart.

Salvador.

By the time Javier found his footing and was turning around to see what caused the clatter, I was completely under Salvador's control. The look of utter outrage and madness strained Javier's face. I knew he wanted nothing more than to tear Salvador from limb to limb, but that would never happen now.

Now that he had me. Now that he would kill me in front of Javier.

"Javier, Javier, Javier," Salvador said, his voice raspy. "Finally we meet in person. You know, you're a lot smaller than I thought you'd be, even with you way up there."

His chokehold around me tightened and I tried to pry him off with one good hand, giving me a few more inches of breathing room, but the strength just wasn't there. I was slowly losing air.

"Let her go," Javier commanded, his voice steady despite

everything. "Do what you want with me, but let her go. You've already hurt her enough."

"Really? I don't think I have," Salvador mused. "Tell me, Javier, when you were fucking her, did she scream for mercy like she does with me? Did you make her bleed too? You must have. Nice carving job, by the way. For an amateur."

Javier swallowed. I could see how hard he was breathing, how difficult it was for him not to whip out his gun and try and shoot Salvador, promise to the DEA or not. But he couldn't, not when I was a hostage once more.

"Let him kill me." I managed to get the words out to Javier. "Let him kill me, just make sure you kill him. Make him suffer."

"Shut up!" Salvador roared in my ear. "I will kill you, but then he's next. He doesn't even have his gun out. Fucking pussy."

The gunfire in the background had started to die down. The helicopter that we had seen in the distance was now long gone. I wondered what side was winning now. I wondered if they'd come and find us only after it was too late. I could only hope that if Javier and I were dead, the DEA would ensure that Salvador suffered, that he would never get out of jail alive, that our deaths wouldn't be for nothing.

"So what do you want, Salvador?" Javier asked, raising his hands. "Why are you doing this? Just shoot her now if that's what you want."

"You're as fucking crazy as she is," Salvador said, sneering. "Don't the two of you have any respect for death? You of all people, Javier, should know the importance of making a show of it. Of making it last. The true torture doesn't come during death – it comes in the moments before. When you know it's about to happen, but you don't quite know when. Just like now."

Javier's chest heaved. I could see his wicked brain working on overdrive, trying to come up with a way to at least save me if not himself. I could also see he had no options to go on. For all the fury he was carrying, I caught the sorrow on his brow. I saw the soft way he was coming to terms with the end.

But that didn't mean I had nothing. Even if it meant us getting shot, I at least had to try for the both of us. I welcomed the end more than he did. I had nothing to lose.

I held Javier's eyes with mine and then slid my gaze over to the partly-healed gash on Salvador's forearm where I had driven in the piece of glass last week. I couldn't reach around with my own arms and touch it, but that didn't mean I was powerless.

When I saw the nearly invisible hint of recognition in Javier's eyes, I knew it was time. I drew upon my reserves of anger, of injustice, of pure unadulterated rage that I had coiling deep inside me. I let those feelings, those hot, swirling, pulsing emotions wrap me up into an uncontrollable tornado that had nowhere else to go. Then I gave it permission to fuel me, to become my strength.

I screamed, a raw, brutal sound that ripped out of my gut and my throat, and used all my power to twist Salvador's forearm toward me. I bit straight into his wound, tasting the blood, loving the blood, relishing the feeling of my teeth plunging in deeper and deeper, tearing through muscle and nerve and causing so much pain.

The next thing I knew Salvador was screaming, caught off-guard by my violence, and Javier took that moment to whip out his gun and shoot.

He aimed for Salvador's shoulder. He got it.

Salvador spun back, out of my teeth and grasp, but not before he took his own gun and fired it at Javier as he fell.

I thought Salvador's aim would be off.

But it wasn't.

He shot Javier right in the head.

I screamed as Javier stumbled slightly then pitched forward off the roof and facedown onto the balcony, the glass bouncing around us from his impact.

With what strength I had, I kicked Salvador's gun off the balcony, then scampered over to Javier, crying, screaming, feeling like my own heart was bleeding, my breath pulled from me. The pain in my chest was so incredibly great, I wasn't sure how I was going to survive it. I wasn't sure if I wanted to.

I fell to my knees beside Javier, afraid to touch, afraid to roll him over. I wouldn't be able to handle what I so deeply feared to see.

But before I could reach out and touch him, he started to stir.

Alive.

"Javier!" I sobbed, my hands going for his head. I brushed away his hair and saw the wound, a long trail of blood on his temple. His eye opened and fixed on me.

"Fuck," he groaned. "Did he get me?"

I burst into the biggest smile and nearly laughed at the intense amount of relief flowing through me. "Get you? I think you were just shot in the head!"

He reached up and gingerly touched the wound. "Oh." He smiled weakly. "It just grazed me. How is my hair?"

I wasn't sure whether to punch him or kiss him.

But before I could do either, I was suddenly picked up by my shoulders from behind and thrown to the side. My head smacked against the floor, making everything spin and swirl nauseatingly, blackness teasing my vision and keeping me down.

I stared helplessly as Salvador launched himself on top of Javier, trying to choke him. Even with his one arm useless, he was a big man, stronger than Javier, and he was able to squeeze his throat tight with just his one hand.

"Look at you," Salvador sneered at him, saliva dripping down into Javier's face. Javier gasped for breath, his skin turning white. "A traitor to Mexico. You brought in the Americans just to take this whore back. You're a pussy. You're soft over a woman. A girl. You'll be known as the drug lord who became oh so good for no good reason."

"I am not good!" Javier managed to roar, the fight coming back in his face. With all he had left, he managed to kick up under Salvador and get his knife free from his boot. He raised the knife above his head, and just as Salvador looked up in surprise, Javier swiftly drove the knife between Salvador's eyes, plunging it all the way in to the handle. "I am just not as bad as you," he spat out.

Salvador froze up, the knife stuck into his brain. It instantly killed him, and Javier quickly rolled out from under his crushing body. He rapidly crawled over to me and felt along the side of my head. "Are you okay?" he asked, his voice cracking.

I swallowed and tried to talk but couldn't. I burst into tears instead.

"Shhhh, Luisa," Javier said soothingly. "I'm alive, you're alive. The fucker is dead. We're okay." He sat down beside me and pulled me into his lap, cradling me while I let everything loose. Anger, pain, shock, sorrow. He let me cry for as long as I needed. And when my tears started to dry, he said something that made me cry more, only from happiness.

"You should know that I have your parents," he whispered into the top of my head. "They're safe with my sister in Puerto Vallarta."

Even though Javier had never told me he loved me, I still had never known such love. I couldn't thank him enough, couldn't get over how absolutely selfless he had been, and all for me.

We sat like that together, me gathering strength in his arms, until a few DEA agents burst onto the balcony with their guns blazing. One of them I didn't even know was a woman until she took off her helmet and shook out her hair. She stared down at Salvador's body in dismay.

"Honestly, it was self-defense," Javier protested at her disapproving glare before she could say anything.

"But I bet you still enjoyed every moment of it," she said.

He smiled. "Of course I did."

And I did too.

I could tell Javier was nervous though, about what the DEA might do with him since Salvador was dead and he'd broken the one condition. But by the time the medics arrived by helicopter and had treated his head wound and splintered up my broken fingers and applied antibiotic creams to my body, we were told we'd be free to go anyway.

"He may not be alive," the woman, whom I learned was Lillian Berrellez, said, "but at least we were able to dismantle the Sinaloa Cartel. That's not too shabby."

No, it certainly wasn't. Even though there was a cartel that was ready to take its place: Javier's.

The DEA knew that, too. But for now, we were shaking hands and agreeing to walk away from each other.

I knew Berrellez would be back though. And if I was still by Javier's side at that time, I'd be making sure she didn't get far.

In this business, you didn't build empires by being good. And though I'd never truly be able to forget the person I was and could never fully eradicate my morals, I was looking forward to being bad.

I was looking forward to getting dirty.

Very, very dirty.

CHAPTER TWENTY-FOUR

Javier

It was the next day when Berrellez finally dropped us off in Mazatlán. Luisa and I were tired, wounded, and sore, but we were together and the DEA was letting us go free. For now, at least. But that was enough for us. We had each other and we were going home, back to my compound where I would surely scare the shit out of Esteban with my untimely return from the dead.

But even though that was the plan, that wasn't the only plan I'd made. Truth be told, I wasn't sure what the next step was. I felt as if I were being pulled by different hands, and though I knew which one felt right, I no longer knew what *was* right. Perhaps I had never known the difference. Perhaps there was no right or wrong anymore, not in this life.

Once Berrellez left, I took Luisa by her good hand and led her out onto the beach. Like usual on the coast, it was a blindingly beautiful day, the heat stunted by the cool Pacific. We weaved our way through thatched umbrellas, fat tourists on towels, and vendors hawking their cheap shit, until I found a more secluded place away from the hustle and bustle of bloated indulgence.

We sat down in the warm sand and I made a mental promise to myself to try and escape to the beach more often.

It was nice to leave the controlled comforts of home and step into the chaos. I really had been making too many of my men do the work when I should have been doing it myself. Even though it was risky, it was a lot more fun to get my hands dirty.

"I was thinking that this weekend we could make the trip down to Puerto Vallarta," I told her. "To see Alana and your parents."

She beamed at me, her cheeks looking so cute I wanted to fucking bite them. "Oh, that would be wonderful."

"I even have a special present for you there," I said.

"Ooooh," she cooed, clapping excitedly. "What is it?"

"It's a surprise." Boy, was it ever. There weren't many men who'd deliver your lecherous ex-boss's head to you. Then again, there weren't many men like me.

While she sipped a Corona that I bought from a ten-year-old kid with a cooler, I pulled out two passports from my inner pocket and threw them down on the sand.

She eyed them with curiosity. "Where did you get Canadian passports?"

"They're ours," I told her.

She planted her beer in the sand and picked up the nearest passport, flipping it open. There was a picture of a woman that looked almost like her, just a few years older and with different hair, both things that could be easily faked. "Christine Estevez?" she said, reading it. "Who is this?"

I shrugged. "Who knows? It's legit though. I didn't have a photo of you so I had to obtain an actual passport through one of my channels." I flipped open the other passport and pointed at my unsmiling picture, not so different from the actual mug shot I had upon my arrest in the States. "Mine, however, is completely forged. You can't buy anything better though. It will pass all the tests again and again, so long as you can remember who you are. I have birth certificates and driver's licenses, too."

"Javier Garcia," she read off of mine. "I think I like Javier Bernal better."

"Of course," I said, straightening my collar. "He is the best."

She bit her lip, thinking. "So why do we have these? Are we going to Canada? I think I have an uncle there, maybe we could go visit him."

"Darling," I said to her, pulling her to me. I ran my thumb over her lips then ran it over mine, tasting the beer. "We can go anywhere you want to go. And for as long as you want. We don't ever have to return."

She frowned, shaking her head. "I don't understand. What are you talking about?"

I took in a deep breath, my heart beating hard against my ribs. I'd rehearsed this a few times in my head already. For something this serious, this life-changing, I couldn't chance saying the wrong thing. "I risked everything to get you, Luisa. There's no way I can risk losing you again. You say the word, and we can run. Tell me to do it and I'll do it. I'll give all of this up. We can be free out there, out of danger. We can leave all of this behind."

"We can't run away, Javier," she said slowly.

"Yes, we can. We can do anything we want to do."

She smiled patiently and gently kissed my lips. "No, my love, we can't," she said, cupping my face in her hands. "You can never run away from yourself, you'll just go in a circle. There is no escape from this life because this is *your* life and you are what you are. And there is *nothing* wrong with that."

Her words sunk into me like the sweetest blade. Even so. "I can't lose you," I told her, feeling the truth in my bones.

"You won't lose me. I'll gladly live this life with you. I feel that it's what I was meant to do. To be your queen and rule by your side."

I rubbed my lips together, trying not to smile at her beautiful phrase. "It's an ugly life."

She shrugged. "I know. And it's all I've ever known. But at least now I'll have enough power to mask the ugliness."

I grinned. My heart could have burst. "You'll have all the power. You'll have everything."

"And yet all I want is you."

"You have me, my black heart and my dirty soul."

I grabbed her and kissed her forcefully, unable to hold anything back. She'd never tasted better. The smell of sun on her skin, the cool ocean spray, the idea of her ruling by my side, with all her good and all her bad – all of it made my heart spin and my dick throb mercilessly.

"I don't think I've ever wanted you more." I groaned into her mouth, falling back into the sand and bringing her down with me. I pulled her on top of me, gripping her legs so she was straddling my waist. My tongue eagerly plunged into her mouth again and again, stirring the flames that I wasn't able to hold back. I'd dreamt about this for days and days.

"We can always get a hotel room," she said against my mouth, and from the way her breath hitched, I knew she was just as turned on as I was. I could still get her hot in seconds flat.

"Fuck that," I said. I reached between her legs and under her skirt. I pushed her underwear aside and grinned at how wet she was. "My queen, we aren't going anywhere."

She moaned, her eyes fluttering. "But there are people on the beach. We'll get arrested."

"Is that so?" I asked, knowing I'd never be arrested in Mexico for anything.

"People will see."

"Tourists will see," I told her, licking her ear. "And let them see. Let them go back home and think that Mexico is a fun place." I bit her neck hard, relishing the feeling of her skin between my teeth. She shivered, loving it.

"I don't know," she said breathlessly, her back arching. I thrust my fingers into her with one hand while unzipping my fly with the other. It was a losing battle on her behalf.

"Look," I said, stifling a groan, "are you a Mexi-can or a Mexi-can't?"

She laughed, throaty and hot. "Quoting movies now? You're bad."

"You love that I'm bad."

She smiled serenely at me. "You know I do." Then her mouth twisted into an "o" as I took my swollen dick out and eased it into her. She was so exquisitely tight, so silky, so perfect. It didn't matter if we were fucking in public and in the broad daylight on the beaches of Mazatlán, or in the confines of my bed, she was everything I needed, everything I wanted.

"Take me home, my queen," I whispered to her. Finally she relaxed, sitting back, and I plunged deep inside of her. We both cried out from the pleasure and pain. It was impossible not to.

I gripped her hips and moved her back and forth in slow, subtle swivels. We were barely moving but that didn't mean I wasn't feeling everything, everywhere.

It wasn't long until the yearning I had felt for her, the fear of losing her, the intense sun behind her back, the blue sky and the passing people murmuring their disapproval and admiration, built up to a thunderous climax. I came hard into her, making sure her clit was well fed at the same time. While she clenched around me, squeezing me dry, she called me her king.

I don't think the words had ever sounded so right.

After our escapades on the beach, I went and got a rental car that I would never be returning, and we headed off on the highway that lead to Durango. It would have been a shorter trip home but my sexual appetite had been reawakened by all the violence, adrenaline, and the fact that we had almost lost each other. We pulled over twice: once because I craved the taste of her pussy so bad that we ended up going down on each other in the back of the car, the good ol' sixty-nine. The other time, I wanted to be back inside her warmth so she climbed on top of me while I was driving and started riding me that way. I only went about ten feet before I nearly crashed the car. Seemed I was good at most things but fucking and driving at the same time wasn't one of them.

Eventually we made it back home to the compound around sunset. The guards at the gate seemed shocked at my return, but they were smart enough to look happy about it. When it came down to it, there were worse bosses than me.

I parked the car right outside the front doors and looked over at Luisa, sitting serenely in the passenger seat. She seemed to glow.

"This is your home now, you know," I told her.

She smiled. "I know."

"It's your castle."

She leaned over and quickly kissed me. "And it will be a golden one."

We got out of the car just as the front door swung open to Este staring at us, completely dumbfounded. I relished the faint strain of disappointment in his brow. It served him right for me to prove him wrong.

"I don't fucking believe it," he said in quiet awe.

I raised my arms. "The ghost of narcos' past has returned to fuck you up the ass."

He grinned. "Lucky for me, I haven't had time to screw anything up. How the hell did you pull this off, Javi?" He continued to look between the two of us in amazement.

I shrugged. "What can't I pull off?"

I put my hand on the small of Luisa's back and guided her up the stairs. We paused in the doorway, looking Este over. "Esteban Mendoza," I said to him. "Meet your ruler, Luisa Chavez." I leaned into her ear. "You know, he's your employee now. How does that make you feel?"

She grinned at Este before she stared up at me. "Makes me feel like I should keep a Taser gun on me at all times. You know, just in case he misbehaves." She then winked at him and went inside the house.

I laughed at the look of fear in his eyes. I patted him on the shoulder. "She's not kidding either. She killed a man back there. I think she's gotten a taste for it."

We left the bewildered Este out on the steps, and I quickly led her straight up to our bedroom, where I would bring her fire and she would bring me peace, that beautiful peace.

I was her king.

She was my queen.
And we had a fucking empire to rule.
After we were done fucking, of course.
After all, I was still Javier Bernal.

ACKNOWLEDGMENTS

Some books are easy to write, others are hard. *Dirty Angels* has the distinction of being an incredibly easy book to write considering the very hard circumstances I found myself in while writing it.

First of all, I actually came up with the concept of Javier's book back in February of 2013, when I had just finished writing *On Every Street*. Though I knew he wasn't the man for Ellie at that point, I also knew that I wanted to explore his story later. The man utterly fascinated me – and I knew I wasn't the only one under his spell.

Second of all, I started writing a big chunk of the book back in December of 2013, though the book had to be put on hold for various reasons. Starting and stopping with a book can be extremely difficult, though I was later grateful for this because when I did sit down to finally start writing again . . .

. . . I was planning a wedding. Yes, I wrote this book while I planned my wedding and finished it less than a week before the ceremony. I will be editing on my honeymoon. It's just the way things go when you're an author. But had it not been for Javier Fucking Bernal and my love for that crazy sexy psycho, I wouldn't have been able to do it. Somehow, despite all the outside stress, I wasn't stressed at all when writing it. It was easy, it was fun, and I had a blast.

But of course that's not to say that I didn't have help. From my best friend, Kelly St-Laurent, to my parents, Tuuli and Sven, to my husband, Scott MacKenzie, and all my friends who rallied behind me and this book (Sandra Cortez, Kayla Veres, Stephanie Brown, Shawna Vitale, K.A. Tucker, Barbie Bohrman, Ali Hymer, Lucia Valovcikova, Nina Decker, Laura Moore, Chelcie Holguin, Kara Malinczak, Chastity Jenkins at Rock Star PR), I had a LOAD of help in all directions, and without them this book could *not* have been possible.

Thank you!

Read on for an excerpt of

Dirty
DEEDS

Book Two in Karina's raw, explosive and electrifyingly sexy series.

The call came at 6:30 a.m. from a voice I recognized but couldn't place. The fact that it sounded familiar was surprising, though. The turnover rate for these guys was exceedingly high. They were shuffled around to different *sicarios* like a game of musical chairs. Sometimes I wondered if the ones giving me the orders – the narcos just underneath the bosses – ever lasted more than a few weeks. Did they go on to have long careers doing the dirty work of the *patrons*? Or were they so good at getting the job done, that they were held on to for a long time, even promoted, just like any assistant manager at McDonalds?

It didn't really matter. I took these calls, I carried out the orders, and I got paid. I was at the bottom of their food chain but as long as I wasn't tied to just one cartel, then I didn't have to worry about long-term security. You didn't want long-term security when working for the narcos. You wanted to stay as distant – freelance – as possible. You wanted a way out, in case you ever had a change of heart.

That was unlikely for me. But I was still a bit of a commitment-phobe. Freedom meant everything, and in this game, freedom meant safety.

The girl next to me in bed moaned at the early intrusion, pulling the pillow over her head. She looked ridiculous considering she was completely naked on top of the sheets.

Was it Sarah? Kara? I couldn't recall. She was so drunk last night I was amazed she even made it to my hotel room. Then again, that's why I was in Cancun. I could pretend to be like everyone else, just another dumb tourist on the beach.

I took the phone into the bathroom and closed the door.

"Yes," I answered, keeping my voice low.

"I have a job for you," the man on the other line said. His English was pretty much perfect but relaxed, almost jovial. Sometimes they gave me orders in Spanish, sometimes in English. I felt like this man was trying to extend a courtesy.

"I assume I've worked for you before," I said.

"For me?" the man asked. "No. For my boss? Yes. Many times. But this has nothing to do with him. Let's just say this is coming from a whole new place."

None of that concerned me. "Tell me about payment."

He chuckled. "Don't you want to hear the job?"

"It doesn't matter. The price does."

"One hundred thousand dollars, US, all cash. Fifty now, fifty upon completion."

That made me pause. My heart kicked up. "That's a lot of money."

"It's an important job," the man said simply.

"And what is the job?"

"It's a woman," he said. "In Puerto Vallarta. She should be very easy to find for someone like you."

"I need a name and I need her photo," I told him. Though the price was quite higher than normal, the man was ignoring the basics. It made me wonder if he had ever done this before. It made me wonder a lot of things.

"I have the first, not the second. As I said, she should be easy to find. You might even be able to Facebook her."

I waited for him to go on.

He cleared his throat. "Her name is Alana Bernal. Twenty-six. Flight Attendant for Aeromexico. I want a bullet in her head and I want it front page news."

It was a common name, which is probably why it sounded familiar. I had wondered what she had done, if anything. Usually when I was sent to kill women, it was because they had been involved with a narco and had overstayed their welcome. They knew too much. They had loose lips in more ways than one.

I was never really given time to think about it. You weren't with these types of things. There were a few minor alarm bells going off in my head – the high price for someone minor, the greenness in the man's voice – but the price won out in the end. That amount of money could get me away from this business for a long time again. I saw a lengthy hiatus on my horizon, one that didn't include fucking drunk chicks on spring break just because I was horny, a hiatus that didn't include bouncing my way from hotel room to hotel room across Mexico, waiting for the next call.

I told the man I agreed to his terms and worked out the payment plan. I wouldn't get the other half until she made the news. Considering how rare shootings were in Puerto Vallarta, I had no doubt it would happen. And I would be long gone.

I hung up the phone, feeling almost elated. The promise of a new life buried that worm of uneasiness. One more job and then I'd be freer than ever.

I came out of the bathroom to see the chick sitting up in bed and looking extremely nauseous. Once she saw me though, her eyes managed to light up.

"Wow," she said. "You're fucking hot."

I tried to smile, hoping she didn't find me enticing enough to stay. "Thank you."

"Did we have sex last night?"

I stood beside the bed and folded my arms across my chest. Her mouth opened a bit at my muscles. I still had the same physique I had back in the military and it still got the same reactions from the women. They never knew the real me – knew Derek Conway – but at least, with the way I looked, they thought they did. Just another built, tough American boy, a modern G.I. Joe.

They had no idea what I did.

They had no idea who I was.

"No," I told her, "we didn't have sex. You stripped and then you passed out."

She looked surprised. "We still didn't . . ."

I gave her a dry look. "Sex is only fun when you're awake, babe." I stretched my arms above my head and she stared openly at my stomach, from my boxer waistband to my chest. Okay, now it was time for her to go.

I told her I had stuff to do in the morning and needed her to move along. I could tell she wanted to at least take a shower, but I wasn't about to budge.

I had a plane to catch.

Alana Bernal was extremely easy to find.

At least, for me. She had a Facebook page under Alana B. Her privacy settings were high but I was still able to see her profile picture, one of her in her Aeromexico uniform. She had a sweet yet beautiful face. Her eyes were light hazel, almost amber, both stunning and familiar at the same time. They glowed against her golden skin, as did her pearly white teeth. She looked like a lot of fun and I could imagine all the unwanted attention she'd get from unruly passengers in the air. She looked like she could handle them with a lot of sass.

Once again I found myself wondering what she had done. And once again I realized I couldn't care.

That wasn't my business.

Killing her was my business.

I drove to the airport and for the next two days, began to stalk the employee parking lot, using a different rental car each day. Most of the flight crew I saw looked a bit like her but lacked that certain vitality that she had. So I waited in mounting frustration, just wanting this job to be over with.

On day three, just as I was driving past for the forty-second time that morning, I spotted her getting out of a silver Honda and wrestling with her overnight bag. I quickly pulled the car around again and parked at the side of the road, plumes of dust rising up around me. There was nothing but a chain-link fence between us as she began the long walk toward the waiting airport shuttle. Her modest high heels echoed across the lot and she tugged at the hem of her skirt with every other step. Not only was she beautiful, but there was something adorably awkward about her.

What had she done?

No, I couldn't care.

I looked down at the bag in the passenger seat and took out the silencer, quickly screwing it on the gun I was holding between my legs.

She only had a few seconds of life left before I put the bullet in her heart.

Get ready for the
Dirty Angels Trilogy . . .

Mexico is lawless. It's lethal. It's scorching-hot.

It's dog eat dog in the world of the drug cartels.

But sometimes, forbidden love can blossom
from poison.

And when it does, you've got to guard it with
your life. You've got to watch your back.

Available from

headline
ETERNAL

headline
ETERNAL

FIND YOUR HEART'S DESIRE...

VISIT OUR WEBSITE: www.headlineeternal.com
FIND US ON FACEBOOK: facebook.com/eternalromance
FOLLOW US ON TWITTER: @eternal_books
EMAIL US: eternalromance@headline.co.uk

You haven't lived 'til you've visited the wild world of The Artists Trilogy . . .

You'll meet a Mexican drug lord, a beautiful con artist and a damaged tattooist.

You'll play a lethal game of cat and mouse, of life and death, of love and revenge.

It's dark, dangerous and deadly.

It's time to buckle in and lose your inhibitions.

Available now from

headline
ETERNAL